WHAT THEY DON'T KNOW

K.V. SCRUGGS

NIGHTLARK PUBLISHING

ISBN-13: 978-0997959925
ISBN-10: 0997959924
LCCN: 2017905991

ACKNOWLEDGEMENTS

Thank you to my parents, who gave me the gift of a safe-space in which to fail when it mattered most.

Thank you to the friends and family—you know who you are—who wouldn't stop asking about the book's progress, thereby making it impossible for me to give up on this dream and still save face. A special thank you to those who read the book in its various stages and gave invaluable feedback and encouragement.

Thank you to my editor, Katelyn Stark, who pulled things out of me I didn't know were in there.

Thank you to everyone at Nightlark Publishing, especially Ryan, who believed in this book, and believed in me, enough to take a chance.

To Justin

For never not believing in me

"A government big enough to give you everything you want is a government big enough to take from you everything you have."

— Gerald R. Ford

CHAPTER 1
Then
August 29, 2018

Cheyenne Rose watched the police officers pace the length of the line that had formed outside Raleigh City Hospital, their heels scraping in unison against the concrete. Their guns were holstered but never far from their twitchy, nervous fingers. She quickly averted her eyes when one of the officers glanced her way. Cops made her feel like she needed to confess to something, even if there was nothing to confess. She had never so much as stolen a pack of gum in her entire life, but maybe they somehow knew she was supposed to be in school today, or that she had almost failed the seventh grade last year because of all the days she'd missed.

Cheyenne gripped the handles of the wheelchair a little tighter and leaned down. "Mom? You still doing okay?"

Sandra Rose was bent forward with her hands propped on her knees like a tripod, her chest rising and falling at a tempo twice as fast as Cheyenne's own. The stifling humidity of the North Carolina summer was making it almost impossible for her to catch her breath. Her thin t-shirt had wet circles underneath the armpits and hung on her as though she was nothing more than a skeleton, which was not far from the truth.

Cheyenne made a halfhearted attempt to smooth her frizzy, red hair before realizing it was no use. "We're learning about the stock market crash in economics." She tried to distract her mother. "Mr. Tremont is a little obsessed."

"Oh yeah?" Sandra suddenly grabbed her chest, her words cut short and her body rigid.

Cheyenne felt her body tense up, too. She wasn't sure how much more of this heat her mom could take. Not on top of everything else. She craned her neck to look ahead of them in line, but saw only the same few heads they had been staring at for the last hour and a half.

After a moment, Sandra relaxed. "So. What are you learning?" she asked a little too casually.

Cheyenne kept a wary eye on her mother as she took in the scene around them. Cars were double and triple parked in the lot, and patients were still joining the line, which was wrapped around the building now. People were crowding closer and closer together as they neared the hospital's main entrance. The double doors opened and closed continuously in response to the weight of the people standing just outside.

"You know how everybody started freaking out and selling their stocks all at once, and how that's what caused the real problem. Seems sort of similar to what's happening now." She didn't understand why, but it didn't take a genius to see that, for some reason, people were flocking to the hospital. Too many people.

Sandra nodded. "Seems like everybody's coming to the hospital just 'cause. People are saying there'll be no doctors at all by this time tomorrow, but I don't know about all that." Sandra's smile was pained. "I sure did pick the wrong day to get sick, didn't I, punkin'?" She strained to force out the last few words before dissolving into a coughing fit.

Cheyenne didn't answer. Her mom had been sick for a long time. She knew that, and she was sure her mom *knew* that she knew. But they never talked about it. It was a continuous cycle of good days and bad. Cheyenne would go to school each morning, her mom smiling and waving at the door as she got on the bus. Then, without any warning, she would get home one afternoon and her mom was in bed, too weak to even sit up to eat the dinner that Cheyenne prepared, usually SpaghettiOs or tomato soup.

This would last a couple of days, Cheyenne having to stay home from school to nurse her mom back to health, and then all of a sudden, life was back to normal for several weeks. Inevitably, once Cheyenne had gotten used to things being good again, the cycle would start all over.

It was just the two of them for as long as she could remember, ever since her dad had died in Afghanistan. She had seen pictures of him, but it was like looking at a stranger posing with a younger version of her mom. There were even a couple of pictures with the three of them. Her as a baby, her mom, and a man who just happened to have Cheyenne's eyes. It was weird seeing that.

The line advanced in front of them a couple of inches, just enough to make Cheyenne feel like they should move forward as well. She knew it was probably from people becoming impatient, moving closer to one another, slowly compressing the line. No real progress. Like going through security at the airport or being in bumper-to-bumper traffic.

She didn't understand what was going on, but she had a feeling that whatever it was, it was bad. The crowd was growing larger by the minute. For every patient allowed into the building, five more showed up to wait in line. And the influx showed no signs of slowing down.

"You'd think a broken pinkie could wait," said a large man in a tank top a few feet ahead of Cheyenne, speaking loudly as if wanting to be heard. "I mean, considering." He gestured toward the line of people.

"Wanna say that to my face?" Another man even further up in the line turned around. "I still have one good fist."

"Mind your own business," someone else chimed in. "We're all here for the same reason. It's not his fault you're having to wait."

"Mind my own business? Are you kidding me right now? That's all I been doing for the last hour. My wife's about to have this baby right here in the parking lot, all just so this pansy can get a couple popsicle sticks taped around his finger?"

For the first time, Cheyenne noticed a hugely pregnant woman sitting in a folding chair facing the man. Her head was bent forward, and her eyes were squeezed tight.

"Brent," the woman whispered. She reached one hand up from where she was clutching her gravid abdomen and batted the air a few times before making contact with his wrist.

"What is it, babe?" He bent down to her level, all his posturing melting away into genuine concern. She said something into his ear, and he stood up like a shot. He looked at her, then at the front of the hospital, then back at her. He said something to her, and she nodded, then slowly stood up with his help. They began to make their way toward the front of the hospital. There was an enlarging dark circle on the back of her dress, and at first Cheyenne thought the woman had wet herself. Then she realized what it was and looked away, her cheeks burning. The woman continued to leak the clear fluid as she limped toward the entrance of the building. Several people stepped aside for them, but when they got to the man with the broken finger, he stood in their path.

"I don't think so." The man's injured hand was cradled in his other palm, and Cheyenne could see it was more than just a broken pinky. There was a large amount of gauze stained with yellow, orange and red fluids that looked several days old. Despite the bandage covering it, she could tell his hand was badly misshapen.

"C'mon, dude. Don't be a douche." Brent tried to step around him with his wife, but the other man reached out with his good hand in a sort of chopping motion. Before Cheyenne knew what had happened, Brent was lying on the ground clutching his neck and coughing. A couple of women rushed to either side of Brent's wife, talking her through a poorly timed contraction.

"You're doing great, sweetie."

"What's your name, anyway? Janet, that's a beautiful name."

"Pick out a name for this little one yet? Boy or Girl? Surprise? How exciting."

Janet's legs started to give out from under her. Someone brought the folding chair to where she now stood, and she collapsed into it.

Brent stood up and rushed the other man, swinging and shouting obscenities. A few surrounding people tried to pull them off of one another, and a few others tried to cut in line. Several more fights broke out ahead of them.

Two policemen ran toward the commotion, their loaded belts bouncing against their hips. The heavy metallic clicking sound reminded Cheyenne of the soldiers she'd seen in movies, trotting across the desert or the jungle, sweat streaming down their faces. The thought made her scoot a little closer to her mom, the sides of their knees touching just enough to remind Cheyenne she wasn't alone.

She closed her eyes and imagined she was in PE class. Feet shuffling, grunts, skin against skin. All the sounds were familiar and harmless, she told herself, until she heard a guttural scream coming from Janet's direction.

Cheyenne opened her eyes just in time to see a paramedic running toward Janet, whose legs were splayed open, a ruined pair of panties on the ground beside her. Bystanders averted their eyes, trying to give her some semblance of privacy. She slumped to the right, leaning on one of the women who had rushed to her aid.

"Alright, Janet. This is it. You have to push now."

"I can't," she sobbed. "Not here."

"Babe!" Brent's voice came from a few feet away. Cheyenne looked over to see him being handcuffed by one of the cops. "Babe, I'm right here. You're doing great. Just breathe like we practiced." He turned to the officer. "Please, man. You don't understand," he said. A bruise was already forming along his jawline. "I gotta be there for her."

"You should have thought of that before starting a fight while a cop was standing five feet away, dickhead."

Cheyenne glanced down at her mom, feeling weirdly protective, hoping she hadn't heard that.

"Seriously, please, do you have kids? What if you had to miss one of them being born?"

The policeman didn't answer, just jerked Brent onto his feet by his armpits as his counterpart handcuffed the other man. "I got bigger shit to worry about than your sorry ass. Look around."

The policemen hauled away both of the men, Brent kicking and screaming and the other man eerily silent. As they approached the far corner of the hospital building, Cheyenne heard Brent's voice degenerate into sobs. She had to look away, tears stinging her own eyes. She didn't think she had ever seen or heard a man cry.

"Where's my husband? Where's Brent?" Janet had just finished another round of pushing and was now looking around in a panic. Someone had found a large sheet and had spread it over her knees.

"Janet, he's fine. He had to sit down. You need to focus, now. You need to push in one…two—"

"Ahhhhh!" Janet bore down, leaning slightly forward and revealing a ring of sweat along the nape of her neck. The dark tendrils of loose hair from her ponytail were matted to her skin.

"That's it; that's it. I see the head. Baby's coming! Next push, guaranteed," the paramedic said as Janet collapsed in the chair, and her head dangled precariously over the edge.

"Good birth control, huh?" Sandra quipped from the wheelchair in front of Cheyenne.

"Mom!" Cheyenne punched her lightly on the shoulder but was secretly glad for the distraction from the garish scene playing out in front of her.

Sandra laughed, then immediately broke into a coughing fit. She clutched the arms of her wheelchair and gasped for air.

"Mom, you okay?" Cheyenne stood patting her mom on the back and fanning her face. She could hear the wheezing from where she stood. Her airways were starting to close up.

"Mom!" She bent down, practically yelling in her mom's face now, but Sandra's eyes had glassed over. Cheyenne had seen this look before. She didn't have much time. She glanced around them, fighting off the panic that threatened to take over. "Help!" she called out to no one in particular. "My mom can't breathe. I need some help, here!"

"Here you go, doll. See if this helps." A thin, plastic tube with two inch-long prongs sticking out of one side appeared as if from nowhere. She'd seen one before, knew exactly what to do with it. She grabbed it and positioned the prongs in her mom's nostrils, wrapping the extra tubing around her ears. Only when her mom's breathing slowed and her own heart stopped racing did Cheyenne look to see where the oxygen had come from.

Just behind her stood a heavy woman with swollen, discolored legs and feet that spread out across her shoes until the sides were almost flat with the ground. She had a soiled bandage on her right shin. Her face was pretty, though. Her makeup was perfect, and her hair was stylish and short. She leaned on her oxygen tank for support, and Cheyenne could see the indentations left behind by the cannula that was now in Sandra's nose.

"I heard there's been looting in New York," she said. Cheyenne looked around but couldn't tell who the woman was talking to. "Pharmacies, hospitals…people are taking whatever they can get their hands on right now. Whatever they think they might need…or be able to sell."

"Will be here, too, I expect. Before too long, judging by the looks of it," another woman responded. "Less than twenty-four hours since the announcement and the line's halfway across the parking lot. It's only gonna get worse."

"Thank you, ma'am. So much." Cheyenne's voice sounded small and timid.

The woman waved her hand. "It's no biggie. Doc says I really only need it when I sleep."

"Well, we really appreciate it. Mom just needed a little help till we get inside. Shouldn't be too much longer, now."

Cheyenne saw the two women exchange a look.

"Um, do either of you know what's going on?" she asked, trying to stand a little taller.

"Didn't you hear?" the first woman replied. "All the doctors are on strike. Say they can't keep their lights on and their water running with the amount they're gettin' paid. Say healthcare reform has bled 'em dry."

"Don't forget all the 'rules and regulations'," the other woman chimed in. "They say doctors might as well be a bunch of computers the way it is nowadays. Say it's not safe for patients. As if this *is*."

Cheyenne glanced at her mom, who was listening intently, before venturing, "Who says?"

The woman shrugged. "They got a spokesperson. Kevin? Karl? I don't know how this is supposed to be better. As of yesterday, when the announcement was made, a third of all the doctors had quit. More are leaving every hour."

"Who knows if there's even any doctors left here," the other woman added, swinging a lazy hand toward the hospital entrance. Her skin reminded Cheyenne of fingertips that had soaked in water too long, only instead of translucent white, it was tan and spotted. She had thinning, brittle hair that she lifted off her neck as she spoke and fanned herself in time with her words. "Maybe we're all just waiting in this line for nothing."

Cheyenne's heart skipped a beat. She hadn't considered the possibility that their patience wouldn't eventually be rewarded, that they wouldn't get to the front of the line sooner or later so her mother could see a doctor. She glanced down at her mom, watching her work for each breath, and felt the panic starting to return. Did they even have a Plan B?

"You think that's true?" She spoke to her mother now, the other women forgotten.

"Don't listen to them, Cheyenne," Sandra whispered, patting the back of Cheyenne's thigh where her arm rested in an awkward embrace. Cheyenne was barely five feet tall, but she still towered over her mom in the wheelchair. "They're just repeating rumors they've heard. The truth is probably much more boring." She took a slow, deep breath. Her voice trembled ever so slightly when she spoke again. "Most of the people you see here are just afraid. Everything is going to turn out just fine. It always does."

Cheyenne wanted to believe her, but she knew her mom had lied to protect her before. She felt like everything she had taken for granted was slipping away. She couldn't look at her mom, afraid she might start crying. Or worse, that her mom would.

"It's a boy!" Cheyenne's gaze followed the voice back to the commotion ahead of them in line. The paramedic now held up an angry, wrinkled baby, as proud as if he, himself, were the father. Janet sat crumpled and sobbing into the chest of a woman who patted her back and stroked her hair.

The paramedic passed off the baby and cut the umbilical cord. Janet was cleaned off and transferred to a wheelchair to be moved inside. It seemed a little late for that, in Cheyenne's opinion, but what did she know?

Cheyenne sat down on the curb of the sidewalk leading into the hospital, ankles crossed and arms resting on knobby knees. She risked a glance up at her mom. From this vantage point, she didn't look so sick.

She thought about what the big woman had said. If it was true, if that many doctors had quit in one day, then that would explain these long lines. It might also explain the fights and the fact that the police were there. But if that was the problem, what was the solution?

She racked her brain and couldn't think of one. And, looking around, it was obvious no one else had any bright ideas, either. How long could this go on before people really started getting hurt? Or worse?

"What do you think is going to happen, Mom?" She wasn't sure whether she was asking about the crisis unfolding in front of their eyes or her mom's illness or—the scariest question of all—what Cheyenne was going to do when her mom was no longer around. Maybe all three.

"I don't know, sweetheart." Sandra answered all of Cheyenne's questions in one exhausted, sad breath. "I just don't know."

CHAPTER 2
Now
June 9, 2030

"When did you know?" Cheyenne felt as if every light in the studio was trained on her forehead, and she willed herself not to break a sweat. No matter how many times she did this, she could never get used to the feeling that she was an ant under a magnifying glass. Even her pre-show vodka tonic wasn't helping much these days. Maybe she needed to up it to two. She took a deep breath. "That is, when did you know everything was going to be okay?"

Danny Reid sat opposite her on the couch of an artificial living room set. He was a caged animal, wary and on edge. He studied the cameras for a long moment then just stared off at nothing. His hands lay unmoving and forgotten in his lap. When he finally did speak, Cheyenne had to lean forward and strain to hear him.

"I still don't know. Every day I look at Ridge, I look at my son, and I think about how close he was to dying. I don't think you ever really come back from that."

"The idea of—" Cheyenne swallowed, blinking back tears. Then she started again. "Losing someone you love, it's life-altering."

Danny nodded, and his shoulders sagged even further, forced down by the weight of the memory. "I thought I'd been through the worst with my accident. Not even close."

He paused again, and the only sound in the studio was the faint, ubiquitous humming of electronics. Cheyenne took him in from across the coffee table. He had a buzz cut and a tan line in the shape of his sunglasses. He carried himself more like a shy third-grader than a blue-collar worker with a family and bills to pay. He should be more hardened, more grizzled. She wondered if he was always this sensitive, never truly cut out for the life he'd been handed. Or was he irreparably wounded by the accident, by his disability, by his inability to provide for the family he so clearly couldn't live without?

Cheyenne felt tears prickle her nose and scolded herself to get it together. She wanted to reach across the table, give him a hug, and tell him everything was going to be okay. Instead, she tried to calm him with her words.

"Ignore the cameras." She sat on the edge of her chair and leaned over, her forehead so close to his that they were almost touching, then put a hand on his knee. "Close your eyes."

Danny obeyed, and the tension melted out of his shoulders instantly. He reached his right hand blindly across the couch toward his wife, Isabella, and she grabbed it. Their two children, Ridge and Hendrix, sat on the other side of her, fidgeting and poking at one another.

"You've already taken us with you on your personal journey," Cheyenne said, "the long recovery after your accident. I saw how difficult it was for you to open up about that, and this must be infinitely more so."

Danny nodded, his eyes still closed.

"But I want you to try to go back to that night in the hospital, the CSM," she continued. "What was the first thing you felt when you were told that Ridge, your seven-year-old little boy, your straight-A student who wants to be an astronaut when he grows up, who loves soccer, who insists on making his mother breakfast in bed every single Saturday—" Her voice trembled. "What was it like to hear that he might not make it through the night?"

Danny took a deep breath and stared at the coffee table in front of him. "I felt powerless. He was dying right there in front of me, and there was nothing I could do."

Isabella shook her head, a stern look on her face. "Baby, you did everything you could. You got him the help—"

Danny's eyes angled toward her, and when he spoke, his voice was uncharacteristically harsh. "She asked how I felt, Isabella. That's how I felt."

Danny seemed to instantly regret his outburst, but not before the hurt had passed over Isabella's delicate features and she had slowly but pointedly removed her hand from his. Now she busied herself with the kids, wiping faces and straightening jackets, as a deep redness started to color her normally pale complexion. She let her dark hair cover her face like a curtain.

Cheyenne heard a few uncomfortable murmurs from the crowd. "I can't imagine how stressful this has been for both of you. I just don't know what I would have done if I were in your shoes," she said. Then she let out an awkward laugh. "I would have been a total basket-case." There was nothing like a little self-deprecation to defuse a situation. She had learned that little tip way back in middle school.

Danny remained facing Isabella as he answered Cheyenne. "It was incredibly hard," he said. He reached an apologetic hand out to his wife and placed it on her knee. "But in the end, it's brought us closer. There's nothing like almost losing someone you love to make you realize what's truly important in life."

Cheyenne could almost feel the collective sigh of relief from her audience members. Isabella studied her husband for a moment then gave him a small, icy smile that Cheyenne would know anywhere. *We'll play nice while we're in front of the cameras, but this is not over. Not even close.*

"So that night," Cheyenne said quickly, "they told you Ridge had a ruptured appendix, that he was in shock and needed emergency surgery."

"Yes."

"Then what?"

"They wanted to transfer him to another hospital, one of the CSMs."

"Ah, yes. The Centers for Standardized Medicine. We've all heard of them, and we all no doubt have developed our own opinions. By now, I'm sure you're quite the expert."

The CSMs emerged from the ashes of the healthcare crisis and had completely revolutionized the way Americans received healthcare, but so little was known about their day-to-day operations. All anyone knew was that you went there when you got sick, and they would take care of you, and somehow, the government was footing the bill.

"Well, I don't know if I would call myself an expert." Danny smiled a rare smile and rubbed his neck where his collared shirt and tie appeared to be a little too tight. He wore a short-sleeve button-down, the sleeves ending right above the permanent farmer's tan that bisected his muscular bicep. He had a demarcation even though he hadn't had a steady job in several years. It was a marker, a tattoo, telling the viewers he was one of them.

Cheyenne nibbled the inside of her lip and tried to focus on Danny, but her thoughts went back to the unmarked manila envelope that had shown up in her dressing room earlier that day. Months ago, she had located an old classmate, Rebecca Stephenson, who worked in the information security department of their regional CSM. It had taken a lot of effort on Cheyenne's part, but she guessed she had finally earned Rebecca's trust.

"I didn't really know much about the centers before that day," Danny continued, and Cheyenne forced her attention back to what he was saying. "But I felt like the doctor was trying to push us out because—" He hesitated then started again. "After my accident, Isabella worked two jobs just to pay the rent and keep the lights on. What few odd jobs I could get, the money went straight to feeding and clothing our boys. Insurance just seemed like an unnecessary expense when we were all pretty healthy, you know?"

Cheyenne nodded. "So, what is the purpose of the CSM program as you understand it now?"

"The way it was explained to me—to us," he looked at Isabella, "is this: certain hospitals that got low MedScores were bought out by the government. Then they used tax money to turn them into the centers."

"Why go to all the trouble of rebranding them as CSMs? Why not just call them hospitals, if that's what they are?"

Danny got a mischievous look in his eye, shrugged his shoulders, and opened his mouth to speak. But before he could answer, Isabella placed a hand firmly on his shoulder, silencing him.

"I think they wanted to separate the CSMs from the low-scoring hospitals in the minds of the patients," she explained. "But all we knew at the time was that they were different and new and they sent uninsured patients there. You can imagine how scared we were. We felt like guinea pigs."

"Who wouldn't? I mean, this is not a stubbed toe we're talking about, here. It's your child's *life*." Cheyenne felt herself getting emotional again, even though she knew the story ended happily. Ridge was sitting there across the table from her, for God's sake. She turned back to Danny. "So, how was your experience once you got to the CSM?"

"I honestly don't remember all the details." He looked at the cameras as if noticing them for the first time and shrunk into himself a little bit. He nodded toward his wife. "She was there by that point." He clenched his jaw and pulled at his shirtsleeve as if it were too tight.

Isabella eyed her husband for a moment before stepping in and taking over the conversation. "Ridge was evaluated immediately and stabilized within fifteen minutes of his arrival. He was taken back for a CAT scan and ultimately to pre-op within an hour of us arriving."

"Sounds very efficient. And how did Ridge do after surgery?"

"It was a little rocky, at first. He required antibiotics for peritonitis—an infection he got because of the ruptured appendix. Then he had a brief episode of kidney failure." Isabella reached a protective arm around her oldest son. He acquiesced to the hug for a moment before wriggling away from her grasp. "But he's here with us now. We couldn't have asked for better care."

"And what did Hendrix think of all this excitement?" Cheyenne smiled at the youngest Reid, who responded by ducking behind his unwilling older brother. A scuffle ensued, and Ridge had Hendrix in a headlock before Isabella could separate the two.

Once Isabella had successfully wedged herself between the two boys, Hendrix buried his face into her side so that only his stick-straight brown hair was visible to the crowd. "Hendrix is a wee bit shy." Isabella laughed. "But they made him feel right at home while Ridge was in surgery. There was a playroom with tons of toys and books. Hendrix didn't even realize we were in a hospital until we went to see Ridge after the surgery."

"That's wonderful. A true success story." Cheyenne leaned once more across the coffee table and took Danny and Isabella each by the hand. "What would you say to the people that still oppose the CSM movement? Oppose the work that is being done by dedicated people, such as the surgeon general, to build more facilities and provide health-care to every citizen of the United States, regardless of their ability to pay?"

Danny glanced at Isabella, whose eyes flashed as she stared into the camera. "We worked hard and followed the rules and paid our taxes. We were good citizens, and we never would have guessed we'd be in the position we are now, but here we are." She gestured to her family on the couch. "If it can happen to us, it can happen to anyone. I truly believe the folks at the CSM saved my son's life. Bottom line. In my mind, there is no debate. There *should be* no debate."

"And yet, the debate continues." Cheyenne stood and walked over to where Ridge now sat between his parents and put a hand on his shoulder. She addressed her audie-nce, forgetting about the cameras for a moment. "Trust me, the world is a better place with Ridge Reid in it." She looked down at him. "We redheads have to stick together, right, sweetheart?"

Ridge grinned up at her, his face flushing a shade of pink that camouflaged his freckles.

At that, Cheyenne gazed into the camera, into America's hopefully tearful eyes, and signed off. "Be sure to tune in next week as we continue our series, *Reid it and Weep*. I've got a big surprise for the Reids that you're not going to want to miss! And never forget, friends: *These* are the stories that matter."

Cheyenne watched as the Reids made their way off the stage. Voices called out from every direction, congratulating each other on another amazing segment. A glass of champagne seemed to come out of nowhere, and she took it. There was a sense of excitement in the air, an electricity that caused her pulse to quicken and her hair to stand on end. She had felt it several years ago when she'd covered her first story, and she'd been gunning for it ever since. She closed her eyes and let herself enjoy the rush. It never got old.

This was their third interview, but she could tell Isabella was no less incredulous than she was the first two times. The carefree attitude that pervaded the studio never seemed to be quite enough to make her forget about all the bills and responsibilities awaiting her at home. Cheyenne knew how she felt. She knew this place—the lights, the noise, the constant motion with nothing really being accomplished—could feel like a bubble. Predictable. Controlled. Yet so easily burst.

Taking a sip of the crisp champagne, Cheyenne stepped out of the building and stopped for a moment to gaze at the Western Boulevard traffic, always moving, always headed somewhere different. Better. The heat and humidity rose off the asphalt parking lot and slammed into her, despite the fact that it was already almost seven o'clock at night. The beads of sweat popped up so quickly that it seemed as though they were there all along.

She squinted at the endless rows of cars, wavy and nebulous in the heat. The Reids had already closed half the distance between the building and their beat-up Corolla. Cheyenne watched as they reached the car, Isabella tugging at the passenger door handle for a long moment before it came off in her hand.

Danny opened her door from the inside, and she sat down as he put the key in the ignition. The engine turned over several times before catching, and then Cheyenne heard the unmistakable chime of their MedScreen coming to life.

Isabella, sitting with her back straight and her hands resting in her lap, looked up and met her gaze with a cool, proud stare. Cheyenne turned away, her face flushing with the hot shame of being caught watching. As she approached the glass doors leading back into the studio, she caught a glimpse of her reflection.

She turned her face to the side and studied her profile: the triangular nose, the pointy chin, the curly red bob that had become her trademark. She knew what people like Isabella thought, that the bouncy hair and carefree attitude was all there was to her. They didn't know what she'd lost to get here, or how hard she worked to keep up the happy-go-lucky persona they saw on camera. They didn't know how close she felt to losing it all.

After a moment, she shook her head and pulled the door open just a little too forcefully. She was met by cool air that enveloped her, taking away any memory she had of the stifling humidity and replacing it with a cold, damp chill.

CHAPTER 3
Then
April 25, 2021

Senator Alexander Montgomery sauntered into the boardroom overlooking uptown Charlotte, fifteen minutes late, and almost walked right into the slight, balding man who stood with an arm full of papers, his other hand outstretched, and a name tag on his chest. Dr. Karl Buchner. Monty stopped just in time to avoid bulldozing him, but they were close enough that Karl's upturned chin grazed his chest.

"Senator Montgomery," the man said, smiling up at him. "A pleasure." The doctor's words reached Monty on an almost palpable cloud of halitosis, and he took an urgent step backward.

"Call me Monty," he said, making a wide circle around Karl and carefully avoiding the proffered handshake. He hesitated when he reached the tall, narrow armchair at the head of the table, eyeing it for a long moment before forcing his backside into the seat. When he met resistance, he angled to one side and crossed his legs, dropping the rest of the way down in a huff. A former defensive lineman, his size was more of an annoyance than an advantage nowadays.

"Let's get this over with," Monty said, running a hand over his shaved head and glancing up to see Karl frozen in the same spot. "For God's sake, have a seat."

Karl did as he was told, sniffing loudly and wiping his chaffed nose with an open palm. "Anxiety-related rhinorrhea." He laughed briefly, then quieted when Monty didn't join in. "It's an honor, Senator. It really is."

"Just start talking."

As Karl launched into his prepared presentation, the slides appeared in the tabletop screen in front of Monty. He pulled the coffee pot toward him, directly over the screen, and poured a cup of coffee into a stained mug. The lack of steam coming from the murky liquid was not a good sign. He took a sip, made a face, then pushed the mug aside. He went for the water pitcher instead and then finally turned his attention to Karl. The guy had the kind of skinny frame that told Monty he had never stepped foot in a gym. Scrawny arms and legs but with a lazy, shapeless gut poking out beneath his nonexistent pecs. As if he could read Monty's mind, Karl stopped talking, folded both hands over his fleshy abdomen, and waited expectantly.

"I'm sorry, can you repeat that?" Monty said, adding halfheartedly, "Coffee hasn't had time to kick in."

"I was just saying that I truly believe the CSM program was an inspired idea. I admire you greatly for your innovation. Always have." The doctor overarticulated each word, effectively making his voice almost as unpleasant as his appearance. "But it's just that the cost savings you projected don't seem to have panned out, sir, Senator—Monty."

"Oh, yeah?" Monty leaned forward, the shoulders of his suit jacket straining against his broad shoulders. "How do you figure?"

"Well." Karl paused, clearing his throat and pressing a button that brought a screen down from the ceiling. "By my calculations, the CSMs are barely paying for themselves. Slide twenty-seven." He gestured toward the main screen where a line graph appeared in response to his voice command. "Much less generating additional revenue."

"A program paying for itself is a remarkable achievement in healthcare. You would know that if you had any experience with this sort of thing. You know, other than just staging doctor's strikes."

Karl's eyes flashed. "The strike brought us here, to this table. I consider that a win." He placed his hands on the table, looked down, and took a deep breath. When he looked up again, his eyes were a blank slate. "I understand this is a lot of information, Monty. But I believe my ideas could help generate some extra capital that we could then reinvest into the CSMs." His fingers tremored right to left, the screen shots following suit until he found what he was looking for. "For example, take a look at my proposed MedScreen initiative. As you can see in the chart here, this program alone should result in a positive cash flow in three to six months, which is unheard of in the healthcare industry. I want to stress that I'm not trying to replace your program." Karl spread his hands out, palms up, and flashed a crooked, yellow smile. "Just improve it a little."

"And *I* want to stress that you don't know the first thing about what goes into running a program like the CSMs."

"True, my background is not in administration, but I'm a quick study. Since I was appointed as the physician representative of the CSM advisory committee, I've learned a lot about the ins and outs. Enough to offer my opinion, I believe." He pulled out a moist, wadded handkerchief and wiped his nose straight upward. The motion lifted his upper lip to reveal an unobstructed view of his buckteeth, a chunk of broccoli—the putrefying source of his offensive breath—wedged between them.

"This looks like more than just an opinion." Monty lifted his hand, palm facing outward, and made an abrupt fist. The screen went blank. "This looks like an overthrow."

Karl shrugged. "Call it what you will, but it looks like we're going to be working together, whether you like it or not. We might as well get used to the idea."

"You don't know what you're talking about." Monty leaned back in his chair. "This meeting was recommended by the president's advisors, and I went along with it. I knew it was going to be a waste of time. Total bullshit. And, Karl, you'd better believe I'm not letting a nobody like you interfere with my legacy. I *invented* the CSMs. I was the savior of the American healthcare system, picking it up like a baby bird and taping its broken wings back together. I am the *unopposed authority* on healthcare reform. I work alone."

"I'm just—"

"So you can take your bad comb-over and your off-the-rack Men's Wearhouse suit and go back to wherever it is you came from." Monty placed his palm heavily over the rest of Karl's precious handouts and shoved them down the table with such force that they knocked over an abandoned coffee mug.

Karl picked up the papers from the quickly spreading brown puddle as if they were made of pure gold and blotted them with a stack of beverage napkins.

Monty stood and exited the boardroom, leaving Karl to clean up his mess.

CHAPTER 4
Now
June 10, 2030

Cheyenne climbed into the backseat of her car, physically and mentally drained. For the last hour, she had tried her hardest to leave but kept getting intercepted. Normally she would have loved the attention, but all she could think about tonight was the ID chip that was now in her possession, the world she suddenly had at her fingertips.

Thankfully, Cheyenne had enough misguided fans trying to get into the studio to meet her that no one had questioned the mousy brunette that had shown up earlier that day with an unmarked package, insisting on leaving it for Cheyenne, and Cheyenne only. Once the package went through the appropriate screening, the staff had merely rolled their eyes and sent an intern to deposit it in Cheyenne's dressing room. Same old, same old.

Rebecca had warned her the level-five clearance attached to the chip wouldn't last forever. There were many layers of security built in, not the least of which was the requirement that security clearance be renewed each week. In person.

It was two in the morning, and Cheyenne had to be back at work at nine, but she intended to make full use of this access while she had it. It wasn't like she would be able to sleep, anyway. She pressed the intercom.

"Roger, I need to make a stop before going home." She sent the address for the CSM headquarters to the car's GPS, and it immediately rerouted them downtown.

"Sure, Miss Rose. Not a problem." He turned on the blinker. "ETA ten minutes."

Cheyenne leaned back against the black leather and closed her eyes as the car drove along Wade Avenue, but her mind raced. Ever since her fifteenth birthday, when her mother had finally succumbed to breast cancer and Cheyenne went from beloved daughter to inconvenient niece in the blink of an eye, she hadn't gotten a full night's sleep without the use of alcohol or pills. Even then, the bursts of sleep that she did get were interspersed with wakefulness and the uneasy feeling she had just awoken from a bad dream.

However, everything seemed to fall by the wayside as each Monday through Thursday was consumed by preparation for that week's segment, and each Friday night was spent rewarding everyone's hard work with a wrap party. Then her weekends were spent editing the show for the Sunday night spot in which it would air, but she didn't mind. She was happy to have the diversion, the ambition to get out of Raleigh and on to a bigger stage, the excuse to avoid a social life. She liked having her surface-level friendships at work that didn't extend past the walls of the studio or past the long hours of her workday. Acquaintances tended to mind their own business. Friends and family did not.

Cheyenne slid off her pumps and felt a blast of cold air on her clammy feet. It didn't matter if she had the most comfortable heels known to man, wearing any shoe for twenty hours straight was just plain wrong. She kneaded her soles until she felt the tension let up a bit. Then she undid the top button of her pants, relishing in the feeling of release. She tried again and focused on relaxing every muscle in her body. She leaned her head back on the seat, closed her eyes, and dropped her hands to her sides.

A moment later, Cheyenne lifted her head. It was hopeless. She rummaged through her bag for the envelope and located the map that Rebecca had the foresight to include. The ID would give her access to the CSM mainframe computer, the only place where confidential patient information was housed since Internet security breaches had become so commonplace. She needed to know exactly where to go once she got through the door, or she was sure to be intercepted before she could get there. She grabbed a glass from the cabinet to her right and filled it to the brim with champagne.

She studied the map and thought about what she was hoping to get out of tonight. The idea that she might blow the cover off a huge conspiracy, she knew deep down that was a pipe dream. Her main objective—the reason she had contacted Rebecca in the first place—was to enhance the Reids' storyline. It was rare nowadays for patients to ever meet the doctors—especially the surgeons—who took care of them. It was just one of the many things that had changed after the crash. And if she knew anything about her viewers, she knew they would be chomping at the bit to see the surgeon who had saved Ridge's life.

When Cheyenne's mom had ended up in the hospital that last time, she went two weeks without a doctor stepping into her room or laying hands on her. Instead, overworked nurses were the front line, and they conveyed information to the doctors, who were running two, three, or even four hospitals from a single remote location. Finally, when it had become fairly obvious that her mom wasn't getting any better, a doctor came in to talk to her about her options. She could choose to be made comfortable or not, but either way she was not a candidate for any further aggressive treatment. Cheyenne had hated that man with her whole being. He had taken her mother away. But now she understood that was what her mother was waiting for. Permission to stop suffering. Permission to leave her only daughter. Permission to die.

At the time, Cheyenne hadn't realized what it had taken for that doctor to come to her mother's room that day. He probably drove over an hour each way to have that conversation face-to-face instead of over a MedScreen. That would never happen today. Everything had become infinitely more streamlined and digital. More efficient but even less personal than a decade prior. Hospitals—CSMs—had become a well-oiled machine, and surgeons were the assembly line workers. They did their surgeries, and someone at a lower pay grade took care of all the messy patient interactions and the paperwork. Or at least, that's how Cheyenne understood it. But you couldn't argue with the success of the CSMs. That's what it really boiled down to, wasn't it? Patient outcomes?

From what she knew of the Reid family, however, she thought they would like to at least be able to say thank you. Plus, it was going to make for some really great television.

Unfortunately, the search was more difficult than she had expected, and accessing the information she needed required a clearance level that Cheyenne did not have. What Cheyenne did have was an extremely persuasive personality and, it turned out, an old high school classmate in a very convenient position.

And now, she held the key to the CSMs in the palm of her hand. It was just a matter of having the courage to use it.

"Miss Rose, we're here." The car pulled to a stop at the curb in front of the huge building that housed the CSM headquarters.

Cheyenne finished off the last of her champagne, threw caution to the wind, and stepped out of the car.

Once in the building, Cheyenne followed Rebecca's map to the mainframe on the second floor. It was located in a frigid room with aluminum walls and a concrete floor. She used her chip to sign in to the computer, and a black screen flashed onto the monitor. She waited, but nothing else appeared. After a moment, she lightly placed a finger on the mouse pad and motioned left-to-right, up-and-down. Nothing.

Her fingers began to tremble as she tried several different combinations on the keyboard with no luck. She knew this was the right computer, and she knew the information she needed was stored inside, but she had no idea how to access it. She blew out an exasperated breath.

"What in the world do you want from me?"

"Hello. What can I do for you today?" A female voice came from nowhere.

Cheyenne froze, and for a few horrible seconds, her heart stopped beating. When she finally took a breath, her chest was on fire. With a sense of dread, she slowly turned to face the room's single entryway.

The room was deserted and dark, and the door was closed. She thought she remembered shutting and locking it behind her, but now she couldn't remember.

"I'm sorry; I didn't get that." The voice spoke again, clearly coming from the computer this time.

"Oh, it's just you." Cheyenne giggled, giddy with relief. "Your voice sounded so natural."

"Thank you."

"Um..." Cheyenne took a few deep breaths and thought about exactly what it was she wanted. "I'd like access to the physician procedure database for the last two years...cross-referenced by patient, if possible."

"Of course. Please allow four minutes, fifteen seconds to complete your request."

An hourglass appeared at the top right of the screen with a countdown just beneath it. As she waited, Cheyenne glanced around the room, really seeing it for the first time. There were shelves lining every wall except where the computer sat. The rest of the room was open except for a long table that ran down the center. The table held a few boxes but was otherwise empty. There was a door on the wall to the left of where she sat.

The timer had gotten down to twenty seconds and she had inserted her flash drive into the computer when she heard the doorknob behind her rattle. After a moment, the doorknob quieted and the person on the other side let out an unintelligible profanity. Then, Cheyenne heard another voice followed by the jangle of a huge keyring.

"Ten seconds," said the voice, echoing off the metal walls.

The two voices were going back and forth in a language that sounded like Spanish, seemingly oblivious to the noises coming from inside, and Cheyenne was thankful for that small blessing. She looked around for somewhere to hide, but the room was so sparse she could see no options.

"Five seconds."

She tried the door to the left of the computer, and the knob turned easily in her hand. It looked like some sort of closet.

A key scraped into the lock behind her.

"Database accessed."

Cheyenne pressed a few buttons, moving the entire file to her USB. Another hourglass appeared, and she prayed there was enough room.

The doorknob turned, and the door started to swing open.

The download completed, and Cheyenne jerked the flash drive out of the computer and lunged into the closet, pulling the door closed behind her just as a supply cart rolled into the room.

Her heart pounded in her ears, and she mentally kicked herself for thinking she could pull this off. She blamed the champagne for the irrational hubris that had gotten her into this mess. But now, she felt all too sober. She realized she was probably committing a federal crime just by being here, much less helping herself to protected patient information.

For five minutes, Cheyenne couldn't stop herself from shaking. She ran through the story in her head a million times, with slightly different iterations depending on who was waiting for her on the other side of the door. Then she realized that whoever had entered the room didn't seem to be looking for her or even know she was there. Her breathing slowed and her head began to clear. She heard the familiar, clumsy sound of a mop as it clanged repetitively into the metal shelves. The brief sense of relief she felt was quickly eclipsed by the knowledge that the cleaning crew would likely be heading to the closet next. And, regardless of their relatively low rung of the CSM totem pole, they would immediately know she didn't belong there.

Cheyenne fumbled in the dark until her hands reached the doorknob, then felt a lock. *Yes, there it was!* She turned the lock closed just seconds before one of the workers tried the door.

"Ay dios mio." A nervous female voice floated across the door to where Cheyenne stood frozen in the center of the closet. "How can we clean the room if the doors are locked?"

"Don't worry about it; it's just a closet." Her cohort, an older man, brushed off her concerns. "We'll get it next time."

The woman responded with a tirade of Spanish, Cheyenne picking up on only the occasional word or phrase.

"Maria, don't get your panties all in a wad. Who's even going to notice? No one ever comes in here, anyway. Consider it a blessing. We still got half the floor to clean, and it's already almost three thirty."

Cheyenne heard the woman continuing to mutter to herself in Spanish, the words becoming softer as she made her way toward the exit. Cheyenne waited a full two minutes after hearing the door close before she ventured out of the closet. She poked her head out into the hallway and, once she was sure the coast was clear, made her way toward the stairwell. Not until she was back in the car and riding toward the freeway did the gravity of what she had done hit her. She tried to pour herself some more champagne, but between her hands shaking and the rumbling of the car's engine, she couldn't aim for the glass. She gave up and drank straight from the bottle instead.

This time, when she finally leaned back on the headrest, her thoughts did not keep her awake.

"Miss Rose? Miss Rose, you're home."

Cheyenne sat up, disoriented and a little headachy. She smoothed her hair down and blinked a couple of times, trying to get her bearings.

"Thank you, Roger. I believe I might have nodded off for just a second."

"Miss Rose, you keep burning the candle at both ends, you're just gonna burn right out." He put the car in park and stepped out of the driver's side.

Cheyenne smiled. Roger said that to her at least once a week. But unlike the majority of her staff, he seemed genuine when he expressed his concern.

The door opened next to Cheyenne, and Roger stood with his hand extended and his eyes crinkling in a warm smile that reminded her of Santa Claus. He didn't have a family of his own that Cheyenne was aware of, and she had come to think of him as the father she never had.

"I know, Roger. Sorry to make you keep my crazy hours. One of these days I'm going to take a vacation."

"I'll believe it when I see it," Roger said. He trailed five or six feet behind her in the parking garage, carrying her work bag and her purse. He never left before she had made the trip across the parking garage to the elevator alone. And on late nights such as this one, he often escorted her the whole way. Secretly, she was happy he did this. She had covered stories about women getting jumped in places just like this. As much as she liked being on TV, she preferred being on her side of the story.

The elevator door opened, and she took her bags from him. "Thank you, Roger. See you at eight fifteen?"

He smiled and shook his head. "Whatever you say, Miss Rose. Whatever you say." His head was still moving slowly side-to-side as the elevator doors closed in front of him.

When they opened again, Cheyenne stepped off the elevator and unlocked the door to her penthouse apartment. As she walked inside, she was greeted by her kitchen MedScreen.

"Good morning, Miss Rose. Welcome home. We need to confirm your pill count for the Zoloft, please."

She pressed the two-way button and said, "I'm just getting in from work." She enunciated each word, glancing at the clock as she spoke. "It was kind of a late night."

"I see."

"I haven't taken my nighttime meds yet. I'll be one off."

"That's okay, we still need to get the pill count for your records. I'll make a note."

Cheyenne fished around in a drawer until she pulled out a pill bottle. "I have three pills left." She popped one in her mouth, swallowing it dry. "Now I have two."

"Okay." The woman looked down, writing something into a notebook. She looked up and smiled pleasantly. "Thank you, Miss Rose. Have a nice—night?"

Cheyenne felt her cheeks redden. "Thanks. Hey, how did you know I'd just gotten home, anyway?"

But the screen had already gone blank. Cheyenne idly waved a hand in front of the screen, then she crossed her eyes and stuck out her tongue. Convinced the woman was no longer watching her, she headed to her bedroom and collapsed onto the bed, not bothering to wash her face or even change out of her work clothes.

Hair and makeup would die if they saw me now, she thought, just seconds before falling into a deep but fitful sleep.

* * * * *

Cheyenne woke up at 6:57 on the dot, as she did every morning.

"Ugh," she moaned, reaching for the bottle of Motrin she kept on her bedside table. For a moment, it seemed like any other Saturday morning after too much champagne. Then she remembered her little excursion the night before.

"Oh, my—"

She crawled out of bed and made a beeline for the foyer, where her purse, shoes, and pantyhose lay crumpled in the corner. She rifled through her bag until she located the USB drive and ID chip, and the memories all came crashing back to her. So she had really done it. She had to admit, she was kind of impressed with herself. Granted, it was a terrible decision, but still. She kind of felt like a badass. But the high Cheyenne felt after her discovery only lasted a few seconds before she sunk back into the fog of her hangover.

She moved like a robot around her apartment, turning on the shower, putting in her contacts, and setting out her clothes for the day. Jeans and a button-down. Editing days were more laid back. Truth be told, she didn't even have to be there for this stage of the editing, but she liked seeing everything—what was cut, what was left in—and having input on the whole process. Part of it was her Type A personality, and part of it went back to her need to stay busy.

It was hard to believe this was her life now. She was disappointed at how unfulfilling her success often felt. She had everything she'd ever dreamt of and more. But it would all be forever tainted by the circumstances surrounding her rise to the top.

In the kitchen, she poured a bowl of Cheerios and leaned against the countertop, barely tasting the cereal. She closed her eyes and listened to the noises in the quiet: the hum of the refrigerator, the trash settling, a bird chirping just outside her window.

"Miss Rose?" A high-pitched, nasal voice forced its way into Cheyenne's thoughts, causing her to jump. She looked toward the voice in time to see her kitchen MedScreen light up. "Miss Rose? My name is Valerie, and I'm with the MedScreen program. I wanted to notify you of a change in your MedPlan."

Cheyenne put down her cereal bowl and pressed the input button. "Is anything wrong? I don't usually get a call from you guys in the morning."

"There's been a change," she repeated. "Given your, um, variable evening schedule, we've talked with your doctor. He'd like to move your medication administration to the morning." The woman smiled. "We believe it will result in a more predictable steady medication state."

Cheyenne blinked at the screen, taking a moment to process what the woman had said.

"Ma'am?"

She shrugged. "Fine with me." She dug around in her purse for her pill bottle. "Starting now?"

"Yes, ma'am."

"Okay. I'm going from two to one. I'll pick up the refill today after work."

"Very good, Miss Rose. Due to the change in schedule, I will be your new care coordinator. Again, my name is Valerie."

"Nice to meet you, Valerie. I guess I'll be seeing you tomorrow morning."

"Yes, see you then. Have a nice day." The screen went blank.

Cheyenne moved her cereal bowl to the sink and grabbed a bottle of water from the fridge. She heard Roger knock on the door and glanced at the clock on the microwave. She grinned. Eight fifteen, like clockwork.

She checked her reflection one last time in the foyer mirror, took a deep cleansing breath, then opened the door to another day.

CHAPTER 5
Then
February 3, 2023

Karl Buchner sat in the hotel bar, trying to remain inconspicuous as he drank a vodka martini and watched himself on the news. All flights were grounded for the night due to weather, so he was stuck in Washington at least until the morning.

His announcement at the press conference earlier that day was met with mixed reviews, and now it was up to the liberal media to put the right spin on things. If the idea wasn't embraced by the American people, then it was sure to fail. If it failed, he failed. Harris had made it very clear to him there would be no second chances. Where Monty was given four years to turn things around before being replaced, Karl would have two at the most. Time was running out.

It was a special form of torture for someone like Karl to watch himself give a speech on national television. Every stutter, every pause to check his notes made him cringe. He was glad he'd opted for the baseball cap tonight. At least his characteristic bald spot was covered, and there was a good chance he wouldn't be recognized.

"Do you believe this guy?"

It took a moment for Karl to realize the bartender was talking to him and another moment to realize he was talking *about* him. He shrugged and took a long gulp of his martini, hoping the guy would move along. No such luck.

"He actually thinks we would let some 1984 shit like that actually happen? Not in America, that's for damn sure."

"I'm sure there's more to it than that." Karl cleared his throat and risked a glance upward at the man, then immediately regretted it. The bartender easily had him by a hundred pounds and six inches. Oh well. He'd already opened his mouth so he might as well insert his foot. "It sounds like it might save money in the long run, doesn't it?"

"It ain't all about money, Richie Rich." The skinny, wrinkled woman to the right of him spoke up, her thinning hair barely moving as she turned to face him. "Or haven't you heard of human decency? The right to privacy?"

These were the arguments he'd expected. If he couldn't convince a couple of drunks in a bar, then how was he supposed to convince the rest of America? He took a deep breath. "But, at the rate we're going with spending, America's healthcare system will be equivalent to a third-world country's by the year 2027." He pulled out a napkin and began to sketch a line graph as their eyes glazed over. "This is not your grandchildren's problem, or even your children's. This is your problem in four short years." He stopped and checked himself. "Dr. Buchner just seems like he's trying to help." His voice trailed off as the two just stared at him. Then the bartender went about his business of pouring drinks, and the woman went about her business of drinking hers. He didn't know if he would consider that a win, but at least it wasn't a complete loss. Karl glanced back up at the TV screen, which had just gone from a clip of his speech to a young Fox News anchor.

"Good evening," she said before diving right into the night's leading story. "Former practicing physician and current chair of the United States Health and Finance Committee, Karl Buchner, made an announcement today that has shocked the nation, an announcement that has quickly earned him the nickname 'Big Brother' and has many people, Democrats and Republicans alike, up in arms about a perceived violation of privacy."

"Oh, geez," Karl grumbled, taking another gulp of his martini. He looked around him in the hopes of finding some solidarity and noticed a young blonde at the end of the bar on her phone. Normally, he wouldn't have given her another thought; she was definitely out of his league, but she was staring straight at him. She squinted in his direction, then nodded and said something into the phone. Her lips moved so quickly he couldn't make out what she was saying. He attempted what he thought was an inviting smile, but she had already looked away from him, pressing a finger into her right ear and concentrating on whatever was being said into her left.

"In his address," the anchor went on, "he cited the high medical noncompliance rate among certain socioeconomic groups as being a main driver of America's astronomical medical costs, costs that still plague this country despite aggressive healthcare reform that first began over a decade ago under the Obama administration and ultimately resulted in the initiation of the CSM program.

"Mr. Alexander Montgomery, former North Carolina senator and founder of the CSM program, joins us tonight to provide his thoughts on today's turn of events."

"You have got to be kidding me." Karl's outburst earned him a few curious glances from people sitting nearby, and he ducked his head, fuming. He hadn't seen this coming, not by a mile. The public loved Monty—trusted him, for whatever reason. He wasn't sure his initiative could survive if the disgruntled former politician was determined to bring it down.

The anchor continued, "Mr. Montgomery has been one of Dr. Buchner's loudest critics since he was supplanted by the doctor as head of the Health and Finance Committee just last year. Mr. Montgomery," she addressed him, "thank you for being here to give us your input on Dr. Buchner's recent announcement."

"Of course, Julie. Thank you for having me, and please, call me Monty." He flashed a toothy smile toward the camera.

"Alright, Monty. Let's cut straight to the chase here. In your opinion, what is Dr. Buchner trying to accomplish with this radical intervention?"

"As far as I'm concerned, this is Dr. Buchner's Hail Mary pass. He is probably getting pressure from above to make the money appear, and he's realizing how impossible it is to change an established system like American healthcare in one to two years. It's a marathon, not a sprint, but no one wants to accept that."

"What kind of problems do you see with the proposed system?"

"Julie, I'm a simple man." His eyes sparkled when he spoke. "But I know an invasion of privacy when I see one. If we let the government into our homes, where does it stop? First it's the MedScreens, then, next thing you know, it's twenty-four-hour surveillance. We absolutely cannot allow this to happen if we value our freedom." He looked straight into the camera. "I know that Americans value their freedom."

Karl motioned a female bartender over.

"Another martini?"

"Make it a double. And can you turn that shit off?" He glanced toward the end of the bar, but the blonde was gone. "Typical," he mumbled.

The woman waved her hand in front of the screen a few times until she came to ESPN. She looked over her shoulder at him. "Basketball okay?"

Before he could answer, Karl saw a light bulb go off as she recognized him from the news.

"Hey, you're Big Brother!" She motioned toward the television with her thumb.

Karl shook his head. "It's not me. I guess I must just look like him."

"No, it's you, alright." She wrinkled her nose. "You got that creepy mole on your chin." Other people were starting to look their way, and the background chatter in the bar had died down.

Karl's hand flew to his chin, and he self-consciously planted a finger over the birthmark. He didn't dare look around, but he didn't have to. He could feel the eyes on him. The morbid curiosity.

He threw a fifty-dollar bill on the bar and walked out as quickly as he could, not looking back. He was on the elevator and had just allowed himself a sigh of relief when a hand jutted through the closing doors.

As the doors pinged back open, Karl closed his eyes and prepared for a barrage of questions.

"Going up?" Her voice was sultry and so quiet he almost didn't hear what she said.

He opened his eyes.

It was the woman from the bar. Up close, she looked like she couldn't be more than twenty-five. She wore a beige tank top tucked into a snug, black pencil skirt and carried a matching blazer draped over her arm. Her collarbones jutted out at the base of her long neck, and Karl fought back the urge to reach out and touch them. She wore her blonde hair in a bob with thick bangs that accentuated her huge green eyes and made her look even younger.

Karl held his hand in the doorway as she walked onto the elevator. He wondered what it would take for him to land a girl like that. The doors closed, and she studied the numbers.

"Oh, twenty-three. Me, too!"

For a moment, Karl thought she was talking about her age, but seconds later, the elevator dinged and the doors opened on the twenty-third floor. Karl let the woman off first, but instead of making her way down the hall, she just stood there, digging through her purse.

"Oh, darn. I think I lost my key."

Karl sent a sympathetic nod her way as he stepped off the elevator and headed toward his room. Then he heard footsteps behind him.

"Would you mind if I—if I used your phone? To call down for a key?"

"Sure." Karl tried to hide his astonishment. "I'm afraid the room's a mess. I wasn't supposed to be staying tonight."

"I'm sure it's fine." The woman sidled up next to him and put a hand lightly on his shoulder. "I'm Tracy, by the way."

Karl stared straight ahead, focusing on walking. He let himself into his room and gestured for her to go first.

"Mind if I use the ladies'? I don't think I can hold it one more second."

"Whatever you need." Karl headed into the room and began to loosen his tie, then thought better of it. He didn't want Tracy to get the wrong idea. He opened the mini-fridge and located the bourbon. He grabbed two, just in case.

He was just emptying the first mini-bottle into a glass when Tracy came out of the bathroom wearing nothing but a nude lace bra and matching panties.

Karl's mind jumped to the first thing that made sense. "Wait a minute, are you a—"

"Prostitute?" She laughed, not at all offended. "No, Dr. Buchner. I'm just someone who's very excited to meet you."

CHAPTER 6
Now
June 16, 2030

Cheyenne couldn't help but laugh as she watched from backstage as Isabella sat reviewing her lines on set, oblivious to Danny trying to corral their two boys. Her lips moved ever so slightly as she practiced her inflection, her facial expressions. Cheyenne had asked them to come early to prep—something she had never done before—and had tried to make it clear this was an important show. And she had asked, in so many words, that Isabella take the lead. Isabella was reliable, predictable. Danny was a loose cannon.

The show's opening music played, and Isabella ran her hands over her middle, smoothing her tunic over snug pants. Cheyenne frowned. What were the people thinking backstage? She looked like she had barely gotten the button snapped. But it was much too late to change it now. Cheyenne downed her drink and set the glass to the side. As she made her entrance onto the TV set, the audience burst into applause.

"Welcome to the fourth installment of *Reid it and Weep*. I'm here with Danny and Isabella Reid and their two sons, Ridge and Hendrix." Cheyenne settled into the cozy, cream-colored loveseat opposite them and smiled. "Let's get right to it, shall we?"

Isabella smiled back. "Sure."

"When we left off last time, you were just telling me about your experience at your local CSM. I believe it's fair to say it was a good one."

"The best." Isabella nodded and smiled again. "It was our first time stepping foot in the door, and I was skeptical at first, but we were treated with nothing but respect the entire time."

Cheyenne shot Isabella a look. She was going to have to loosen up if this segment was going to make the cut. Right now, she sounded like a robot. "So everyone was nice and accommodating. That's wonderful, but I'm sure everyone has been wondering—I know *I* have—how you felt about the quality of the medical care that Ridge received?"

Isabella cleared her throat and nodded. She took a deep breath before speaking again.

"Having never been through surgery myself, I assumed Ridge would have a lot of pain and that it would take a while to feel like himself again." She glanced at her son, who sat listening with his hands folded in his lap. "But the surgery was done utilizing a state-of-the-art robotic video assist procedure. His incision was no bigger than the length of my pinkie." She held up her finger as a visual. Much better.

"I understand that you never met the doctor who operated on your son."

"That's correct." Isabella nodded. The corners of her mouth twitched in the beginnings of another smile, but she maintained a straight face.

"Was that strange for you?"

"Not really."

A murmur went through the crowd. "Well, I mean, at first it did seem a little weird, but the surgery was explained to us by someone very knowledgeable on the procedure—a consent specialist—who was able to answer all of our questions. The surgeons spend all their time in the operating room, and there are medical assistants who do the other tasks necessary in and around the time of surgery, such as getting consent, prepping the patient, and writing the procedure note afterward. It's so much more efficient than the old way of doing things."

"Mmm-hmm." Cheyenne acknowledged Isabella's argument, then her eyes took on a mischievous glow, and she leaned in closer to Isabella. "I'm curious. What would you two have said to the doctor who operated on Ridge if you had been able to meet him?"

"Well..." Isabella looked at Danny for the first time since the interview started. Tears pooled in her eyes. "We both feel very indebted to him or her. I'm sure removing an appendix is probably a routine procedure for a surgeon, but the whole experience was very traumatic for us." Her voice trembled, and Danny reached out to place a hand on her leg. She took a shaky breath before continuing. "It provided us with a little peace of mind to know that Ridge was being taken care of at a good facility by excellent physicians regardless of our...financial status."

"What would you say if I told you that I've tracked down Ridge's surgeon," Cheyenne paused, allowing a few dramatic seconds to pass before adding, "and he's here with us today?"

Isabella put both of her hands to her mouth, and the tears fell. Danny wrapped an arm around her.

"His name is Dr. Hamilton Walker, and he is very excited to meet you and your family. And actually, I'm meeting him for the first time as well." She winked at the boys. "Dr. Walker, come on out!" Cheyenne motioned toward the door that led onto the set from backstage and started to clap. The audience followed suit.

Danny and Isabella stood, prompting their boys to do the same. Isabella leaned down to whisper into her sons' ears. Ridge straightened up and held his hands at his sides, clenching and unclenching his fists. Hendrix moved behind Isabella, peeking out to watch the activity from his safe place.

Dr. Walker did not disappoint. The sound of his quick, confident footsteps preceded his appearance onstage, and the audience fell silent without any direction to do so. Then, the backstage door opened, and the doctor came into view. He carried himself like the tall, handsome surgeon that he was. His otherwise dark hair was graying a little above the ears, and he wore it in a no-nonsense crew cut. His electric blue eyes made everything else in the room seem black and white. Then he smiled, revealing dimples. Cheyenne's weakness.

"Dr. Walker, this is Ridge Reid." Her cheeks were a warm pink as she stood up. She caught her toe on the carpet and pitched toward him for a terrible moment before righting herself. She beamed at the doctor then gestured toward the boy.

The doctor gazed into her eyes a moment longer than necessary before turning his attention to Ridge. Cheyenne caught her breath. She remembered that feeling so well. The giddiness, the weightlessness. The feeling that everything was about to change. She placed a tentative hand on Dr. Walker's shoulder and led him toward center stage, where the Reids all stood at attention.

Isabella watched them with a steady, unblinking gaze until they stopped in front of her son. Then she knelt down and spoke again in Ridge's ear.

Cheyenne spoke to the doctor again, ignoring the cameras. "You performed an emergency appendectomy on Ridge two years ago and saved his life."

Dr. Walker once more tore his gaze away from Cheyenne. He walked right up to the boy, kneeled down in front of him, and said, "Hi, Ridge. It's a pleasure to meet you."

Ridge responded to the doctor's authoritative voice by standing a little straighter. He held his trembling hand out, and Dr. Walker gripped it and shook. Then he stood up and clapped Ridge on the back twice. The child gave him a huge smile.

"And these are his parents, Danny and Isabella."

The surgeon then greeted Danny. "Sir." Another handshake. He looked at Isabella. "Ma'am."

Before he could extend his hand to her, she collapsed into his arms. "I'm sorry, I'm sorry." She was half laughing and half crying. "I don't know what's gotten into me. I'm so sorry."

He stood still for a moment then placed his hands on her upper back in a half-embrace. He didn't speak, just held her and waited for her to let go first.

Finally, Isabella pulled away from the doctor, wiping her eyes. "I had no idea I was going to do that. That's so embarrassing."

Everyone in the audience and onstage laughed, feeling that they were part of something meaningful and important. Feeling thankful for their own good health and their children's.

Isabella hung back, a peaceful air about her that Cheyenne had never seen. The hard edge Cheyenne had assumed was just part of her personality was gone, replaced by a softness that was very becoming.

Cheyenne stood back and allowed the moment to unfold without interfering, and when the magic had dissipated, she invited everyone to take their seats.

"That was truly something. Dr. Walker, I'm sure that was out of the ordinary for you."

"Please, call me Hamm."

"Hamm." Her lips closed over his name in a way that was both sensual and subdued.

"And yes. With the system the way it is now, it's easy to forget how validating it can be to hear from patients. It's why we do what we do, after all. To help people."

"Do you feel that's a deficiency of the system?"

Hamm paused a moment before answering. "I feel there's been a necessary give-and-take. I don't believe at the end of the day there was much of a choice in the matter."

For the rest of the interview, Cheyenne was on autopilot. She could have done the interview in her sleep. Judging by how distracted she felt in Dr. Walker's presence, it was a good thing.

And it appeared Isabella was right there with her. She watched closely as the doctor used his hands to explain his surgical technique. He had a special suture tie that he used on every patient and swore he would recognize if he ever operated on the same patient twice. He sheepishly admitted that he called it the “Hamm Hock” because its triangular shape resembled the piece of meat by the same name, and the audience exploded with laughter.

Cheyenne liked the way he appeared shy and confident at the same time, and she relished her time in the interview seat. Dr. Walker made deliberate eye contact with her and grinned as she phrased each question, making her feel as if what she was saying was the most interesting and profound thing he had ever heard.

For the first time, it wasn’t Cheyenne that the audience found their eyes glued to. She was a professional, and she used that to her advantage. Regardless of whatever personal feelings she was experiencing, she was still able to use Dr. Walker to get her message across, loud and clear: the CSMs are safe, they are good for the country, and they need our support.

And when the taping was complete, the studio sat in complete silence as if waiting—hoping—for Hamm to say something else. Finally, when it became clear the interview was over, the guests slowly stood up from their seats and milled about, waiting to be told to leave.

“Well.” Cheyenne felt her cheeks flush once more as she addressed Hamm for the first time with the cameras off. He was easily a foot taller than she, and their height difference was noticeable even when they were sitting down. “I would be honored if you would join me for the wrap party. I feel like there’s so much more to discuss. You can only go so deep on national television.” She placed a hand lightly on Hamm’s arm and smiled up at him invitingly.

“Thank you for the offer, but I should probably get going.” Hamm didn’t budge from his seat. “Early day tomorrow.”

“I insist you stay for one drink. I promise I won’t keep you out too late.” Cheyenne stood up as if the matter was settled. “Even surgeons need to have fun every once in a while.”

"Touché." He laughed, tugging absentmindedly at his ear lobe. "Okay, I'll stay for a drink on one condition: that the Reids grace us with their presence as well."

Cheyenne let out her breath in a huff, feeling like a spoiled teenager but not caring. The Reids never stayed after the taping.

"I don't know," Isabella said. "I've got an early appointment tomorrow, and it really can't be rescheduled."

"One drink?" Cheyenne knew her eyes conveyed her desperation, but she couldn't help herself.

"Okay," Isabella said. "We'll stay for one drink."

* * * * *

"So let me get this straight." Cheyenne was on her third glass of wine, and things seemed to be going really well. Hamm had only had one beer, but he had finished that an hour ago and didn't seem to be in any rush to leave. Most of the staff had gone already, so it was just the six of them in the deserted greenroom. "You do ten surgeries in a day? I can't even answer ten emails in a day."

He tilted his head toward her and smiled. His expression said he didn't believe her for one second. "Obviously you're doing something right, Miss Rose."

"Please, call me Cheyenne."

"Okay, Cheyenne. Back to your question, the system really is remarkable. Like you said, Mrs. Reid," he turned to look at Isabella, "it's amazing someone didn't think of it sooner. As surgeons, all we want to do is operate. All the other stuff, the busy work, was the bane of our existence in the old system. Now, I scrub in, someone tells me what surgery I'm doing, and I do it. Someone else writes it up. It's a beautiful thing! And so far, it's looking like there are far fewer medical errors than in the old system. We still need a little more data to say for sure."

"And it sounds like the CSMs are raking it in," Danny said. He, too, was a bit more talkative after a couple of beers.

"Let's just say they're holding their own," Hamm said.

"Think about how many jobs the system has created." Cheyenne was always looking for the angle. "The consent teams and the documentation specialists—these are jobs that didn't exist in the old system. They were just done by already overworked physicians."

"Exactly. Physicians who should have been doing what they were trained to do, not a bunch of scut work." As if sensing a presence, Hamm looked down to see Hendrix staring silently up at him. "Well, hey there kiddo. What's up?"

Hendrix didn't say anything, just stood looking at Hamm and rubbing his eyes intermittently. He hiccupped twice, never taking his eyes off the doctor.

"Someone's got the hiccups."

"Someone's *always* got the hiccups these days." Isabella rolled her eyes. "I tell him to eat more slowly, but he doesn't listen."

"Hmm. Those eyes are pretty swollen, too, little guy. Have you been to the doctor about that?"

Hendrix shook his head no, letting out another little hiccup.

"Should we take him? We've been giving him Benadryl, and it seemed to be helping." Isabella's eyes darkened. "We just assumed he has allergies like his daddy."

"That's probably all it is." Hamm didn't sound convinced. "I would get him checked out just to make sure."

Alarmed, Cheyenne looked at Isabella, whose face had gone white. The energy in the room had been sucked out in an instant, replaced with a sickening sense of foreboding.

Hamm reached into his wallet and pulled out a business card, handing it to her. "Just come by the office. We'll take care of him." Then, turning back to Hendrix, he said, "Would you like to come visit my friends at work?"

Hendrix nodded yes.

"It's settled then. You'll bring Hendrix in next week?" Hamm looked at his watch. "Good grief, how'd you let me stay here so late, Miss Rose? I thought we had an agreement."

"It's Cheyenne." She flashed him a smile, trying to shake the feeling of dread. "And I'm sorry. I lost track of the time, too. I hope you don't have to work too hard tomorrow."

"I always work too hard." He took her right hand in both of his and looked deep into her eyes. "But we must do this again. I forgot how nice it could be to share a lady's company."

"Well, I think it's time for the Reids to be going," Isabella interrupted, taking each of her children by the hand and heading toward the door. "Thank you so much for having us, Cheyenne." Then, remembering herself, she slowed and half-turned back toward Cheyenne and Hamm. "And Dr. Walker, we can never thank you enough."

"You can thank me by bringing Hendrix by the office next week, Mrs. Reid."

She nodded, her eyes fluttering closed for a moment before meeting his gaze. "I will. Thanks." She herded her family out of the greenroom and toward the exit.

CHAPTER 7
Then
April 10, 2023

Karl woke up to the sound of running water and grinned before opening his eyes. The sunshine peeked through the blinds into his bedroom, a streak of light falling across his face, temporarily blinding him. He rolled over and saw the covers pulled back on the other side of the bed, *her* side of the bed for the last two months, and enjoyed his favorite time of day: when he realized that Tracy wasn't a dream. She was actually here, with him. By choice.

He stretched and padded his way toward the bathroom but stopped short of the door. He could hear her whispering, and something in her voice stopped him short. He strained to make out the words.

"Now? Are you sure?"

There was a pause.

"Okay, but we only have one shot at this. Everything we did to get here..."

Karl hated himself for his insecurities. For not trusting her. He cleared his throat and pushed the swinging bathroom door inward. A cloud of steam enveloped him. "Morning, hon." He avoided eye contact, guilt washing over him like the steam.

Tracy had already ended the phone call and looked at him with wide, innocent eyes. "Mom says hi." She dropped her robe and stepped into the walk-in shower, her back to him, humming softly as she lathered her hair. He pulled off his t-shirt and pajama pants and opened the door.

"Oh!" Tracy wrapped her arms protectively around her breasts. "You scared me."

"Sorry, sweetheart. I was just thinking I would join you." He felt exposed as he stood outside the shower, her body blocking his entrance.

"Sorry, not today. I have to hurry. Big meeting." She turned her back once more and finished her shower. A few minutes later, she opened the door wide and plucked her towel from a hook on the wall. "It's all yours," she said, stepping out onto the shower mat to dry off. He was able to admire her pink, post-shower skin for a moment before she wrapped the towel around herself and moved to the sink.

Karl stepped into the shower by himself, immediately scalded by the water. "How do you stand it so hot in here?" he called out as he turned down the temperature, but Tracy had already left the bathroom.

Fifteen minutes later, Karl stood helplessly in his closet, trying to pick out a tie.

"Here, wear this one. It brings out your eyes." Tracy held a bold blue and red striped tie to his chest. Her silk robe was partially open and gave him view of the Tiffany necklace she had picked out for their two-month anniversary, plus a tiny glimpse of what was underneath.

He took the tie from her and wrapped it around his neck.

"Pookie?" She stood behind him now, her hands on his shoulders and her eyes trying to make contact with his in the mirror.

"Mmm-hmm?" He half-listened, struggling with his tie.

"My cousin, Daniel—you've heard me talk about him, right? Anyway, he's been following your career and really admires you."

Karl stopped what he was doing and looked at her in the mirror. "Oh yeah?"

"Yeah." She turned him around to face her. "So, he has a business degree, and he really wants to work in healthcare, like you. He has some interesting ideas and wanted to get your opinion on some of them. I think he's hoping to get his foot in the door."

Karl turned to face Tracy. "I don't really have any say as to—"

Tracy stepped back, pulling her robe tightly over her chest. "You know, he's the only reason I even knew who you were that night at the hotel bar. He's the one who talked me into introducing myself. He just wants to meet you. Can't you spare fifteen minutes to talk to him?"

Karl felt her pulling away from him and desperately wanted to get that closeness back. "Sure, babe. That's no problem. As long as he knows—"

"He knows." She released her hold on her robe, took his face in her hands, and pecked his cheek before rushing out of the closet. "I'll let him know," she called out over her shoulder. "He's going to be so excited!"

Karl sighed, turned back to the mirror, and resumed work on his tie, shaking his head. He smiled like a schoolboy at his reflection. He could never say no to Tracy. Why would he ever want to?

He would have never thought he could be with a girl like Tracy, but here she was. He would do whatever it took to keep her.

* * * * *

Karl waited impatiently at the restaurant bar. It was a nearly six, and he had been there for twenty minutes already. He still hadn't seen anyone that matched Tracy's vague description: tallish with dark hair. At least, no anyone that seemed to be looking for him. He was becoming annoyed that he had left work early for some kid who didn't even have the decency to show up on time.

"You Karl Buchner?"

Karl looked up to see the bartender who had served him a beer when he first sat down.

"Who's asking?"

The guy shrugged and dropped a paper bag in front of Karl. "Do I look like your freakin' secretary?" He had turned his back and was walking toward the other end of the bar, ending the conversation before Karl even had time to ask a follow-up question.

He turned his attention to the bag. Inside was a nondescript, black cell phone. It started ringing just as Karl picked it up, prompting him to look over his shoulder into the restaurant behind him. Was someone watching him?

The phone went silent after a few rings then almost immediately started up again. He flipped it open and put it to his ear.

"To your right, there's a hallway," an unfamiliar voice told him. "Down that hall, there's a door leading to the alley. Go out that door. I'll be waiting for you."

Karl heard a click, and he slowly lowered the phone from his ear. He glanced to his right for a split-second then stared straight ahead, processing what he had seen. There was a hallway, and he thought he had seen the outline of a door at the far end. He took a deep breath and emptied his beer. He was nervous and excited, the excited part winning out by a minuscule fraction. Even though he knew he would probably regret walking down that hallway, he actually found himself considering it. He felt a smile creeping onto his face.

He threw a ten-dollar bill onto the bar and stood up, draining his beer. He started to set the bottle down, then thought better of it. Better take it with him. He put the phone in his front pocket, glanced around the restaurant one last time, and headed toward the door.

Once outside, Karl found himself on a small landing. Three steps led down to street level. He squinted in both directions, but saw no one. He turned around to go back inside, realizing too late there was no door handle on the outside of the door. He was locked out.

He shook his head and turned to go down the stairs. He had just started down the alley toward the cross street when he heard a car drive up behind him. He stopped, trying to get the courage to turn around. The car stopped, too. He heard a window roll down, then a voice.

"Dr. Buchner, I presume? Please, join me."

Karl slowly turned around to see a dark sedan with tinted windows. The rear window facing him was rolled down several inches, and he could just make out a shock of dark hair inside the car.

"Daniel."

The man opened his car door in response, and Karl stepped inside.

"Phone." Daniel held his hand out, and Karl dropped his phone into his palm without a second thought. Daniel turned it off and placed it on the seat between them. "I've been watching you quite a while, Dr. Buchner. Truth be told, I nudged Tracy into your path that fateful night a couple of months ago, but she doesn't really know why. We think it's better that way."

"We?"

Daniel ignored Karl and continued. "I have a financial proposition for you, a way to make your little MedScreen project show a billion dollar profit in the first two years. *Profit*. But first, I will share the ground rules with you."

"The ground rules?"

"What we discuss in this meeting is confidential. If you say anything to anyone—anything to anyone—I will find out. And it will be very, very bad for you."

"Okay…" Karl was starting to feel claustrophobic. He slowly reached out for the door handle, then heard the lock engage. He dropped his hand back into his lap as the car crept through the alley and entered traffic.

"You will employ a cadre of employees whose sole purpose it is to maintain the confidentiality of our agreement, and you will do what it takes to justify their employment on paper."

"I, uh, don't think I—"

"In turn, I will make you one of the most powerful men in America."

CHAPTER 8
Now
June 25, 2030

Cheyenne hadn't been inside a CSM hospital for two years, but the tile floors, the calming music, and the cheery, yellow walls brought her right back. Then the stabbing pain in her chest started, and she felt like it was all just yesterday when he had taken his last breath and her entire world had crumbled around her for the second time in her short life. But she was here for a different reason today. She had stopped at the front desk, had gotten directions to the children's ward, and now stood outside Hendrix's room, clutching a bouquet of balloons and trying to gather herself before knocking on the door. She wasn't sure what to expect, wasn't sure how she would handle it.

"You here to see Hendrix?" A nurse appeared at Cheyenne's side. "I'm heading in to do his vitals. Come on in."

"Thank you. I—they may not be expecting me."

The nurse nodded and winked at her, then knocked on the door. "Time for vitals, Mr. Hendrix, and you have a visitor!"

"Cool, who is it?" The tiny voice floated toward them.

"It's me, buddy," Cheyenne said, stepping around the door frame. "It's so good to see you." She was careful to keep the smile on her face as she took him in. He was alone in the room, his tiny body impossibly small against the hospital bed. Both arms lay straight out beside him and were connected to IV tubing. An enormous machine stood on one side of his bed, churning and beeping as it funneled liquid into and out of his body. A MedScreen was positioned at the foot of his bed, and a red line scanned his body from head to toe in a continuous repetition.

He followed her gaze. "Pretty cool, huh?"

"Yeah, Hendrix. It's really cool. It's awesome." She'd never seen a dialysis machine, but she knew what it was immediately. Why hadn't Isabella said anything about this?

"I got the candy and the toys. Thanks."

"Sure," she said.

Everything had happened so quickly. The day he went to Hamm's office for blood work, they'd seen something so abnormal he was sent straight to the CSM, and he had been here ever since. Cheyenne had not been invited to come see him, but she couldn't stay away any longer.

"Cheyenne." Isabella stood in the doorway, holding a milkshake. Her hair was pulled back into a messy ponytail and her clothes were wrinkled. She looked like she hadn't changed clothes or slept in days.

"Hi, Isabella." Cheyenne felt ridiculous holding the balloons but didn't know what else to do with them. "I just wanted to come by and let you all know I'm thinking of you."

"We know." Isabella looked pointedly at the ostentatious gifts Cheyenne had sent daily since Hendrix was admitted. "We appreciate the gesture, Cheyenne, but it's really not necessary."

Cheyenne felt her cheeks burn as she took in the balloons, the stuffed animals, and the enormous gift baskets. "I just wanted to do something."

Isabella had moved to Hendrix's side and was feeding him the milkshake through a straw. "We're just trying to figure out *life* right now, Cheyenne."

Cheyenne nodded. They stood in silence for a moment while Hendrix sucked at the straw.

"And Danny and Ridge?" Cheyenne finally asked. "How are they?"

"They're fabulous. Really great. We all are."

Cheyenne took a step backward, startled by the anger in the other woman's voice. When Isabella scowled up at her, it was with a face that had aged ten years in ten days. Shadows had settled beneath her eye sockets, wrinkles blanketed her forehead, and her eyes were completely empty.

Cheyenne let go of the balloons and they floated to the ceiling. She backed out of the room, mumbling a quick goodbye to Hendrix, and practically ran to the elevator. She didn't fully breathe until she had stepped out of the building and onto the curb. It was only four thirty, but with the sun hidden behind a huge storm cloud, it might as well have been eight or nine. She gulped in the muggy air that always seemed to come before a big rainstorm until her breathing had evened out.

She made her way to her car, telling herself it wasn't personal. That Isabella was dealing with her grief in her own way. That there was no right way to face your own child's mortality.

She told herself not to go to that place, that nothing productive would come of it, but she was already on her way. She gripped the steering wheel and tears rolled down her face as the memories came rushing in. Watching them turn off the machines. Watching his skin mottle and his legs twitch. Just a reflex, they told her. Then that terrible moment at the end, second-guessing everything. Begging to take it back.

She hadn't been able to stop it then, and she couldn't now. All the gift baskets in the world wouldn't change what the Reids were going through, what they were in for.

She turned on her blinker and pulled into a gas station just as the rain began to fall. She bought a twist-top bottle of wine and had already opened it by the time she got back to her car.

CHAPTER 9
Then
May 3, 2025

Karl strode into the boardroom, and everyone stood to acknowledge his arrival. *Damn, that never gets old*, he thought. He took a moment to look at the faces around the table. It was the same room in which he had sat—cowered, if he was being completely honest—four years prior when he had first been promoted to the head of the Health and Finance Committee. At that time, he hadn't known anyone except Monty, and Monty absolutely despised him.

My, how the tides had turned. He was sitting at the head of the table, and everyone was reporting to *him*. It was intoxicating.

After the meeting was called to order and they had reviewed the old business, Karl turned to the man immediately to his right. "Bennett, catch everyone up."

"My pleasure, Dr. Buchner." Bennett pushed his thick glasses up his angled nose and tapped his finger several times on a screen he held with shaking hands.

"Today, Bennett."

"Yes, here it is." He cleared his throat and placed the device on the table in front of him, his hands now gripping the edge of the table. He stared straight down at his personal screen, despite the fact that the electronic content was now displayed at eye level for everyone to see. "Dr. Buchner's MedScreen program has reduced healthcare spending by twenty percent—much more than projected. The program was recently approved for use with a much wider range of diagnoses, and the screens are projected to be in nine out of ten homes by the end of the fiscal year." Bennett glanced up then bowed his head again to continue shuffling through his presentation. "All proceeds have been funneled right back into the CSM program, either for research, building new centers, or supplementing the purchase of new MedScreens." Now he looked up from his papers and grinned. "The CSMs are functioning one hundred percent on their own. No government money is being used to help the centers provide care. It's unprecedented."

Karl looked around the room at the nodding heads and looks of approval, mentally patting himself on the back. It was once more the golden age of healthcare in America, and, at least on paper, it was because of Karl's MedScreen initiative.

However, even in the wake of his colossal success, he couldn't seem to get away from Alexander Montgomery. The arrogant prick had dug his heels in deeper with each of Karl's accomplishments, trying his best to vilify him in the media and casting a shadow over his career that Karl couldn't seem to shake. He had run out of ideas to try and shut Monty up, so today was about swallowing his pride and offering up the proverbial olive branch, as much as it sickened him.

Karl cleared his throat. "Alexander, you're probably wondering why I asked you here today."

"Monty," he corrected.

"The CSM program has really blossomed in the last year or two, and the number of centers is becoming too much to be managed under the umbrella of the Health and Finance Committee."

"No shit," Monty muttered under his breath.

Karl ignored him. "You have continued to stay relevant by staying in the media spotlight, even though it seems your agenda has mostly been to defame me."

Monty scoffed at that, glancing around the room as if looking for someone to laugh with him. Everyone looked down at their notes or toward the door. One man reached for his water glass, noticed it was empty, and took a sip anyway.

Karl continued, "I'd like to bring you on in a new position, Director of the Centers for Standardized Medicine. You would take over responsibility for the day-to-day workings of the CSMs." Karl paused, swallowing hard and forcing a smile. "I could think of no one better qualified for the position."

Monty's body had stilled, and he leaned forward, cocking his head a little to the right. The two men stared at one another. No one spoke.

Monty checked himself, leaning back in his chair and folding his arms behind his head, his impressive size exaggerated even more than usual. "So, you need me back, huh?"

Karl was silent.

"Requested me personally."

"You're the best person for the job." Karl could tell Monty was pleased at that.

He nodded. "Of course I am. I know the CSMs in and out. Better than you. Better than anybody. I've got some ideas that'll blow your mind, as long as you're not afraid to get a little dirt under your pretty fingernails."

Karl clenched his jaw and stared Monty down for a few long seconds before responding. "Of course you do. They were wrong to ever squeeze you out. That's why I'm asking you back. I hope it's not too late."

Monty seemed satisfied with that. "How much?"

Karl paused. "Enough."

Monty studied Karl's face then nodded slowly. "Benefits?"

"Same as before."

Neither Karl nor Monty moved a muscle. The room was silent except for the occasional sound of a page turning or a throat clearing. Finally, Monty opened his mouth to speak.

"Send me the contract."

* * * * *

"I still don't know if I completely understand you, Mr. Bradford." Karl walked briskly down the hall away from the boardroom with the phone gripped tightly in his hand, feeling his heart constrict in his chest. He wasn't sure whether the alarming sensation was from the uncharacteristic amount of exercise he was getting or just a sense of impending doom. Ever since delivering on his initial promise, Daniel had made more and more demands, demands which Karl was in no position to ignore.

Daniel now had an official title within the CSM organization and was calling practically all the shots behind the scenes. However, this request was unusual, even for Daniel. Karl couldn't figure out the end game.

"You don't need to understand right now, Karl. You will soon enough."

"So, what now?" Karl was starting to feel like he might vomit. He glanced around for the nearest bathroom.

"You address the confidentiality issues—we're talking system-wide control of all medical information, accessible on a need-to-know basis, only. Need. To. Know. Then, we embark upon phase two, and you stand to make a significant amount of money for your…country." The way the man said it, as if the word insulted him, left no question in Karl's mind what he thought of Karl. A puppet. A pawn. The man must not know what it felt like to command the attention of some of the most influential men in America. To be hailed as a miracle-worker everywhere he went. No, money wasn't his objective at all. It was never about money.

"Well?" Daniel was growing impatient.

"Fine. I'll figure out a way to deal with the medical records," Karl said. "I give you my word. You just make sure things move forward as planned. Now more than ever, it's important that we maintain our momentum."

"I could not agree more, Dr. Buchner. Could not agree more."

CHAPTER 10
Now
June 29, 2030

Cheyenne glanced up just in time to see Hamm approach the hostess stand at the 42nd Street Oyster Bar. Her heart sped up as she watched his lips move, then his eyes follow the direction the hostess pointed to Cheyenne's table.

She took a gulp of her wine and stood to greet him, hand extended. "Dr. Walker. Thank you for coming."

"Hamm." He took her hand but instead of shaking it, brought it to his lips.

Heat rose from her chest toward her face, and she was glad she had chosen a modest, high-neck sleeveless dress.

"Something to drink?"

"Don't mind if I do."

They settled into the booth and ordered dinner. Conversation flowed as freely as the wine. Their knees touched every once in a while and neither pulled away. Before long, it became intentional, their legs intertwined and their eyes locked as their conversation became more suggestive. Cheyenne took a long sip of wine, exposing her neck in a way that made her feel like a Playboy model. Then she pressed her lips together and released them, seeing his eyes go there like she knew they would. "So."

"So." Hamm took her in like he was starved for her. "We'll do this again, Miss Rose."

"Cheyenne."

"Soon." He stood up and offered his arm.

Oddly pleased and also disappointed he wasn't going to try to extend the evening, Cheyenne couldn't shake the feeling that she'd forgotten something.

"I'm only sorry you beat me to it," he said. "I did want to approach you, but you're oddly intimidating for such a tiny lady."

Oh yeah. She had asked him here for a specific reason. Cheyenne stopped walking and turned to him, placing her other hand on his forearm.

"This is me." She nodded toward the car as Roger pulled up to the curb in front of the restaurant, right on cue. "Before we part ways, I do have a favor to ask."

"Anything." He took a step closer, pressing her back against the car door.

"I went to visit Hendrix in the CSM. Isabella—she's angry, and she's freezing me out. I know he's got everything there he could possibly need medically, but I also know they're struggling at home."

He hesitated, the amorous look clearing from his eyes. "I can't talk about my patients, Cheyenne."

"I know. I'm not asking you to. I just want to make sure they're taken care of. Those boys…they're special. I can't explain it. I just—I just want to know that they're okay."

"They are pretty special." He slipped his arms around her waist but looked uncertain.

She leaned into him. "I'll have someone contact your office and set up a direct deposit. The money can go toward anything—childcare, time off work, someone to clean the house, whatever helps. Just don't tell her it's from me."

"She'll know."

Cheyenne shrugged. "Even if she knows deep down, as long as she can pretend…she'll take it."

They stood in silence for a few moments. Cheyenne closed her eyes and focused on his solid chest and on his arms surrounding her like a life preserver.

"It's not you; it's her," he murmured.

"Hmm?" Cheyenne gazed up at Hamm.

"Isabella. It's obvious when she looks at you, talks about you. She feels she was meant for greater things than life handed her."

Cheyenne nodded. She knew that feeling, that burning for something more. “Ambition can be a dangerous thing.”

Hamm put his fingers under her chin and tilted it upward. The kiss was at first tentative and then assured, forceful and tender, hot, yet strangely chilling. It left her wanting far more.

CHAPTER 11
Then
November 13, 2025

"It's another great day in the CSM!" Dr. Aaron Isaacs burst through the operating room door with his rear end after scrubbing in. He held his hands up in the air, arms bent at the elbows, as water dripped down his forearms. "Okay, what are we doing here?"

"Right liver lobectomy." The documentation specialist, Barry, answered him from his seat on the far side of the operating room.

Dr. Isaacs' scrub nurse held out the sterile gown for him to slip into. He put on his sterile gloves. The ritual that had once felt so tedious was now second nature. He would have felt out of sorts without it.

"Indication?"

"HCC." Hepatocellular carcinoma.

"Staging?"

"Stage one."

Dr. Isaacs smiled. It hadn't spread. If they could get this one spot in the liver, the patient would be cured. Damn, he loved his job. Ever since he had joined the CSM, he got to do even more surgeries and less of the busy work that used to be the bane of his existence. Now, that was Barry's job.

He looked around. There was a nurse anesthetist at the head of the bed. His scrub nurse, Rachel, to his right. Barry sat across the table from him with the patient's electronic MedChart in his lap. Beside Barry was an OR tech who would take care of whatever other needs arose during the procedure. "Alright, if everyone's present and accounted for, let's get to it."

Barry spoke up. "This is patient 01409. We are performing a liver lobectomy. Whenever you're ready, Doctor."

"Rachel, where's my music?"

"Sorry, Dr. Isaacs. What are you in the mood for today?"

"Something old school."

She spoke into the air. "Play music, 2000s mix."

The OR was filled with the sound of rain and the first few notes of Justin Timberlake's *Cry Me a River*.

"Oh, yeah. That's the stuff," he said, starting to dance a little. Everyone laughed, lightening the mood in the operating room to a level that Dr. Isaacs approved of. "Alright, now we can get this show on the road. Scalpel."

Rachel obliged then rested her gloved hands on top of the patient's body until she was needed again.

Dr. Isaacs went about his work, occasionally singing along with the music, occasionally asking for equipment. Within fifteen minutes, he had exposed the liver. He paused.

"Which lobe are we taking out again, Barry?"

The documentation specialist checked his tablet. "The right."

"Okie dokie." Dr. Isaacs went back to singing, intermittently using the suction or electrocautery to improve his visualization. He tied off the blood supply to the right lobe of the liver and took a closer look. "Barry, can you confirm we are taking out the right lobe of the liver? I don't see an obvious mass here."

Barry's expression betrayed some mild annoyance, but he indulged the doctor, looking down at his device once more and swiping a finger across the screen several times before answering. "Yes, Doctor. It definitely says the right. I checked the pre-op note and the radiology report." When Dr. Isaacs still didn't proceed, he asked, "Is there a problem?"

The surgeon examined the other lobes of the liver very carefully. "No, Barry, no problem. I just wanted to make sure I wasn't leaving in a diseased liver. The part I'm taking out looks pretty darn healthy."

"Yes, sir. Per the notes I have, the mass is only one centimeter by a half centimeter. Very small. And it's located centrally, so there is a good chance you would miss it on gross examination."

"Okay, just checking." Dr. Isaacs went back to his work and had performed the rest of the lobectomy within another ten minutes. He held the specimen out to the OR tech, who held out a basin for him to drop it into. "Get that to pathology."

The tech nodded, then headed out of the operating room with the discarded tissue.

Dr. Isaacs hummed as he closed up the patient's small incision. Within another ten minutes, he was on to his next case.

CHAPTER 12
Now
August 24, 2030

"So, have you talked to Dr. Leuman? Wasn't the appointment today? How did it go?" Cheyenne barraged Hamm with questions as he strolled toward her. She sat outside at Table, a restaurant that was quickly becoming one of their spots, basking in the glow of the late summer sun. He was joining her after his day at the office.

Hamm sighed. "Cheyenne, you know I can't talk about patient information."

"Isabella's still not answering my phone calls." She tore her napkin in half, then into quarters before finally looking up at Hamm. "I'm asking you as their friend. You're not even his doctor anymore, right?"

He sighed and gazed at her for a moment before giving in. "I can never say no to you. Dr. Leuman said it went as well as can be expected. I think they knew what was coming. They had to know."

"Yeah. But still, it's got to be so hard. I can't imagine making a decision like that, then having to bring your other son into it." Cheyenne shook her head and took a sip of her prosecco.

"They've decided not to involve Ridge. Not yet, anyway."

Cheyenne furrowed her brow. "So what are they going to do?"

"Try cadaveric renal transplant."

"Did Dr. Leuman's assistant tell them their chances of finding a match are less than—"

"Yes." He sighed. "He told them everything. Can we talk about something else?"

"Sure, geez." Cheyenne raised her eyebrows. "You need a drink." With a swipe of her finger, she activated the screen embedded within the table and accessed the menu. "What do you want?"

"Just a Coke."

She pressed the screen several more times. "Okay. Coming right up." She interlaced her fingers beneath her chin and leaned forward, giving him her undivided attention. "So, what do you want to talk about?"

"How's the new segment coming along?"

Cheyenne wiped away the condensation on her glass. "They're no Danny and Isabella Reid, that's for sure."

"What's the story?"

"She was thrown in prison—sorry, the North Carolina Correctional Institution for Women—for allegedly murdering her last husband, but she adamantly denies she did it. He is a prison guard who fell in love with her. They want to get married." She felt ridiculous saying it out loud. "It's not my best work."

Hamilton's eyes sparkled, and his crow's feet had come out in full force. "But, Cheyenne, 'These are the stories that matter'!"

"Go to hell, Walker," she muttered, but she had trouble hiding her own smile. Two months with this man and nothing seemed to carry the weight it had previously. For the first time in a long time, she was letting herself imagine a future, and that future was with the handsome, intriguing, kind man sitting across from her. She hoped to God he felt the same way.

Cheyenne looked up just in time to see Hamm's eyes turn serious. "I came across this the other day when I was looking for something in your nightstand drawer." He drew his hand out of his pocket and deposited a wrinkled newspaper clipping on the table between them. He might as well have pulled the pin out of a grenade and dropped it on her plate. "I didn't realize this was you," he said softly.

She dismissed the article with a shaky hand and picked up her glass, taking a big sip before speaking. "That was a long time ago, Hamm. Why even bring it up?"

"It would make a great story. You know, a *Where is everyone now* kind of piece."

She stared at him. "You have *got* to be kidding."

He stared back.

She shook her head, her shoulder-length, red curls developing a life of their own as a result of the motion. "I lived through that once. Never again."

Hamm leaned back in his chair, crossed his arms over his chest, and tilted his head as he studied her. "I just remember bits and pieces, but everyone in the medical field thought you were a hero. There was a big push for organ donation after—"

"After my fiancé died? Yeah, I remember. It's how I got my big break." She spat the foul words, couldn't get them out of her mouth fast enough. She turned her glass up again. She knew from the heat in her chest she was drinking too fast, but she didn't care.

Hamm looked shocked at her reaction. Hurt, even. She closed her eyes and took a deep breath. She didn't want to fight with him, but she didn't know how to separate her feelings, her regret, from this conversation. She hadn't talked about that day to anyone, ever.

She felt his hand on hers and slowly released her grip on her fork. She opened her eyes.

"Let's get out of here." He swiped his credit card through the reader, pressed the screen a few times, then stood up and offered Cheyenne his hand. She took it.

They walked in silence for several minutes around a pond that provided scenery for several outdoor restaurants. They stopped and leaned their elbows on a fence overlooking the water.

"His parents never forgave me. They said I killed him."

"I remember."

"They said I used him."

Hamm looked at her out of the corner of his eye. "For money?"

"Fame." She watched a bird land on the fence beside her arm then fly away. "Look at me; look at where I am. They're not wrong."

"Oh, c'mon. Just because you are well-known in Raleigh doesn't—" He caught himself, backtracked. "I mean, it's not like you set out with that intention."

"Does it matter?"

"Yes." Hamm gripped her arm and turned her toward him. "Of course, it matters. You fought for his rights. His wishes. If his parents couldn't accept that…well, that's their problem."

"I didn't have to cover the story myself."

"No one else would have done it justice, and you know it." Hamm reached out to take Cheyenne in his arms, and she let him. "Besides, who ever said it was bad to want something good for yourself?"

CHAPTER 13
Then
December 4, 2025

"Tell me again why I'm wasting my time with this?" Monty asked.

"Why *we're* wasting our time?" Karl corrected him. "Because it's what the higher-ups want, and we answer to them. At least for now." The two men sat at a table in Karl's large, glass-walled office, their backs to a window overlooking the street fifty stories below. They faced the door, a stack of folders towering in front of them.

Monty poured himself some water, leaving Karl's cup empty. "You think I don't know what you're up to, but I've heard the rumors about you being considered for surgeon general. So I have to kiss ass for you to get ahead?"

"You have to do your job. You think I don't have a million other things to do today, with the finance committee constantly breathing down my neck? If I go one day without the CSMs turning a profit, they're ready to shut the whole operation down." Karl spoke through clenched teeth as he smiled and waved his secretary in.

"First candidate's here."

"Thanks, Julia. Mr. Montgomery and I have about twenty people to interview today, so we'll need to be efficient. In and out, okay?"

"No problem, Dr. Buchner." She closed the door silently behind her.

Karl sighed and reached for the folder on the top of the pile. He was probably dreading this even more than Monty. Today was the day they would choose the recipient of the first annual CSM Research Grant. The person they selected would receive an exorbitant amount of the program's money—way too much, as far as he was concerned—to use on research that would theoretically help the program in the long run. Karl had tried to squash the idea, but someone much higher on the totem pole had pushed it through. So, here he was, spending his entire day with Alexander Montgomery and an assembly line of socially inept scientists.

Nine grueling hours later, the final nominee was ushered in and took a seat before them. Karl rested his elbow on the table and took a sip of his coffee. If the rest of the day was any indication, all the coffee in the world wasn't going to make this presentation any more stimulating. The last remaining folder lay untouched on the table.

The man didn't introduce himself or make small talk of any kind. Instead, he launched right into his presentation. He spoke with a thick German accent, his words leaving his mouth like molasses, slow and velvety. "How would you like to forget that last public speaking engagement when you blanked on what you were going to say mid-sentence? Or better yet, how would you like to make your wife forget that night you came home at three a.m. with your wedding ring in your pocket?"

Karl cocked his head to the side, glancing out of the corner of his eye to see Monty picking his fingernails.

The man smiled, his eyes crinkling. "Of course, I jest. These are minor issues that typically affect us in very trivial ways. But what about the patients with post-traumatic stress disorder, severe social anxiety, or major depression? Wouldn't those patients benefit from being able to selectively eliminate memories from their short- and long-term recall?"

As the hairs on the back of Karl's neck stood on end, he focused on maintaining a calm exterior. "It's an intriguing proposition," he said. "What is your proposal for achieving this—this amnesia effect?"

"Surgical intervention, to put it simply. Of course, it's much more complicated than that."

"Please elaborate."

The man sat on the edge of his seat, looking more like a child on Christmas morning than a graying, forty-year-old man talking about his scientific research. "You see, the technology is already there to isolate emotions and memories using functional magnetic resonance imaging, and the ability to perform noninvasive surgery using radio waves has been well-established. I'm simply proposing we put the two together."

Monty abruptly glanced up from his fingernails. "It sounds good on paper, Dr…" He consulted his notes. "Dr. Claus. But tell us, how would that work practically?"

Shut up, you imbecile, Karl thought. *Let the man talk.*

"Well, the procedure itself is a form of image-guided stereotactic brain surgery. However, instead of simply using cross-sectional imaging, such as computed tomography, we use functional magnetic resonance imaging. The surgeons are not aiming for a visual abnormality in the brain but instead, a functional one. We just bring out the undesirable recollection, then the doctor sees the associated brain activity on functional MRI, focuses the laser, and—*zap*—it's gone."

Monty had moved on to picking lint off his slacks.

"It makes so much sense." Karl clutched his coffee mug and tapped his foot underneath the table. All of a sudden, he had more energy than he knew what to do with. He struggled to keep his voice calm. "Why do you suppose it hasn't already been done?"

As if sensing his nervous energy, Monty stopped what he was doing and stared at Karl through narrowed eyelids. Then he regarded Dr. Claus with the same scrutiny before picking up the folder and idly flipping through the pages.

"I'm glad you asked, Dr. Buchner." The doctor pulled a binder out of his briefcase and slid it across the table toward Karl. "Mental health research has long since taken a backseat to other types of medical research in this country. Add to that the controversial history of psychiatric surgery in America, and you can understand why people would be hesitant to fund my type of research. I believe that now is the time for that to change. Mental health is an important and potentially curable cause of overall morbidity and mortality in our country. Who better to send that message than the national government? By way of the CSM program, of course."

"And what is your five-year plan? How do see your research being applied in the real world?"

"Clinically, our focus will initially be on those most likely to benefit and who have very specific memories that need to be erased: rape victims, war veterans, and the like. Once we've perfected the procedure, the sky's the limit, and the beauty is that it's an outpatient procedure. The patient can have breakfast with their family, get dropped off for surgery, and be home by dinner."

"Where are you in your research?" Karl asked. He realized he was holding his breath and began to let it out in a slow, steady stream.

"We just finished some preclinical studies in rats. It's complicated, of course, since they have no prefrontal cortex, but they do have pleasure centers. Our studies consisted of exposing the rats to either a pleasurable or a frightening stimulus then performing the surgery. On follow-up, the rats no longer responded to the stimulus in the same way. It was quite remarkable, really. One hundred percent of the rats confirmed our hypothesis. We are prepared to begin phase two trials in humans as soon as the funding is made available."

Karl had heard all he needed to. "Well, thank you very much for your time, Dr. Claus. Yours was one of many intriguing presentations today. We'll be in touch." He swiped the binder Dr. Claus had produced into his briefcase before standing up and dismissing the doctor. He held the glass door open for him. "Julia can validate your parking on the way out."

Monty joined Karl at the door, a huge stack of paperwork under his arm, and they watched Dr. Claus disappear behind the doors of the elevator. "Well, today was a huge waste of time. I guess I'll go through this shit tonight and try to pick whichever one sucks the least."

Karl nodded. "It would be best to choose someone quickly. Get it over with."

Monty nodded. "What did you think of that last guy?"

Karl felt Monty's eyes burning into him and tried to be nonchalant. "It might be a good thing to put the CSM money behind. Mental health is a hot topic right now." He shrugged. "Realistically speaking? I seriously doubt there will turn out to be any real-world applications. It's good stuff for a movie." He opened the door wider to let Monty out. "But it's your call."

Karl watched Monty leave. Once he had rounded the corner, Karl walked around to his desk, picked up his phone, and dialed.

"Daniel? It's Karl. You know those logistical concerns you expressed at our last meeting?" He couldn't suppress his wide smile. "Well, I think I may have just come across a solution."

CHAPTER 14
Now
September 28, 2030

Cheyenne eyed Isabella nervously as she entered the greenroom with her family. Trying not to stare, she took in the finished product now that the stylists had finished her makeover. Cheyenne had insisted on it, as Isabella looked even more haggard when she appeared at the studio today than Cheyenne had expected, even after Hamm's warning.

The woman was like a stick figure of her former self, her clothes no longer snug and squeezing her in all the wrong places. Instead, the dress she had arrived in hung from her body, highlighting the awkward angles of her shoulders and eclipsing her hips altogether. At least now Isabella was wearing a blouse and slacks that actually fit her, hugging her narrow waist and thighs and accentuating her minimal curves. The new outfit, combined with highlights and a little bit of makeup, had made a world of difference, but nothing hid the empty, lost look in her eyes.

The last month must have been absolute torture for her. She had watched one child's health decline to the point that she had no choice but to offer up her other son to save him. To send him off to surgery for his brother, to a battle that wasn't his to fight, when he had already cheated death once.

"Coffee?"

"Sure," Isabella said. "I could use some caffeine."

"Help yourself." Cheyenne pointed Isabella in the direction of the beverage table then turned her attention to Ridge. "Young man, I swear you've gotten a foot taller since the last time I saw you. What are your parents feeding you?"

Ridge stood a little straighter, and his cheeks flushed as he fought back a smile. "I dunno." He kicked at the ground and scratched the back of his neck behind his collar.

"You look very handsome today. Every bit the hero."

Ridge looked up at his father.

Danny nodded. "Go ahead. Just like we talked about," he said.

The boy glanced down at his feet then angled his neck up to look Cheyenne in the eyes. "You look very pretty."

Cheyenne's hands flew to her chest as she basked in the compliment. "What a sweet thing to say."

Danny ruffled Ridge's hair, winking at Cheyenne. "I think she likes you, son."

Cheyenne playfully hit Danny on the shoulder. "You stop teasing him, Danny Reid."

But Ridge was already halfway across the room, legs shuffling double-time trying to put distance between himself and the embarrassing scene that had just unfolded.

"I think he's got a little crush." Danny grinned at her. "All he's talked about for the past week was telling you how beautiful you are. 'Ravishing', I think, is the exact word he used." He chuckled. "I don't think things went exactly as he planned."

Cheyenne shook her head, hands still clutching her heart. "No, that was perfect." She glanced behind her to where Ridge now sat with Hendrix, digging his knuckles mercilessly into his little brother's skull, no doubt trying to regain some semblance of manhood.

Isabella walked up. "What just happened? Why is Ridge trying to decapitate Hendrix?"

"I'll take care of it." Danny didn't look at Isabella before heading to break up the two boys.

Isabella watched him go then turned to Cheyenne. "So, we're almost done here."

"It's hard to believe. The last few weeks have been an absolute whirlwind."

"You can say that again."

"I appreciate you letting me cover the surgery. And letting me get Hamm involved. I can't believe it's tomorrow."

Isabella nodded, staring at a spot on the wall.

"America loves you guys. They've been with you every step of the way. I can't tell you how many emails I've gotten, asking about you. 'How can I help?' 'What do they need?' These days, people want to be a part of something, want to feel human. They need it."

Isabella nodded. "I get that. I just wish it was somebody else's tragedy for once." She finally turned from the wall and looked pointedly at Cheyenne. "We appreciate you helping with expenses," she said. "I wouldn't have been able to go back to work if you hadn't."

"I was happy to, Isabella. As weird as this may sound, I feel connected to you. To your family. Telling your story, being part of it…it's the most meaningful thing I've done since—" Cheyenne stopped herself. "I just, I finally feel like I'm here for a reason. Like everything that happened before…"

"Was justified?" Isabella had that faraway look in her eyes again, and Cheyenne had the distinct feeling they were no longer talking about the show.

"You look great." Cheyenne changed the subject, gesturing to Isabella's outfit.

Isabella cocked her head, confused for a moment. Then she looked down at herself. "Oh, this. Yeah, the girls did a great job."

Just as the silence began to get uncomfortable, Danny strode up. "Crisis averted, and all for the low price of an ice cream on the way home."

Isabella tensed. "I wish you would've talked to me about that first, Danny. I don't like for the boys to have sweets after eight o'clock."

"Sucks, don't it?" he shot back. "One person making a decision that affects all of us."

"Not now, Danny," Isabella said through clenched teeth.

Cheyenne took a step back in response to the sudden hostility in the air. "I'm going to go see if the boys have any questions before we go on." She left the two with whatever issues they were dealing with and headed toward the boys. As she walked up, she noticed Ridge was eyeing his parents with concern. Hendrix sat reading a book, oblivious.

Turning to Hendrix, she asked, "How are you feeling, sweetheart?"

"I feel okay." His downturned face was round and a little swollen. Between the fluid retention caused by the kidney disease and the steroids he was on as a treatment, she hardly recognized the scrawny little kid she had met just over six months ago. He watched his feet dangling above the tile floor and kicked them back and forth in the air. "I can't wait till I don't have to go to diasis anymore."

Diasis. You couldn't write this stuff. She made a mental note to repeat that exchange when the cameras were on. "How about you, Ridge? Are you nervous about tomorrow?"

"No way." Ridge turned from the scene unfolding across the room and looked at Cheyenne. "I've had surgery before. It's awesome. You get all the ice cream and suckers you want."

Danny and Isabella's voices grew louder. Cheyenne tried not to listen, but she couldn't help it as the argument became more heated.

"If you had just talked to me—"

"And how would that have been any different, Danny?"

"It wasn't just your decision to make."

Both of the boys now sat completely still, staring at their parents.

"You know what?" Cheyenne said, "I was going to save this for the show, but what the heck. Can you two keep a secret?"

The boys looked at her, wide-eyed, their concern forgotten for the moment. They nodded in tandem.

"Then come with me," Cheyenne whispered.

Cheyenne led the boys through a side door and into the backstage area. She could tell by their silence they were intrigued. What boy didn't like to go on a treasure hunt? She smiled to herself as she turned on the lights in the huge closet.

She knelt down and faced the boys. "See that display over there? The one with the sheet over it? That's for you guys."

Hendrix ran over to it, but Ridge stayed behind, looking skeptical. "What's that for, Miss Cheyenne? It's not our birthday or nothin'."

"Birthdays aren't the only reason to give presents. Sometimes you just want to say thank you."

Ridge walked over to join his brother, who had already pulled the sheet off the display. Beneath it were several life-size Disney figurines, Cinderella's Castle, and Epcot's Spaceship Earth.

The boys immediately began tearing apart the display, pulling down the figurines and initiating an intricate sword fight between Cinderella and Goofy.

Cheyenne contentedly watched the boys play for a moment before sensing a presence behind her. She turned around to see Danny and Isabella standing in the doorway.

"Had a little surprise for you guys. Thought I would show the boys, since we had some time before going on set."

Isabella walked over to the boys, placing a hand on each of their shoulders. "What do you say?"

The boys looked up at Cheyenne, pausing momentarily to mumble a synchronized, "Thank you, Miss Cheyenne."

Isabella did a double take when she saw the miniature Mickey Mouse was holding four plane tickets and four brightly colored bracelets. She put her hands over her mouth, looking shocked and a little distraught. "Cheyenne, you didn't. You shouldn't have."

Danny had caught on now. He ran up to the boys and gave them each an enthusiastic high five. All three chanted, "Disney World, Disney World," as they jumped up and down in a group hug.

"We couldn't possibly," Isabella was saying. "When would we even…"

Cheyenne smiled broadly, determined not to let Isabella's sour mood destroy everyone else's good time. "Nonsense. Look how happy the boys are. There's no way you could turn this down."

Cheyenne kneeled down, and the boys ran into her arms. She closed her eyes and hugged them back.

She knew once Isabella had time to digest the news, she would be excited, too. She just had too much on her plate right now. But after tomorrow, after the surgery, their lives would begin to return to normal. Thank goodness.

Cheyenne didn't even want to think of what would have happened to the Reids if it weren't for the CSMs.

CHAPTER 15
Then
March 25, 2026

"I still don't understand," Aaron Isaacs said, shifting his attention from the portable screen back to Alexander Montgomery as the flashy presentation came to a close.

Monty closed his eyes and took a deep breath, no longer even trying to hide his frustration. Ever since Buchner had saddled him with getting this Career Renewal Package bullshit off the ground, it had been nothing but headaches. He had just spent a good fifteen minutes explaining the process to this moron, Dr. Isaacs, but he might as well have been talking to a brick wall.

He opened his eyes and looked across the table at the doctor, speaking slowly and clearly. "It's a *good* thing. Think of it as a reward for all your hard work. A token of our appreciation."

Dr. Isaacs looked again at the display in front of him, slowly clicking through the information once more. Behind him, in his office, there were two large bookshelves overflowing with journals and textbooks that looked like they hadn't been touched in a decade. In front of the books on each shelf sat numerous trinkets that must have been given to him over the years by delusional patients. Who else would think a doctor would want a plastic stethoscope filled with M & M's?

The doctor closed the notebook. "I have to admit, this all-inclusive resort sounds pretty nice. As hard as I've been working lately, I could certainly use a little down time. But why me?"

"The program is relatively new. We can't afford to send everyone who qualifies. So we put all the nominees' names in a hat and—voila! You were the lucky winner."

Dr. Isaacs eyed Monty coolly. "So, this doesn't have anything to do with the lawsuit? Or the concerns I brought up recently about the—"

"This only has to do with your ability as a surgeon," Monty said. "Your *outstanding* ability." Karl had told him he might have to butter this guy up, but this was getting ridiculous.

The doctor placed his hands on the desk, one on top of the other. "Four weeks in this resort. A few afternoons participating in a research project, one afternoon of CME, and the rest of the time I get to relax?"

"Exactly. So, what do you think?"

"And I'm not allowed to bring my wife?"

"No spouses or children allowed. This is meant to be a time for you to recharge your batteries without any distractions. That's why we call it a Career Renewal Package. You can tell your wife it's an honor even to be nominated."

Dr. Isaacs lifted his eyebrows and nodded slowly to himself.

Monty eyed the man sitting across the desk from him, looking him over from head to toe. His hair was a little too long, so he either couldn't spare the time or didn't care enough to schedule regular appointments. He wore a bow tie, so either he was trying to be ironic or his wife picked out his clothes. Both options were equally depressing to Monty. Last but not least, he had a slight paunch, which just strengthened the initial hair argument. He couldn't see the man's pants or shoes, but he didn't need to in order to know Dr. Isaacs desperately needed a vacation.

"So, when do I leave?" the doctor asked, placing his hands palms-down on the table and looking Monty in the eyes.

Monty bit back a smile. He knew it was just a matter of time before the poor bastard gave in. Monty leaned forward, maintaining eye contact with the doctor across the table. "How quickly can you pack your bags?"

* * * * *

Dr. Aaron Isaacs stepped out of the car and into paradise. Everywhere he looked, there were palm trees and water fountains. An exotic woman greeted him with a smile and a drink—something in a coconut with an umbrella straw. He took a sip. Not his usual cup of tea, but hey, when in Rome.

He wasn't exactly sure where this place was located—he hadn't been able to see much through the heavily tinted windows, and he had slept for most of the drive, anyway—but he didn't really care. He had already felt his blood pressure drop about twenty points.

"Dr. Isaacs."

He looked in the direction of the voice. Another woman was smiling warmly at him. He smiled back.

"We've been expecting you." She took his arm and led him toward a large, open building. "Once we get you checked in, you'll be free to roam around the grounds, get your bearings."

"Whatever you say." He felt like Dorothy approaching the gates of Oz. His eyes didn't seem big enough to take everything in.

The check-in process was like butter. His escort walked him right up to the empty counter. Again, the receptionist seemed to be expecting him and had his room key ready. She tapped her computer screen a couple of times and smiled. "You're all set, Dr. Isaacs. Sheila will show you to your room."

The woman on his arm led him out of the lobby and toward the elevators. She pressed the up button, and they waited in silence.

After a few moments, Aaron stole a glance at Sheila. She was staring straight ahead at the gold elevator doors. "Everyone seems to know who I am here."

She smiled. "Yes."

"I'm not really used to that."

"Well, you should become accustomed to it. At least while you're here, Doctor."

He nodded but couldn't shake the feeling he was missing something.

"I think you will be very happy with your room, Dr. Isaacs. It is one of our suites. Plenty of room for guests."

What kind of a place was this, anyway?

"Will your wife be joining you?"

He relaxed, laughing a little at himself. "No, Sheila. Unfortunately, not this time. I'm here for work. Maybe I'll bring her back at some point. This place is beautiful." The elevator arrived, and they stepped in.

"Yes, it is."

Neither spoke as the elevator ascended. They stopped at the top floor and stepped off in unison. Sheila led him down the hall to a door at the very end of the corridor. She took his key—an actual key, not a flimsy card—and unlocked the suite.

The door opened to a large two-story foyer that doubled as a living area. There were two large couches with a coffee table in between. The wall at the far end of the room was glass from top to bottom, and the floor was a creamy beige tile. There was a platform behind the sitting area that was separated from the rest of the room by two stairs. A baby grand piano sat in one corner and a stocked bar in the other.

A man in a tuxedo addressed him from the bar area. "Can I pour you a beverage, Dr. Isaacs? I'm sure you're parched after your trip."

He looked down at the large, embarrassing coconut in his hand. He set it aside. "Yes, a bourbon. Neat. And please, call me Aaron."

"Of course."

A moment later, the glass was in his hand.

Sheila offered to give him a tour of the rest of the large suite. To the right were the bedrooms. The master bathroom was trimmed in gold and had a large Jacuzzi, towel warmers, and a shower with eight showerheads coming from all different directions. She told him the bathroom also had its own entertainment system with a TV built into the mirror and surround sound speakers. Everything—"no, literally everything"—was operated using hand motions or voice commands and, she assured him, the system was extremely intuitive.

"Check this out," Sheila whispered conspiratorially. She raised her voice, "Watch TNN."

The glass went from being a mirror to a big screen TV. Then she lifted her hand, palm facing up, toward the ceiling. The sound seemed to come from all around him. Aaron had never seen—or heard—anything like it.

The master bedroom had a king-size bed with white, fluffy bedding and a similar entertainment set-up. He watched as she moved her hand back and forth, and the bed unmade and made itself over and over again. There was also a separate sitting area with a chaise lounge, coffee table, and lamp. Next to the sitting area was a screen door that led out to a furnished porch. The guest bedroom was equally impressive, if a little smaller.

Sheila and Aaron crossed back through the foyer to the other side of the penthouse, where the kitchen and laundry room were. As expected, the kitchen was huge and filled with the most state-of-the-art appliances available. Sheila showed Aaron how he could command each appliance to do almost everything for him.

"Apparently, no one has figured out how to make them prepare the food as of yet."

Aaron laughed at her joke, but when he glanced her way, he saw her face was serious. He lifted his eyebrows and continued to look around the kitchen in silence. "What happens if I can't figure out one of these appliances?"

"Just ask for help."

"Hmm?"

"Just speak your question into the air. There are speakers everywhere. We have voice recognition software that will register your speech and identify whether you have a question, complaint, et cetera. Then it gets routed to the correct office, and someone will contact you within five minutes."

Aaron had been studying the convection oven but straightened up to look at Sheila. "You don't say?"

"It's really quite revolutionary. The suite contains the highest level of technology available to us."

"What if I...wanted some privacy?"

"Of course." Sheila walked over to a small door embedded in the wall. Aaron hadn't noticed it before. "Just press this red button." He did so, and an electronic voice came over the sound system.

"Initiating System Disconnect."

"Just don't forget to reconnect when you are ready."

Aaron stared at her, his hand inside the control box, finger still resting on the button.

"Bruce will be standing by to help out with anything you need as well. He also plays the piano beautifully." She nodded to the butler, who walked over to the baby grand, sat down, and flipped the tails of his suit coat behind the stool. Music filled the large apartment as he began to play Beethoven's *Moonlight Sonata*. The acoustics were amazing.

"I want to show you one last thing. Then you can have some time to get settled before dinner."

"Okay."

Sheila led him to the center of the foyer where the coffee table sat, the least remarkable piece of furniture in the whole place. "Push that button."

Aaron did as he was told, pressing a button on the corner of the table. The center of the table separated, and a space opened up within the table. He looked through the gap and could see that the floor was opening as well. Through the opening, a large device began to rise. When it had reached its final position, the bottom flush with the coffee table, Aaron could see that it was a double-sided gas fireplace.

He laughed. "You have to be kidding me."

"Now, push the other button."

He did. The fireplace disappeared, and in its place rose two back-to-back television screens.

"You'd better go, Sheila. I don't think I can take any more surprises today."

"Alright, Dr. Isaacs. I'll just swing by tomorrow to see if you have any questions about the suite's features."

He did have a question: who in the world was paying for all this? But he was sure Sheila didn't have the answer. She started to let herself out the front door, then she stopped and turned back toward him. "If you need anything at all, please don't hesitate to ask."

Dr. Isaacs stared at the closed door for a long moment after she left. In the background, Bruce continued to play the piano. He had moved on to another piece, Debussy's *Clair de Lune*. It made Aaron feel melancholy and strange, but he didn't ask him to stop playing. If felt like the absolute best song for the moment, for what he was experiencing.

Something strange was going on here. He couldn't put his finger on it, but he had to admit he didn't hate how it was making him feel. He sat down on one of the couches and propped his feet up on the coffee table. He took another sip of his bourbon, then he took a deep breath and let the sense of well-being wash over him as the plaintive notes of *Clair de Lune* moved slowly from his consciousness to his subliminal mind.

CHAPTER 16
Now
September 29, 2030

Cheyenne woke up at five fifteen. Today was the day. The surgery.

It was still dark outside, and she wasn't sure whether it was a noise or her uneasy stomach that had awoken her. She lay in bed for a moment, eyes closed, trying to will herself to nod back off. Then she heard footsteps coming from the bathroom, and any hope she had of getting an extra thirty minutes of sleep faded into the background.

She hadn't meant for him to stay the night, had told him it would knock her off her game.

"Morning." He stood in her bathroom doorway, one towel around his perfect waist and another in both hands, drying off his hair. He could be very persuasive.

Cheyenne let herself enjoy the view for a moment before throwing the covers back and placing both feet on the floor beside her bed, her nightgown hem riding up her thighs. *Two can play at that game*, she thought. She rubbed her temples, willing away the heaviness of too little sleep. "I can't believe you talked me into letting you stay last night."

Hamm laughed. "That's not what you were saying a few hours ago."

"I suppose I did change my tune about halfway into that bottle of Merlot." She stood and walked over to him. She placed both hands on his bare chest and leaned in for a kiss. "What did you expect? You refused to help me with it."

"I have a big day today." He kissed her back—a longer, more lingering kiss. The kind of kiss that had impaired her judgment the night before.

"None of that," she said, stepping away from him with her hands on her hips.

He pulled the towel from around his waist and dropped it to the floor at her feet. "Lucky for you, I have to be at work soon. No time for hanky-panky."

"Good," she said, feeling less resolute by the minute.

"Good." He circled around her and headed to an armchair in the corner of her bedroom. He reached for the day's clothes, which he had draped over the back of the chair the night before. She hesitated for a moment then shuffled into the bathroom for a shower.

A few minutes later, Hamm poked his head into the steamy bathroom. "Bye. See you in a few."

"See you," she called into the mist. She closed her eyes and smiled.

Cheyenne's phone was ringing as she turned off the shower, and she answered it without even looking at the caller ID. "Hey you," she said in her best raspy sex-kitten voice. "Just can't get enough, can you?"

"Good morning, Miss Rose." The woman's voice was crisp and clear.

"Oh, my gosh, I am so sorry. I was expecting it to be someone else."

"Miss Rose, I'm calling on behalf of the surgeon general, Dr. Buchner."

What? She dug her fingernails into her palm, trying to stay calm. "Oh. Well, in that case." She tried to sound nonchalant. "What can I do for you, Ms…?"

"I'm calling to tell you that Dr. Buchner has been following your career with interest." She cleared her throat. "He wanted you to know he appreciates your coverage of the CSMs. You've had a very positive impact on the country's perception of the centers. Too many people are trying to uncover 'dirt' or find the 'next big story'. Your approach has been very…refreshing."

"Thank you." Cheyenne shook her head. "You're welcome." Damn it. Her mind was still cloudy from the wine the night before.

"He believes that you could be a wonderful asset to our program. From the inside."

"Oh."

"He'd like to talk with you about a public relations position within the CSM program. When things calm down a little bit for you, that is. He's looking for someone to make sure the focus is kept on the right things within the program. The position would be an adjunct to your current role in the media."

Cheyenne blinked. "Thank you. I don't know what to say. I'm flattered."

"I won't keep you. We'll be in touch. Good luck today."

"Thank you. Wait, how did you—?"

"Goodbye." She ended the connection.

"Bye," Cheyenne said into the silence that followed.

* * * * *

"Welcome, Miss Rose." A woman greeted her in the cavernous lobby of the CSM. "My name is Loretta. If you need anything today, I'll be your point person. Follow me."

Cheyenne and her cameraman followed Loretta. The sharp click of her heels echoed on the tile and then ceased as the flooring changed to carpet. They walked to the end of a hallway, and Loretta opened a door for them.

"Dr. Buchner called me personally. He asked me to make sure you were comfortable." She swept her hand across the room. "Of course, I was happy to oblige."

The area was to serve as a makeshift greenroom and recording studio. It had a table with snacks and drinks in one corner and a large open space on the opposite side. The cameraman headed that way to set up his equipment. Several rows of metal chairs were pushed to the far wall and were stacked on one another. The Reids sat in four cushioned chairs that looked like they were brought in separately. There were three more vacant chairs nearby.

Ridge's complexion was even paler than usual, and Hendrix looked like he would literally disappear into his chair if that were an option. He was slouched over, shrunken into the cushion and staring at the ground. Cheyenne would have to get their minds off the surgery if she was going to get anything worth airing today.

"Hey, guys. Have you thought about when you're going to take that trip to Disney?"

Both the boys stared at the carpet in front of them, their hands gripping the sides of their chairs. Finally, Ridge's head shook in answer to her question.

Cheyenne glanced at Danny and Isabella, who didn't look much better. Isabella attempted a smile.

"So, Isabella." Cheyenne smiled back. "What's the first thing you are going to do as a family when all of this is over?"

Isabella stared blankly at her. "I guess—we hadn't really thought about it." She looked at her husband. "What do you think, Danny?"

"We just want things back to normal. *Our* normal."

Cheyenne nodded. "I can understand that."

Just then, Hamm swept in through the door. Cheyenne would have been happy to see anyone enter the room at that point, but the fact that it was Hamm was an added bonus. She resisted the urge to throw her arms around his neck.

She turned to her cameraman. "Ronnie, are you all set up? I'm sure Dr. Walker only has a few minutes."

Ronnie nodded, and Cheyenne turned to Hamm.

"Alright, Dr. Walker. Are you ready?" She hoped that once she and Hamm got the ball rolling, the others would relax a little bit.

Hamm sat down in one of the chairs in front of the camera and raised his eyebrows playfully. "I was born ready, Miss Rose."

Cheyenne felt her face heat up and turned away from the Reids before they could see her blush. Damn, he made it so hard to concentrate. She took a couple deep breaths and made a futile attempt to smooth her curls. They were operating with a skeleton crew, so she had no hair and makeup team. She was also acting as director. Her supervisors hadn't been convinced she would get anything worth airing today, but she was determined to prove them wrong. She held up her fingers and silently counted down for Ronnie. *Three, two, one.* Then she situated herself and plastered on a smile.

"Thank you for giving us some of your valuable time this morning, Dr. Walker."

He nodded. "Sure."

"Let's get right to it, shall we? Can you walk us through the procedure you have planned today?"

"Well, Miss Rose, what we are doing this morning is unprecedented." He looked into the camera lens. "Imagine everything you think you know about surgery, and completely erase it from your mind. Today, Ridge and Hendrix will be in the same operating room. The entire surgical staff will be performing double duty, so to speak. Including me."

"Please explain. And dumb it down for those of us who aren't surgeons."

"Well, during an organ transplantation, it goes without saying that the recipient cannot receive the organ in question before it has been harvested from the donor."

"Not *that* dumb." Cheyenne batted her eyes at Hamm.

He chuckled. "So, Ridge's surgery will be done before Hendrix's starts."

"Okay."

He paused, waiting to see if Cheyenne would ask a follow-up question. When she didn't, he continued. "Our team has gone through a dozen or so practice runs, anticipating any and all possible complications and coming up with strategies to address them."

"So, the Reids have nothing to worry about."

"Well, there's a certain perioperative risk associated with any surgery. We can't eliminate that risk, but we can minimize it."

"How in the world did you get this approved if it's so different from how things are normally done?"

"I had to file what's called a 'petition of efficiency' to do both surgeries in the same OR at the same time. It will end up saving the system about thirty thousand dollars to do it this way. Not to mention all the pre-op testing we were able to forego since both boys already have a clean bill of health, except the obvious, of course. And the fact that the organ won't have to be transported—will spend less than *fifteen minutes* without blood flow—dramatically reduces the chance of transplant failure." Hamm was getting into it now, leaning forward in his seat and gesturing to the camera. "It's groundbreaking."

"Sounds as if this is pretty beneficial for all parties involved."

He shrugged, allowing himself to relax a little bit. "We are always trying to figure out new, better ways to do things. If it works out well, then great. Maybe we're onto something."

"If it doesn't?"

"I would never put the boys' well-being at risk, if that's what you're asking. The worst-case scenario today is the surgery doesn't go as smoothly as planned, or we have to call in reinforcements. We're prepared for that possibility."

"Well, I'm sure that puts their parents' minds at ease." Cheyenne looked over at Danny and Isabella, who sat listening intently in their separate chairs. They were stock still, as if afraid to even breathe, white-knuckled hands gripping their armrests. It was nothing they hadn't heard multiple times before, couldn't recite word-for-word, but, nonetheless, they hung on every syllable.

"The actual procedure is very straightforward. It's one I perform not infrequently." Hamm's phone beeped, and he looked down to read the message. "I'm getting paged back for my chole." Then he looked back at the camera and smiled. "That means I gotta go take out a gallbladder."

He turned to Cheyenne. "It'll take an hour at the most." Then he called over to the boys. "After that, I'll meet you guys back there to rearrange your organs, okay?"

Ridge wrapped his arms protectively around his abdomen. "Hey, wait just a minute—"

Danny and Isabella looked sharply at their son, but when they saw him smiling, they let themselves laugh along with him. Hendrix giggled at his parents' reactions, and, before long, the entire family was doubled over.

Cheyenne took advantage of the moment. "Alright, boys. You're up!"

The next hour flew by as Cheyenne interviewed each member of the Reid family. Even though a lot of the tension had dissolved, everyone was still distracted, and Cheyenne worried whether she had gotten anything worth airing besides the interview with Hamm. Maybe her producers were right.

Before they knew it, the boys were being called back to be prepped for the surgery. Two nurses stood waiting with wheelchairs as Danny and Isabella hugged the boys.

"Don't worry, Mom," Ridge whispered. "I'll take care of him. I always do."

"I know you do, Ridge." Isabella bit her lip and hugged her son closer to her chest. "What would Hendrix do without his big brother watching over him?"

The boys sat down in the wheelchairs, their bodies impossibly small in the adult-size seats, and each was given an ID bracelet before being rolled back to surgery.

Now there was nothing left to do but wait.

CHAPTER 17
Then
April 17, 2026

Aaron stepped off the elevator and onto the plush carpet of the fourth floor of the Research and Development building. Intended to look like any other building in the resort, it was the most unlikely research center he had ever seen. Ten-foot ceilings, crown molding, priceless art hanging on the walls. The scent of fresh lilies had to have been piped in from somewhere, because Aaron had yet to see any flowers.

Aaron rapped on the door at the end of the hall, and it swung open. He stepped into the room and called out, "Anybody home?" He got no response. "It's Dr. Isaacs."

The lab was empty except for the rows of computers and workbenches lining the walls and several pieces of futuristic looking equipment at the center of the room. He walked further into the laboratory, running his hand over some of the more impressive machinery and pressing the occasional button. This was his third and final afternoon with the research team. As far as he could tell, they were doing some sort of advanced brain mapping. He wasn't sure what the practical application would be, and he was only a little ashamed to say he didn't really care. He was merely here to fulfill his twelve-hour requirement.

"Dr. Isaacs, yes, thank you."

Aaron jumped at the voice coming from behind him and jerked his hand back from a computer screen.

"Come in. We were expecting you." The woman spoke in a thick, Eastern European accent. "My name is Isolde. My partner, Stuart, and I will be guiding you through the experiment today."

It was a woman he had seen working in the lab the past two times he had come in, but he hadn't paid much attention to her before today. She had limp, brown hair that looked to be in desperate need of a wash and impossibly thick glasses she perpetually squinted through. If that weren't enough, she had the build and intermittent male-pattern hair growth of a high school football player. Now she stood in front of him with her hand extended, wearing a dingy, over-size white lab coat. Aaron reluctantly shook it.

"I believe this is my last session."

"Oh, it is?" She furrowed her brow and leaned over a nearby computer, her fingers swiping across the screen so fast Aaron couldn't keep up. His pulse rose by about ten beats per minute. Surely they weren't going to try and rope him into another four hours.

"Yes, I came—"

"Oh, yes. Here it is. Yes, thank you, I see. Today is the last session. Very important."

"So, do you think it will take the whole time? I kind of have a thing." He had only been here three weeks, but he already felt himself getting used to this bizarre lifestyle, questioning it less and less and enjoying it more and more. He certainly didn't want to spend any more time in this windowless room with Isolde than he absolutely had to.

The woman looked up from studying her paperwork. "I'm sorry?"

"Is it going to take the whole afternoon?" Aaron repeated himself slowly.

For the first time, she gave him her undivided attention. "Well, Dr. Isaacs. I suppose that depends on you." Without another word, Isolde seated herself at her workstation, leaving Aaron standing alone in the center of the room. There were a few seconds of awkward silence as the woman looked back and forth from her two computer screens, occasionally typing in a couple of characters.

Aaron stood with his hands in his pockets and cleared his throat in the silence. He wondered if she was expecting an apology.

Without looking up from the screen, the woman said, "Dr. Isaacs, please go ahead and have a seat now."

Aaron walked toward the center of the room and made his way up the three stairs onto the platform that looked out over the lab. He sat down in the single armchair and looked up. Suspended in the air above him was a gigantic helmet-shaped piece of equipment. It looked like some sort of space-age mind-reading contraption. Which, in a way, he guessed it was.

The technology for functional magnetic resonance imaging had been around since the late twentieth century. It allowed radiologists to visualize the blood flow to the brain and, therefore, actually see which parts of the brain were activated by certain emotions. It was used widely in neurologic research since its inception but had few clinical applications that he was aware of.

The previous two sessions had consisted of the research team stimulating emotions in him—showing him a picture of a puppy, talking about a senseless hate crime, that sort of thing—and marking which areas of his brain were stimulated by his response to those things. He assumed the information was being gathered for educational purposes. Who knew? Maybe a picture of his brain would end up in a textbook or something.

"Okay, Dr. Isaacs. If you're ready, we will begin."

"Sure."

He heard a low hum, and the helmet descended toward his head. It clicked into place. Now, all he could see was the inside of the device. There was a screen there, but it was turned off.

"Okay, Dr. Isaacs," a man's voice addressed him. He, too, had an accent. It was more subtle than Isolde's and harder to place. "My name is Stuart. I'm going to take you through a couple of last minute equilibrations, then we'll be good to go." He paused. "Okay, whenever you are ready, please think of something that makes you very happy."

Aaron pictured himself back in his suite, drink in hand, Bruce playing the piano behind him. He couldn't help but smile.

"Okay, hold that thought," the voice said into the microphone. Then, to the side, "Sections 586 and 587."

"Okay, now something that makes you worried."

Aaron did as he was told.

"Section 233. Okay, now imagine you've been lied to."

Once more, Aaron complied.

"Whoa, 367 through 370."

Aaron waited for the next instruction.

"Dr. Isaacs, do you remember performing a liver lobectomy on a patient about one month ago? The indication was hepatocellular carcinoma." The man's tone was conversational.

"Yes, I remember. I thought the liver looked normal, but the cancer turned out to be centrally located."

"Whatever came of that case?"

"Oh, uh, let's see. The liver was sent to path. It came back HCC, as we expected. Clear margins."

"Oh. Good news for the patient."

"Yes."

Aaron heard some murmuring followed by a low hum and a click.

"Have you ever had a case before in which you had a bad patient outcome?

"Yes. Several, unfortunately. It's the nature of practicing medicine."

"Tell me about the most recent."

"Hmm, let's see. I recently operated on a twelve-year-old child with an abdominal tumor—"

He heard another hum and click that stopped him mid-sentence. "Do you guys hear that?"

"Hear what?"

"It sounds like, I don't know, some machine or something."

"No, I'm sorry. I don't hear anything. Please continue."

"Well, now I've forgotten what I was saying."

"I asked you if you've ever had a case in which a patient did poorly."

"Oh." Aaron thought for a moment. "Not recently. As a matter of fact, I can't think of any specific instance right this second."

"Nothing?"

"Not that I recall. Sorry."

Aaron heard more murmuring.

"Okay, thank you. Now, if you'll bear with me, I have some routine questions for you. Can you tell me your full name?"

"Dr. Aaron Isaacs."

"Your birthdate?"

"December ninth, 1990."

"Your wife's name?"

"Elizabeth."

They continued that way for another forty-five minutes. By the time they were done, Aaron was pretty sure Stuart and Isolde would be able to take a credit card out in his name if they so desired. But, still, he was out in just a little over an hour, which meant he could stop by the suite for a little nap before his golf game. His stride was quick and purposeful as he headed to the elevator and pressed the call button.

Now the only thing standing between him and a relaxing final week at the resort was a general surgery reentrance exam. Totally unnecessary, but if they needed to document he hadn't lost his surgical proficiency in the mere month he'd spent at the resort, he would humor them.

He couldn't quite explain it, but he almost wished they'd asked more of him. For someone who had to work for everything he'd gotten in life, it was a little uncomfortable to be treated like such royalty, especially since he didn't really know who was footing the bill, or why. He almost felt like he was getting away with something.

He just wished he knew what that something was.

* * * * *

Aaron stared over the surgical dummy at the sweaty man who stood clutching a clipboard and pen. His upper lip beaded with sweat, but he resisted the urge to wipe it with his sleeve.

"Whenever you're ready, Dr. Isaacs."

He squinted, searching his memory until his head hurt. "I'm sorry, Peter," he said. "You asked for McBurney's incision?"

"Yes, Dr. Isaacs." The man peered at Aaron through bifocals before dropping his eyes to his paperwork and scribbling something in the margin. "As I said before, we are in no rush. Take your time."

Aaron reached across the dummy and picked up a scalpel from the surgical tray. His normally steady hand trembled as he placed the tip over the middle of the abdomen, watching the examiner out of the corner of his eye. A quick jerk of Peter's head told Aaron he was in the wrong spot. How had he forgotten so much after only four weeks off of surgery?

McBurney's incision. He frowned then slowly moved the scalpel toward the body's right side, and the tension in the other man's jaw began to release. A barely perceptible nod told Aaron when to stop. He sunk the blade into the mannequin's rubbery skin and followed a path straight down the right side toward the hip. He left the scalpel partially submerged and took a step back from the table, grinning across at Peter. When their eyes met, he immediately regretted his showboating.

Peter capped his pen and shoved it in his shirt pocket, tossing the clipboard on top of the body. "I think that's enough for today."

"I imagine so." Aaron finally wiped the perspiration on his upper lip. "We must have been at this for a few hours at least."

"Forty-five minutes."

"No kidding. I guess it just felt like longer." Aaron plucked the scalpel out of the incision and tossed it back onto the tray. It clanked loudly in the otherwise quiet room. "This kind of stuff, it's like riding a bike, you know? It'll come right back once I'm back in the OR."

Peter nodded. He now had his back turned to Aaron and was dictating softly into a small TabScreen.

Aaron shoved his hands in his pockets, jingling the loose change he always kept there. "So, when do I get my score, or results, or whatever you call it?"

Peter stopped talking and glanced over his shoulder at Aaron. "Uh, soon. Somebody will be by your suite to talk to you. Probably this evening." He ducked his head back down and returned to his recording.

"So I just let myself out, then?" Aaron jabbed his thumb behind him in the direction of the door.

Peter waved a dismissive hand toward Aaron, not even bothering to look at him this time. Aaron stood watching the man for a moment longer, then headed toward the exit.

As he made his way to the pool, he couldn't shake the feeling that something about his performance on the reentrance examination didn't add up. Sure, he hadn't had to lift a finger for himself this past month, but he hadn't forgotten how to drive or chop vegetables. Why were his surgical skills so rusty?

He made a mental note to ask whoever came this evening to give him his test results. Surely they had dealt with this kind of thing before. They probably even had a system to retrain physicians when needed. Worst-case scenario, he might have to take some sort of refresher course.

In the meantime, he only had a couple more days at the resort, and he certainly didn't want to let this experience ruin the rest of his time here. He approached the cabana, smiling a greeting at the familiar girl who handed him a towel. Then he made his way to his lounge chair where a margarita already sat waiting for him.

There was nothing he could do for the next few hours to change what had happened this afternoon. He might as well enjoy himself while he still could.

CHAPTER 18
Now
September 29, 2030

Hamm whistled to himself as he burst through the double doors of the frigid operating room. The boys had already been put to sleep and prepped. Their bodies were silent and still, waiting patiently for him to begin. Their heads hid behind a curtain, reminding Hamm of a guillotine. It was a little twisted, yes, but true. The anesthetist sat behind the curtain like the Wizard of Oz, pressing buttons and turning dials to control each breath their lungs received, responding to each beep or whir with another adjustment. Sterile, blue drapes covered them from neck to toe except for a square of white skin exposed on each boy's torso. For Ridge, it was to the right of his belly-button. For Hendrix, his pelvis.

After getting gowned and gloved, Hamm took the scalpel from his scrub nurse, Brenda.

"I'm timing you, Doc. No slacking."

He glanced at her. The mask covering her nose and mouth hid any hint of a smile and, as usual, her eyes revealed nothing of her mood.

"Got somewhere to be, Brenda?" He made the first incision, enjoying the brief view of clean, pink tissue before blood began pooling into the space. "A hot date, maybe?"

"What business is it of yours? You jealous?"

Hamm chuckled. "You and I both know you're too much woman for me."

Hamm began dissecting away the fascia to better visualize the kidney. They would take the right one, so he was using the same point of entry they had for the appendectomy. Same scar. It would be like he was never here—a second time, at least.

After several minutes, he had exposed the retroperitoneal space, but the anatomy didn't look quite how he expected. He stopped for a minute, stepped back from the table, and stretched, letting the peritoneal fluid and blood fill in the spot where he was working. Then he went back in with the suction, once more clearing bodily fluids out of the way to get a better look at the space. He searched again for the organ—kidneys were small and could be evasive, but he usually had no problem finding what he was looking for. After all, he knew the inside of an abdomen like the back of his hand.

"Is everything alright, Dr. Walker?"

"Yes, Brenda." Hamm paused to glance up at her. She was peering through her glasses at him, trying to read his expression. "This kidney is just trying to get the best of me, but I'm going to show it who's boss. Don't you worry."

"Alright, Doc. Just let me know if you need some help in there."

He gave her a quick, meaningful look. *Not now*. She raised her eyebrows then went back to sorting the equipment on the surgical tray. They were like an old married couple that way.

Then he saw it, the reason for his difficulty. He was looking in the right spot—the adrenal gland was right there. He could follow the main vessels to where they should be feeding the kidney, but the kidney was absent. Surgically absent.

His eyes shot around the room. His staff went calmly about their business, with no idea anything was wrong. Even Brenda seemed engrossed, now, in what she was doing. The order of the OR, normally so reassuring, made Hamm feel even more unsettled. He grabbed a blue towel from the tray, patted his forehead, and dropped it onto the floor beside him.

He went back in, sure that he was mistaken. Once again, his search for the kidney came up short.

This couldn't be happening. He had studied all of Ridge's records prior to scheduling the surgery, and the boy had not had a nephrectomy. Why *would* he? He was a previously healthy kid who was unlucky enough to get appendicitis.

But there was no denying Ridge's kidney had already been taken. There was just no record of it. Hamm applied the suction again to get a better look, and then he saw it: the Hamm Hock, his trademark knot, tying off the renal artery.

He was the one who took Ridge's kidney. He had performed a nephrectomy on a kid with appendicitis, and there was no documentation of it. How was this possible? Reeling, he placed both hands on the table, taking deep breaths one after another until his vision began to tunnel inward. Then he held his breath, and his head filled with pressure.

"Dr. Walker, what's going on?" Brenda stared across the table at his now, looking worried.

Her voice echoed in his head. She probably thought he was having some sort of nervous breakdown. He kind of felt like he was, but he knew he couldn't let himself go like that. He needed to get his act together. He stretched his neck back and shook his head from side to side several times, hoping to clear it. He had been in situations much more critical than this. He just needed to figure out the next step.

"Greg."

The documentation specialist looked up from where he calmly sat typing in the corner of the operating room.

"Greg, check the record again for two-four-seven-eight-two. Is there documentation of a nephrectomy?"

The young man searched his file. "No, sir. You only performed an appendectomy according to these records."

"That can't be." His voice was strained. "Check again."

"Dr. Walker, what in the world is going on?" Brenda's voice had gone from worried to bordering on hysterical.

Just then, the OR's MedScreen flashed to life.

"Doctor, is everything okay in here? We detected some unusual activity."

"Oh, there's been some unusual activity, all right. There has been a major documentation error, which has resulted in a patient undergoing surgery to harvest an organ that he *doesn't have*."

"Calm down, Dr. Walker. We will get to the bottom of this."

"Do not. Tell me. To calm down." Hamm was so angry he could barely speak.

Unfazed, the MedScreen operator looked around the room. "Everyone except for Dr. Walker will exit the operating room at this time. We will need to conduct interviews to gather information about the event while the memory is still fresh in everyone's mind."

"Nobody leave," Hamm addressed the others. Then, looking at the operator, he said, "What am I supposed to do without my staff?"

"We will bring in reinforcements," she assured him. "For now, they leave." She turned to the rest of the people in the room, all of whom were frozen in their spots, not sure whose orders to obey. Brenda looked at Hamm, her expression one of utter confusion.

He squeezed his eyes shut for several moments, then opened them and nodded almost imperceptibly. "Go."

The staff quickly stripped off their sterile gear, dropped it on the floor around them, and filed out the single exit.

Hamm looked at the woman who was projected, larger than life, onto the MedScreen. She sat in some office somewhere, while he was here with these two helpless children. He couldn't see a way for this to end well. "Now what?"

She looked at a computer screen that Hamm couldn't see, typed a few characters, then looked up at him. "Protocol says that we—"

"Protocol?" He yelled at the screen in disbelief. "There is no way there's a protocol for this."

The operator ignored his outburst. "Protocol says we have two options. You can harvest Subject A's left kidney, and the patient will arrest. The operative note will reflect that there was an unexpected complication, we ran a code, but unfortunately, the child expired. The other option is allowing Subject B to die on the table. Similar chain of events. We'll take care of the documentation, of course. It's nothing you need to concern yourself with."

Hamm felt himself spinning out of control. The floor was opening up and swallowing him. This was not happening. He did not live in a world in which there was a—a *protocol* for this situation.

There was an obvious solution. Hamm knew there was a way out of this, if only he could think. Option 1—Ridge dies. Option 2—Hendrix dies. But what if they had never gone to surgery today? Ridge would be alive and… so would Hendrix. He would still be getting dialysis.

"I'll just close them up. We'll comb through the records, figure out how this could have happened. Make it right. And Hendrix will go back on the transplant list."

"Dr. Walker, that is not one of your options."

"What do you mean, it's not one of my options? It's the obvious solution." He picked up a needle driver and suture and began sewing Ridge's incision back up.

"Dr. Walker, step away from the patient."

He continued working, ignoring the woman, thinking if he could only get the incision closed up, this would all go away. He was halfway through when he felt a hand on his back. He looked over his shoulder, his hands frozen in midair above Ridge's abdomen.

"Dr. Walker, step away from the table." The command came from a man Hamm didn't recognize. He wore a sterile gown that was hastily thrown on over his suit and tie. He carried an unused respirator in his left hand.

"Who the hell do you think you are?" Hamm felt his last bit of control over the situation slip further through his fingers. This was so much bigger than him, but he wasn't going to give up without a fight. Ridge and Hendrix deserved better than that. They deserved a chance.

He shrugged the man's hand away and turned to face him, his back now to Ridge in a protective stance. He gripped the needle driver like a weapon. "What the hell is going on?"

The man took several steps backward. "My name is Ian. I work with the Quality Control Department." His eyes were cold and gray. "If you do not step away from the table right now, both children are going to die. It's as simple as that. I recommend you relinquish your equipment." He held out a gloved hand for the tools. Hamm sized Ian up, figuring he had the man by at least thirty pounds and four inches.

"If you think I'm going to just hand this over to you, you're more of an idiot than you appear to be. These kids—and their parents—they trusted me with their lives. That's something I take very seriously." He took one step and then another toward Ian.

The man didn't acknowledge the insult at all. Instead, he looked up at the screen and nodded his head in a silent command. He placed the respirator over his nose and mouth.

Seconds later, Hamm heard the sound of gas escaping and felt his eyes begin to tear up. He had just enough time to realize what was happening before losing himself to the blackness.

* * * * *

Cheyenne sat listening to the clock tick in the otherwise silent waiting room. Danny and Isabella sat across from her in a couple of the room's drab, olive green chairs. Two untouched cups of coffee were on the table in front of them, exactly where Cheyenne had placed them an hour before.

A man entered the waiting room, someone Cheyenne had never met. He was wearing business clothes, not scrubs like she would have expected. His face was clean-shaven, and his hair was short. Although he was probably in his mid-thirties, he had childlike features that would have people asking how old he was until well after he was old enough to appreciate the compliment. He sat down on a chair facing the Reids.

"Hendrix is doing well and is in the recovery room. You can go see him just as soon as we're done talking here."

Danny let out a deep forceful breath. Isabella dropped her head and whispered, "Oh, thank God."

"But I need to let you know there was a complication during Ridge's surgery."

Isabella's complexion paled, and she was completely still, a statue except for the occasional shallow breath.

The man continued, "Dr. Walker was able to harvest the kidney from Ridge, but the stress of the surgery caused Ridge to go into cardiac arrest."

"What? Why?" Cheyenne blurted out.

Danny and Isabella just stared hard at him, their eyes like lasers that Cheyenne could imagine penetrating the man's skull and coming out the other side.

The man glanced at Cheyenne, barely acknowledging her outburst, then focused his attention back on the Reids. "It appears his heart was not strong enough for the stress of the anesthesia and surgery. Perhaps something happened during the first surgery two years ago that weakened his heart. Or perhaps he had a congenital abnormality that we are not yet aware of. We attempted resuscitation for forty minutes, but unfortunately, we were unsuccessful. Ridge expired on the table."

Isabella continued to stare at the man, as if willing him to be a figment of her imagination. Cheyenne felt so much pain for her in that moment that she, irrational as it was, began to think of alternate realities. Maybe the man had gotten things mixed up. Maybe it was a different patient he was talking about, and Ridge was fine. Of course, that was it. It had to be a mistake.

"No. Stop." Isabella shook her head.

The man hesitated. "I'm sorry, Mrs. Reid."

“Stop saying that. Tell me the truth. Tell me Ridge is okay.”

Cheyenne tried to slip an arm around Isabella’s shoulders, but she shrugged her off. Isabella stood up and walked toward the door the man had come through.

“Hamm!” she called out, her voice hoarse. “Hamm, I’m coming in there. You’ve had plenty of time. You should be done by now. I’m coming to get my boys.”

The man stood up and tried to block Isabella from reaching the door. She kept walking as if he weren’t even there, and he grabbed her arms from behind.

“Get your hands off my wife!” Danny came out of nowhere, pulling the man from behind and throwing him against the row of chairs. “Honey, you can’t go in there.” His voice was soft, calming, as if he were speaking to a rabid animal. “Come here.” He held her close. It was the first physical contact Cheyenne had seen between the two in weeks. “We’ll figure this out. We’ll figure out what’s going on. Just stay with me.”

Isabella’s legs crumpled beneath her, and she collapsed into his arms. He let her down to the ground, never taking his arms from around her. They stayed there on the floor, locked in an embrace, and the man left the room. He never even told them his name.

Cheyenne looked over at Ronnie, who was recording the whole exchange. “Turn that thing off, for God’s sake.”

Turning to Danny and Isabella, she said the only thing she could think of. “I’m so sorry.”

Isabella looked at her, a coldness and detachment in her eyes. “You. You said Ridge would be fine. You said this was what he would want. Are you happy now? Hendrix has a kidney, but at the expense of our other son’s life.”

“Isabella, I—”

“Get. Out.” Isabella spit the words out, her voice deep and unnatural. She was no longer looking at Cheyenne. Her gaze was trained on the floor as she kneeled there on all fours, her body slack and her heart broken beyond repair.

CHAPTER 19
Now
October 16, 2030

Cheyenne's head was killing her. She didn't remember going to sleep the night before, but at least she had managed to change out of her clothes this time. She gingerly opened her eyes and was surprised to see the sun was out in full force. What time was it? What *day* was it?

She sat up in bed, and an empty vodka bottle rolled toward her. So this was what rock bottom felt like. She heard a throat clear, then she noticed Valerie's face on the monitor at the end of her bed. She pressed the input button. "Good God, Valerie, how long have you been there?"

"Not long. I pushed your morning appointment back a little since your…schedule has changed."

"Oh, okay." Cheyenne hadn't noticed. She took the pill bottle from the nightstand and swallowed a capsule. "Down the gullet."

She was feeling a little lightheaded, so she lay back down on her pillow without even bothering to dismiss Valerie. Surely by now the woman knew her way out. Cheyenne laughed at that thought, then immediately regretted it. Clutching her head, she rolled over into the fetal position.

Cheyenne planned to do something today. She was done with sitting around her apartment feeling sorry for herself. She had no right to feel this way over Ridge's death, not when Isabella had lost a child.

Over two weeks had passed, and she still hadn't heard from Hamm, either. She had even tried to call him once, but he hadn't answered. Truth be told, it was probably better this way. He had proven himself to be a huge jerk, and worse, a coward, leaving her to clean up his mess without so much as a goodbye.

Her hand reached out and gripped the neck of the vodka bottle, then she slung it across the room. It made contact with the wall before landing with a deeply unsatisfying thud on the carpeted floor. Cheyenne sighed and swung her feet over the side of the bed.

She planned to do something today, but she had no idea what. She had nothing to occupy her time. After the news broke of Ridge's death, she was placed on indefinite leave from work, until everything got "sorted out." The surgeon general had retracted his job offer and distanced himself from her in every way possible.

Cheyenne had not been able to avoid the temptation to numb the pain with an almost continuous infusion of alcohol. Pills had always been a close second for her, but with the care coordinators constantly breathing down her neck, it was getting harder and harder to accomplish any meaningful effects through that route. So far, booze had remained blessedly unregulated.

Cheyenne stood up and started to walk toward the bathroom. Her head pounded, and she once again felt the blood rush to her feet. She leaned against the door frame until the moment passed. After brushing her teeth, she headed to the kitchen. She needed coffee if she was going to be productive. As the cup brewed, she checked her refrigerator for creamer. When she found the carton, she poured a little into the sink. It came out in clumps.

"Damn it." The stuff had expired a week and a half ago. "What else is there around here?" She opened cabinets and drawers with no success until she finally came across a bottle of Bailey's Irish Cream. It was a bit early in the day to start drinking, even for her, but just a teaspoon or two couldn't hurt. It hardly had any alcohol in it. Plus, the caffeine in the coffee would counteract it.

Cheyenne poured a generous amount of Bailey's into the steaming mug of coffee. Just as she had taken the first heavenly sip, her doorman buzzed the door.

"Miss Rose, there's someone here to see you," her doorman said through the intercom.

Cheyenne's heart fluttered for a second, and she smoothed down her hair, tucking the loose strands behind her ears. Then she checked herself. Hamm had a lot of explaining to do. She couldn't just throw open the door and welcome him into her arms, as much as she might want to. She needed to be strong, aloof. Not look too eager.

She pressed the buzzer and said, "Give me five minutes, Paul. Then send him up."

Cheyenne took a few more gulps of lukewarm Baileys and coffee before getting to work. In her bedroom, she pulled her hair back into a relatively neat ponytail and changed from her pajama bottoms to a pair of worn jeans. She looked at her reflection in the mirror. At least it appeared she had gotten dressed for the day, even if she *was* wearing yard sale clothes.

Cheyenne smiled at that, despite herself, as she made her way back to the front of the apartment. Hamm always used to tell her she had two kinds of clothes: business clothes and yard sale clothes. Nothing in between. She wondered if he would remember that, if he would say anything today.

She raced around the kitchen, clearing the countertop of empty wine bottles, glasses, and takeout containers. After a frenzy of activity, she stopped and surveyed the end result. It would have to do. She dug a candle out of a drawer and lit it, closing her eyes and inhaling the scent of pumpkin pie.

The doorbell rang. She placed the candle in an inconspicuous spot, made her way to the door, and looked through the peephole.

Cheyenne felt as if she were going to throw up the coffee she'd just downed. It was too late to say she wasn't in, so she took a deep breath and disengaged the lock.

The emaciated woman who stood before her looked no more like Isabella than Cheyenne herself did. Cheyenne hadn't thought it was possible for her to lose any more weight, but somehow she had. A lot of it.

Cheyenne backed away from the entrance, holding the door open for Isabella and trying not to stare. "Come in."

Isabella strode past her and into the apartment, also avoiding eye contact. She made her way straight into the living room and took a seat on the couch. She stared up at the blank TV screen.

Cheyenne slowly closed the door, standing in the entryway for a few seconds, searching her brain for something to say to fill the silence and coming up short. She followed Isabella into the living room and sat across from her in an armchair.

"I think he's going to leave me." Isabella's voice was flat, but it seemed to echo in the silence that followed, the words repeating themselves over and over in Cheyenne's mind.

Well, aren't we just a pair? Cheyenne thought. Out loud, she said, "Would you like some coffee?"

Isabella nodded and scooted herself further back on the couch.

In the kitchen, Cheyenne studied the two mugs of coffee—each with a generous hit of Irish cream—before adding a splash of vodka to hers. It was practically noon, anyway. She took a test sip, closing her eyes and taking a deep breath as the warmth of the coffee and the liquor made its way down her chest.

When she returned to the living room, Isabella was studying a painting above the fireplace. It was an abstract. Cheyenne had bought it because the artist was "so in right now." She had no idea what it was even supposed to be.

Isabella took the coffee from her. "I wake up every morning and for a moment, I've forgotten he's gone." Her eyes shot to Cheyenne. "Ridge," she clarified.

Cheyenne nodded, sipping her own coffee and taking her seat in the armchair.

"Then I remember." Her voice cracked. "And I live that day over and over again. Every terrible moment. I do that every day."

Cheyenne's eyes watered, and her nose tingled; she blinked her eyes to keep the tears from falling. "And Danny?"

"He says he can't move on—I think he means with me. He can't get over it, not after what I did."

"What do you mean, after what you did?"

Isabella's hand went to her belly for the briefest of moments before sliding back into her lap. Her eyes met Cheyenne's briefly before she squeezed her eyelids shut and dropped her head into her hands. "What were we supposed to do with another child? Another mouth to feed? How was I supposed to know—?"

"Oh, Isabella." Cheyenne's chest ached for her. The confession went a long way toward explaining the recent tension between Danny and Isabella and explaining why she had shown up there today, of all places.

Isabella had experienced enough loss for several lifetimes in the span of a few months. It made Cheyenne feel petty and small for the dramatic way she had reacted to Hamm's absence. She moved onto the couch next to Isabella and tentatively wrapped her arms around the woman's shoulders.

Isabella broke down. Her head in her hands, fingers gripping her hair so tightly Cheyenne thought she might pull it out, Isabella shook with sobs that sounded like they originated from her very center.

"This is not supposed to be my life," she managed to get out between gulps of air. She cried for several minutes before finally losing steam. "I'm s-sorry. I couldn't think of anywhere else to go."

"You can stay as long as you need." Cheyenne rubbed a hand up and down Isabella's back. It felt strange to be so intimate with this woman who had been determined to remain strangers for so long. "How's Hendrix holding up?"

"He blames himself." Isabella looked at Cheyenne, her eyes bloodshot. "This is going to haunt him forever, change who he is, who he was supposed to be. How do I convince him it's not his fault?"

Cheyenne's heart broke for Isabella, for Hendrix. She knew too well how it felt to hold onto blame. "I'm sorry I—I don't know how you let go of the guilt. I wish I did."

She thought back to that last day in the hospital with her fiancé.

He had put her in charge well before the accident. Had told her what he wanted done if he was ever unable to speak for himself. But even knowing he was already dead, the act of withdrawing life support had a sort of finality to it that had surprised her. That finality was what made it so hard to move on. She had been sure it was the right decision...but what if it wasn't? There were no do-overs. And, at the end of the day, she was responsible for his *death. She* was responsible for his *death.*

She pitied Hendrix. She knew how he felt, how he would always feel. In every big moment, every moment he should share with his older brother, Ridge wouldn't be there. The wound would tear open again, the memory as fresh as that day two weeks ago.

Isabella took a couple of deep, shaky breaths. When she looked up at Cheyenne again, her eyes were red and swollen from crying, but the tears had dried up. "I didn't mean to fall apart like that. That's not why I came here."

Cheyenne put a hand on Isabella's. "Don't apologize. Please. I'm glad you came."

Isabella took a deep breath. "How have you been? How is Dr. Walker?"

She felt an ice pick jab through her heart. "Uh, Hamm and I—I think we broke up."

Isabella gazed at her sympathetically, her expression betraying not an ounce of sarcasm. "Why?"

Cheyenne shrugged her shoulders. “I’m not sure, Isabella. He just—I haven’t seen or heard from him since that day. I called and left a message. He didn’t call back. He obviously doesn’t want to see me.”

“Why do you think that is, all of a sudden? He seemed pretty enamored with you last time I saw you together.”

That day, Cheyenne thought. It looked like Isabella was thinking that, too.

“Guilty conscience? Maybe he knew I would demand an explanation for what happened—” Cheyenne cut herself off, standing up from the couch. “More coffee?”

“Sure.” Isabella handed Cheyenne her mug then stood and followed her into the kitchen. “What do you think *did* happen in there? In the operating room, with the boys?” Her voice trembled.

Cheyenne focused on preparing the coffee, trying to figure out what to say. She had no right to feel such self-righteous anger toward Hamm, not when Isabella had lost a child because of him. Finally, she spoke. “I’m afraid we may never know.”

Isabella nodded, her lips pressed together in a thin line. “Have you been by his house? His office?”

At first, Cheyenne thought Isabella was joking, but one look at her face told Cheyenne she was dead serious. “Isabella, we had only been dating for a few months.”

“And?”

“And it’s over. The end.”

“You know, Cheyenne, I could really use a distraction. Something to take my mind off everything.”

Cheyenne didn’t like where this was going.

“What if I rode over to his house with you? Just a quick little visit, see if he’s home.”

Cheyenne shook her head, depositing a refilled coffee cup into Isabella’s hands. “No, Isabella. I’m sorry, I just don’t think that’s a good idea.”

“Hendrix is in school today. It’s his first day back. Danny’s not speaking to me.” Isabella placed a hand on Cheyenne’s forearm, her eyes pleading. “What about if we just go by his office? I don’t know what else I’m going to do with myself.”

Cheyenne sighed and grabbed her jacket from where it lay draped over a stool. “Fine.” She tried to squelch the tiny seed of hope that had begun to germinate. “We can go by the office, but that’s it.”

CHAPTER 20
Then
April 23, 2026

"Exactly what did he say about collateral damage?" Karl was growing uneasier by the second as he listened to Monty's version of his meeting with Dr. Claus earlier that day. They were only a couple of months into this, and already there were complications.

"Call the guy yourself, Karl," Monty said, throwing what few notes he had made onto Karl's desk and knocking a canister of pens over in the process. "I'm done being your little errand boy."

"This is your responsibility, Monty." Karl felt himself starting to lose his control of the situation and of Monty.

"No, the CSMs are my responsibility. Whatever this shit-show is, this is all you. As soon as you decided to override my choice for the grant in favor of this guy's weird mind control research—even though it had no 'real-world applications'—it became your problem. So if you have questions, feel free to call him your own damn self." Monty almost tipped his chair over as he stood up and made his way to the door. He stopped with his hand on the doorknob and turned around to face Karl. "I can't quite put my finger on it, but something's not right about that guy."

After Monty was gone, Karl sat motionless and unblinking behind his ornate desk, drumming his fingers on the mahogany tabletop and staring at the empty chair Monty had just vacated. He could almost see the stench that followed the man everywhere he went rising up from the seat cushion. He didn't know whether it was the smell or the topic of their conversation, but his mouth watered, and he thought he might be sick. He swallowed several times and waited for the moment to pass. Then he leaned over to unlock his bottom left desk drawer.

The file was thin and unassuming, and only Karl knew of its existence. Only Karl understood its importance. The only electronic copy was on his home computer, which no one—not even Tracy—had access to. He slowly turned the pages, studying each until he was once more convinced this was something worth protecting no matter what the cost. He was finally getting a break, finally getting the appreciation he deserved. No way was he letting this minor hiccup interfere with everything he had worked so hard for.

He pressed the intercom button on his desk. "Natalie, are you still here?"

"Yes, Doctor." His receptionist's voice came over the speaker, a singsongy lilt that grated at Karl's nerves. "What can I do you for?"

He rolled his eyes. "Get Dr. Claus on the phone, please."

"Coming right up."

He listened to the phone ring through the surround sound speakers in his office as he examined a framed photo of Tracy. He knew their relationship was born of mutual benefit rather than true affection, but what successful relationship wasn't? And now that there was serious talk of him being appointed as the next surgeon general, she had actually started to seriously consider his marriage proposal.

Karl was about to abort the call when he heard a barely perceptible click.

"Hello? Dr. Claus here."

"Dr. Claus. Karl Buchner calling."

"Oh, hello, Dr. Buchner. I assume you have spoken with Mr. Montgomery."

"Yes. I have some concerns about the direction your research has taken. I hope you can alleviate them."

"I will do my best. However, as you know, research is a very fickle mistress. If it always went the way we thought it would, there would be no reason to do it, now would there?"

Karl didn't feel like making small talk. "He tells me that trial participants have been able to regenerate their erased memories."

"Well, no, not that we've directly observed. That is a theoretical possibility, a desirable one, in the cases where our memory treatments have been less precise than we would have preferred."

"Dr. Claus, the point of the research, the reason the review committee felt your work was so promising, was the possibility of a permanent treatment of PTSD and other such disorders." Karl grabbed a pen and began to doodle. "If the procedure is so easily reversible, then why not just give these patients medications?"

"As you know, psychotropic medications have side effects, some of which can be very serious. And the cost of taking a daily medication for the rest of one's life is not insignificant."

"That's what these patients will end up doing if you can't provide better results." Karl drew large figure eights on the back of a manila envelope.

"We're working on it, sir. With all due respect, it's a process. We are still in the trial phase. We are actively identifying the bugs in the system and addressing them."

"What about the current patients' memories? What will you do if they regenerate?"

"Dr. Buchner, if I may be so bold, why would you care about the trial participants' memories? We are dealing with small, inconsequential parts of the memory center in healthy volunteers at this stage."

Dr. Claus was right. There was no good reason Karl should care. He took a deep breath and picked up the phone's handset, taking their conversation off the speaker system. You could never be too cautious.

Karl lowered his voice. "Of course, you're right, but you are going to be monitoring the participants for memory regeneration, correct? It will be important to know if and when it occurs. For future patients."

"Yes, sir. We plan to follow them with monthly phone calls and monitor them closely for any change from their baseline memory at the end of the program."

"Worst case scenario, if the memories do occasionally regenerate, what other options are there?"

"Well, there are your typical treatments such as antidepressants and atypical antipsychotics, which can mitigate some of the symptoms that result as a response to these distressing memories."

Karl's figure eights had degenerated into forceful zigzags, then just a straight line back and forth. He realized he had torn through the envelope and looked absently at the pen before replacing the cap and tossing it in a drawer.

"Dr. Buchner?"

"Yes, I'm here," he said. He rubbed his temple with his free hand.

"I'm not sure how relevant it is, but there are also some medications completing phase three trials right now that target the memory center of the brain. They are very non-specific but could be used in extreme cases."

"Such as?"

"Well, to keep a patient from harming themselves or others, primarily. The drugs would numb the emotional reaction to the distressing memories and, in general, allow behavioral control of patients who may be violent or have the potential to be. The trade names are Memorine and Amnesopam."

"Clever."

"Yes. Memorine is a tablet for once daily administrat-ion. It is intended for patients who have a family member or other caregiver who can assist with medication administration. Amnesopam is a long-acting depot injection, similar to the birth control shot, Depo-Provera. It is administered once monthly as an intramuscular injection. This is obviously a better option for those with behavioral problems, such as patients being cared for in an inpatient psychiatric hospital."

"Okay. So if we needed to use them for a patient, we could?" Karl found himself lowering his voice further.

"Not exactly, not right now."

"Why?"

"First of all, there are some significant side effects: paranoia, agitation and very severe amnesia at times. The medications are strictly to be used as a last resort. Our current patients—if you can even call them that—have no indication for these medications, particularly given the side effect profile. Secondly, the approval process can take months."

"What if we—I mean, a patient—needed the medicine sooner than that?"

"If a doctor felt that there was truly no other option, then I suppose there's always compassionate use. It's usually reserved for cancer drugs, but I suppose you could invoke it for anything. Basically, you can apply to use the drug before FDA approval if you feel that your patient needs—"

"I know what compassionate use is, Dr. Claus," Karl said. "Tell me about the other complications you've come across. The 'collateral damage'."

"As I mentioned to Mr. Montgomery in our recent meeting, one of our trial participants—his name is Dr. Aaron Isaacs—has had a bit of a complication." He paused and cleared his throat. "As you know, each surgeon is being asked to complete a reentrance examination before returning to work."

"Yes. Totally unnecessary in my opinion."

"Apparently not. Dr. Isaacs seems to have failed it. He will need further hands-on training before returning to the field."

Karl dropped his forehead into his hand, waiting a long moment before responding. "Why do you think that is?"

"Well, the trial memories we were asked to target were very close in proximity to those memories used in his everyday line of work. Some of the collateral memory loss appeared to be very relevant to his career. As I said before, we believe the effects to be completely temporary and reversible, and as our treatments get more precise—"

"This is extremely concerning, Dr. Claus."

"I can't reiterate enough, I believe this extra memory and skill loss to be inconsequential."

"I'm sure Dr. Isaacs doesn't feel the same. Dr. Claus, I don't want to take over this project." Karl pressed his lips together in a thin, white line. "But I will if I have to."

"I—we understand, sir, that this is a significant issue," he said. "We are working on it at this very moment."

"As usual, keep me apprised of any and all updates."

"Yes, sir."

Karl ended the call before Dr. Claus could say any more. He took a deep breath and began going through a stack of mail on his desk.

Dr. Isaacs was part of a test run. A trial. And it appeared the trial had already failed. Granted, there was still work to be done and there were idiosyncrasies to be figured out, but that didn't help Dr. Isaacs—or Karl—one bit right now.

It looked like Karl was going to have to take matters into his own hands. He once more pressed the intercom button on his desk.

"Natalie?"

"Yes, Doctor?"

"Get Bradford on the phone."

CHAPTER 21
Now
October 16, 2030

Cheyenne pulled her electric convertible into a parking spot right in front of the office that Hamm shared with several other physicians. She followed Isabella through the front lobby, trailing behind her by a few steps.

When the office door jingled, the girl at the front desk lifted her gaze from her phone long enough to register the ladies' presence, then immediately turned her attention downward again. The waiting room was empty except for an elderly couple in the corner, the man snoozing with a magazine resting facedown on his belly and the woman squinting through thick glasses at a crossword puzzle.

Cheyenne and Isabella walked up to the desk and waited politely for a minute. Cheyenne stared at the receptionist's electric blue eye shadow, generous eyeliner, and clumpy, sparse eyelashes. The woman chewed gum, blowing the occasional bubble and letting it explode loudly, each pop echoing in the empty waiting room. Her bra straps showed on both shoulders, peeking out from beneath the wide neckline of her low-cut top.

Finally, Cheyenne cleared her throat. The girl—her nameplate read "Welcome! I'm Maggie"—looked up at them. The expression on her face made it obvious they were anything but welcome. "Can I help you?"

"Yes," Isabella said, taking the lead. "We're here to see Dr. Walker."

"Do you have an appointment?"

"No," Cheyenne said. "We were just in the neighborhood, and we're—"

"He was my son's surgeon," Isabella said. "I thought Dr. Walker might like to know how he's doing."

"Okaaaay." The receptionist started pecking at her computer keyboard with long, flashy fingernails. *Click, click, click.* "Dr. Walker isn't in today. Would you like to make an appointment?"

"No," Cheyenne said, backing away from the desk. "We'll just—"

Isabella elbowed Cheyenne so hard it stopped her mid-sentence. "Yes. I would like to make an appointment for my son next week." She leaned over the counter, taking up the entire window and blocking Cheyenne's view of Maggie. "Not with his assistant. With him."

The girl rolled her eyes. "I'll see what I can do, but I can't make any promises."

Cheyenne halfway listened to the conversation between the two women as she took in the lobby. The elderly couple was called back, and now there were no patients, just deserted magazines and empty pamphlet receptacles.

Click, click. "He's not in next week."

Isabella took a deep breath in and out then leaned even further in toward the receptionist, articulating each word she spoke. "How about you just tell us what days he's available, and we'll go from there."

The girl started clicking a little faster on the keyboard. Cheyenne raised her eyebrows at Isabella then wandered farther away from the counter.

The women continued going back and forth, their voices low and urgent. Maybe they were finally getting somewhere. Cheyenne noticed a door to the right of the front desk and tried it, surprised when it swung forward into the back hallway. She glanced behind her to where Isabella still had Maggie tied up, then she stepped through the door and let it close softly behind her.

She took a look around her. A hallway extended before her with several doors on either side, all closed. She could hear Maggie's voice to her left, louder now, but couldn't see her through the partition that separated the receptionist's office from the clinical area.

Cheyenne made her way further in, trying to appear as if she belonged. A woman in scrubs exited one of the rooms and passed by her, in a hurry to get somewhere else. She nodded and smiled at Cheyenne, but she didn't slow down.

At the end of the hallway, the corridor continued to the left. On the right, she noticed a closed door with a nameplate. Hamilton Walker, MD. Her heart skipped a beat.

Cheyenne knocked lightly, waiting for only a minute before turning the doorknob. She met resistance and had just started to release her grip when the knob gave beneath her hand. She looked behind her and down the hallway from where she had come and saw no one. Before she could change her mind, Cheyenne swung the door open and disappeared inside Hamm's office.

She squinted into the sunlight coming through the window on the far wall. Dust floated through the air, and a fine layer had settled over the desk and other furniture. She ran a finger idly over the desktop. A clean line trailed behind her hand. A charger for a missing electronic device snaked out from behind the wall. It seemed out of place, somehow. Wrong. She cocked her head and stared at the cord for a second before moving on.

She went for the desk drawers, rifling through them, not quite sure what she was looking for. She came across a notebook, but when she opened it she only saw diagrams of the human body and notes he had jotted down about various surgeries. She came across the pair of sunglasses he never went anywhere without, as well as his keyring. The unsettled feeling she had experienced a moment ago returned, and she couldn't shake it this time. Why hadn't he brought this stuff with him? Why was it here gathering dust? She had just turned her attention to the trash can when she heard a voice.

"Can I help you find something, ma'am?" The nurse from the hallway stood above her. "You must be lost."

Cheyenne pushed the trash can back into its spot and stood up from where she had been kneeling over it. She shoved her hands in her pockets.

"Yes, thanks. I must've taken a wrong turn."

"Are you a new patient?"

"Yes. Well, no, not really. I'm an acquaintance—a friend, I mean—of Hamm's. Dr. Walker's. Is he around?"

The woman's eyes darkened. "We've been told he is on leave. Didn't he tell you?"

"Oh, yes. That's right. He did say he was going to be gone for a bit. I just, I thought he would be back by now." Cheyenne started to inch toward the door.

The woman moved to block the exit with her body. "Dr. Walker won't be back for a while yet. I suggest you call first next time. That way you don't waste a trip, Ms.—"

"Meredith. Call me Meredith." Cheyenne smiled up at the nurse. "You'll tell him I stopped by?"

"Sure." The woman stepped out of the doorway, her eyes never leaving Cheyenne's face. She motioned down the hallway the way Cheyenne had come. "You know the way out?"

Cheyenne nodded and made her way toward the lobby, feeling the woman's eyes on her back until she had gone through the exit door at the end of the hall.

She walked up to Isabella, who now stood with an elbow resting on the counter as she stared down at Maggie. The receptionist was shaking her head.

"I'm sorry, I just don't have access to that kind of information."

"There's got to be someone we can call," Isabella said. "You must have a supervisor?"

"It's okay." Cheyenne grabbed Isabella's arm and tugged. "We need to go. We'll try back again soon."

Isabella looked at Cheyenne, her face expressing annoyance followed by confusion, then understanding.

"We'll try back later," Isabella called to the receptionist as Cheyenne pulled her toward the exit.

Back in the car, Cheyenne sped down the highway. Her foot was heavy pressing down on the gas, almost like it had a mind of its own. She tried to wrap her head around what she had just learned. Isabella had caught her up on the rest of her conversation with Maggie, and it was more of the same. Hamm was gone and no one knew where he was or when he would be back. Either that or they didn't want to tell.

She gave Isabella a sidelong glance. "So, what do you make of all this?"

Isabella shook her head slowly. "I have no idea. It's definitely not what I was expecting."

"What were you expecting?"

"I assumed he was avoiding you because of everything that happened. I thought we'd find him there and be able to clear the air."

"Yeah." Cheyenne's smile was forced. "I guess I was starting to believe that, too."

"This doesn't mean Hamm doesn't care." Isabella turned her body toward Cheyenne as much as her seat belt would allow. "He's been out of work since the surgery. What if he's been suspended for some reason? What if he's not *allowed* to contact you?"

"I don't know." Cheyenne furrowed her brow. She really wanted to go along with Isabella's fantasy, but she needed to be realistic, if for no other reason than to maintain her sanity. "What kind of suspension, or rehab, or whatever, would require you to completely fall off the face of the earth?"

"You never know," Isabella said. The spark had returned to her eyes. "Why don't we go by his place?"

"Now *that's* stalking." Cheyenne laughed and glanced at Isabella. "Wait. You're serious?"

"I need this, Cheyenne. I need to look him in the eyes and hear from his mouth what happened to my son in that OR. He owes me that much."

"What if he doesn't know?"

She shrugged. “Then at least I tried.”

As much as she wanted to ignore Isabella and keep driving, Cheyenne had to admit a spark had been lit in her, too. That morning, she had woken up thinking Hamm didn’t want to hear from her, and now—well, now she had no idea what to think. But she knew one thing: even if she got her heart broken all over again, it would be better than not knowing. She sighed and put on her blinker to exit off the beltline, toward Hamm’s house. “Damn it, Isabella. Has anyone ever told you how stubborn you can be?”

Isabella looked at her, wide-eyed and innocent. “I have no idea what you’re talking about.”

* * * * *

Cheyenne cringed from where she stood in the corner of the wraparound porch as Isabella pressed on the doorbell for the third time. When they had turned onto Hamm’s tree-lined driveway and his house had come into view, a sour taste of bile had made its way up Cheyenne’s throat. It was still there at the back of her tongue, no matter how hard she tried to swallow all the feelings she was trying to avoid. She braced herself on the porch rails and looked around at the familiar surroundings.

The early twentieth-century farmhouse rose toward the sky as if lifted up by the trees that surrounded it on all sides. Hamm had spent the last ten years renovating it, and he had managed to maintain the character of the place while ensuring it had all the modern conveniences one would expect from a brand new home. Seeing the house was like seeing Hamm. She felt his energy all around her and hated how it made her feel. She needed a drink.

“I don’t think he’s home.” Cheyenne started to walk down the stairs toward her parked car but paused when Isabella didn’t follow her. “There’s nothing more we can do.”

Isabella turned around to look at Cheyenne, her eyes wide with purpose. “Do you have a key?”

"What? No. We'd only been dating a couple of months. Even if I did have a key, I wouldn't use it to break into his house."

"It's not breaking in if you use a key." Isabella stood with her hands on her hips. "Do you know where he keeps a spare?"

Cheyenne's gaze automatically went to a potted plant perched on a table to the right of the front door. It was only a split-second slip, but it was enough.

"Aha!" Isabella lifted up the pot.

"No, Isabella. I am not going to break into his house. I'll look like a desperate fool."

"Aren't you worried there might be something wrong?"

Cheyenne looked up at the sky. She was starting to tire of this new, energetic version of Isabella. "Hamm can handle himself. He's an adult. Besides, I'm the *last* person he needs trying to take care of him." She was starting to feel the anxiety building and wondered how Isabella would feel about stopping for a glass of wine on the way home. That is, if she could ever talk her into leaving in the first place.

Cheyenne headed toward the car again, this time with more conviction. Behind her, Isabella huffed. Cheyenne heard the bottom of the ceramic pot scrape against the table as Isabella replaced the key then followed her down the steps.

"You know, I think you missed your calling, Isabella. You should have been a detective." Smiling, Cheyenne looked over her shoulder at Isabella. She stopped. "What are you doing now?"

Isabella now stood at the end of the driveway and was staring at the mailbox.

Exasperated, Cheyenne started toward Isabella, whose hand now rested on the door of the mailbox. "Do not open that." Cheyenne felt like she was trying to talk the woman off a ledge, like any wrong move would send her friend free-falling to her death. "Don't do it. Taking someone's mail is a federal offense."

"I'm just going to take a peek. When did you become such a nervous Nellie?" Isabella opened the mailbox and cocked her head, confused. The look on her face made Cheyenne close the rest of the distance between them to take a look inside.

The mailbox was completely full, stuffed to the point it would be hard to remove any of the mail that was in there. There was a tag from the US postal service explaining that the rest of Dr. Walker's mail could be picked up at the post office with an appropriate photo ID.

Isabella's face had gone from confused to worried as she registered the meaning of what she was seeing. "Cheyenne, something's wrong. Something's definitely wrong."

For the first time, Cheyenne believed her.

* * * * *

Cheyenne took a long, delicious sip of her Chardonnay and sighed, sinking further into the booth across from Isabella, relishing the dark, smoky anonymity of the dive bar they had chosen at random. She knew it was impossible, but she thought she could already feel the heady rush of the alcohol hitting her brain. She always thought better after a glass or two of wine, and right now she desperately needed to think.

"So." Isabella got right to business, leaning forward and putting her elbows on the table. The dim light in the bar accentuated the dark circles beneath her eyes. "What are the possibilities here?" She had a notebook and pen ready. Her red wine sat off to the side.

"Vacation."

Isabella gave Cheyenne a look. "Be serious, Cheyenne."

She shrugged her shoulders. "What? We're trying to make a comprehensive list here, right? That's a real possibility."

"Fine, I'll put it on the list, but I'm sure Hamm would take care of his mail if he were planning a trip like that. And he'd probably let his girlfriend know, too. I'm going to add abduction."

"Who would abduct Hamm?"

"That's what we have to find out."

Cheyenne rolled her eyes. Isabella was turning out to be quite the conspiracy theorist. Cheyenne had the feeling she was enjoying the distraction, maybe too much. She had to rein Isabella in, or this was going to go nowhere fast. "Maybe he got relocated."

"Okay, good. But, again, wouldn't he at least give you the courtesy of a phone call? And forward his mail? And they certainly didn't seem to know anything about that at his office."

"Amnesia." Cheyenne was trying to make a joke, but Isabella's eyes widened and she quickly added it to the list.

"Yeah, what if he's wandering around out there somewhere? Doesn't know his name or where he lives?"

"That would explain a lot," Cheyenne said, taking another huge gulp of wine.

"Or what if he's got a secret life? Another home somewhere, a family?"

"Hmmm."

"Died in a car accident and his car ran into the ocean. Body and car were never found." Isabella was now scribbling feverishly on her writing pad.

"Uh-huh." Cheyenne flagged the waitress down for another glass of wine.

"Why wouldn't anyone be looking for him?" Isabella cocked her head and looked at Cheyenne.

"Huh?" Cheyenne realized she hadn't heard the last few things Isabella had said.

"Why isn't anyone looking for him?"

"Oh, yeah. I hadn't really thought about that, but it kind of makes sense. His parents are both dead, and he was an only child. He had a few acquaintances that he occasionally hung out with, but he was pretty much an introvert. Kept to himself." She pursed her lips. "I guess it's feasible no one's missed him yet. Except me, of course."

"And work. Apparently, his work schedule has been cleared. But no one seems too worried about that."

"Then it's either something work-related," Cheyenne thought out loud, "or he at least gave an explanation to someone at work about his absence."

"We need to talk to someone at the CSM who knows what's going on."

Cheyenne shook her head. "I don't think they're going to tell us anything. They could probably get in big trouble for violating confidentiality." The waitress dropped off her second glass of wine, and she intercepted it in midair with a grateful, close-lipped smile.

"What if he authorized them to give *you* information? It sounds like you were the closest thing to family he had."

Cheyenne shook her head. "If he wanted me to know where he was, he would've told me. That's what I keep trying to get through to you, Isabella. It's over. I've accepted it. You have to, too."

"We can't. Not yet. It just doesn't add up. There has to be another way to find out if any of this has to do with his job."

Cheyenne started to shake her head again, but then she remembered Rebecca. If nothing else, talking with her might satisfy Isabella's curiosity once and for all. "Well, I do have a friend in the CSM headquarters, where they keep all the records. She was the one who helped me find Hamm in the first place. She can probably tell me if there's a change in his professional status. At least, it would be somewhere to start."

"Great! When can you talk to her?"

"I'll call her tonight. But, Isabella, if this is a dead end, please tell me you'll let this go. I really appreciate that you care so much, but this is not healthy. I think the best thing is for me to move on."

"Fine but let's see what your friend has to say, first."

"Deal." Cheyenne smiled and finished off her wine. She got the check, and they headed out to the car.

When they pulled into Cheyenne's parking garage, Isabella turned to Cheyenne. "It's about time for me to pick Hendrix up. Thanks so much for putting up with me today. It was great to occupy my mind with something besides—"

"Anytime, Isabella. I'm really glad you came by."

They hugged, and Cheyenne watched as Isabella headed to her car, the day's strange events really hitting her for the first time. She locked her car and stepped into the elevator, pressing the button for the tenth floor. As she watched the numbers slowly climb, she realized she felt more peaceful than she had in a long time. She didn't think it was because of the wine. She was actually looking forward to getting some closure.

Back in her apartment, Cheyenne took her shoes off and padded to the living room with a bottle of red wine. She poured herself a generous glass, took a sip, and smiled as she leaned her head back on the couch. Tomorrow this whole mess would get cleared up. She would finally get some answers.

The warmth of the wine spread over her chest and into her belly, then made its way into her arms and legs. When it reached her head this time, she closed her eyes and gave in to it.

CHAPTER 22
Then
May 5, 2026

Monty looked up just as his secretary was letting Tracy, Karl's inexplicably hot live-in girlfriend, into his office. He was on the phone, but he gave her a welcoming smile and pointed to a cozy armchair.

"Just a minute," he mouthed, holding up an index finger. He rolled his eyes and pantomimed a babbling mouth with his free hand. She giggled and settled into the chair, her skirt riding up a little as she crossed her legs.

He ended the call, then walked around his desk to sit in the armchair next to hers. He had only met Tracy once or twice, but from what he knew of her, she would be the perfect asset. Ambitious, yet mercifully small-minded.

"The lovely Tracy." He gave her his best lady-killer smile and let his eyes trail down her legs to her Louboutin heels and back before continuing. "Thank you so much for coming here today."

She blushed. "Well, when you said it had to do with Karl's career—"

"I sure do hope he appreciates you." Monty shook his head and flashed her a grin. "Because if I ever hear differently, I'm going to have to have a serious talk with that guy."

"Karl takes very good care of me." Tracy gave Monty a tight smile and absentmindedly fingered a diamond tennis bracelet that dangled from her delicate wrist. She cast her eyes downward for a moment, then met his gaze. "How can I help?"

"As you know, Karl's in the running to become the next surgeon general."

This time, her smile was genuine, and her eyes sparkled. "Yes. We're very proud and excited." She laughed. "A little nervous, too."

Monty couldn't help but take in the generous cleavage spilling out from the button-down blouse she had probably chosen in an attempt to dress conservatively. With some effort, he brought his eyes up to her face before speaking.

"You should be proud. You and I both know he wouldn't be where he is today without such a strong, beautiful woman by his side. It's our job, yours and mine, to make sure he continues to look good throughout this process."

She nodded, but Monty could see the blank look in her eyes.

He started over. "For the last two weeks since the announcement, I've done nothing but field calls about Karl. The media wants to know if I have any information about him, any dirt."

"Of course, you've said no."

"Of course, but that's not exactly the point, now, is it? Everyone has skeletons in the closet. I have skeletons. You have skeletons. Even the Pope has skeletons." He leaned closer to Tracy and lowered his voice. "We just have to make sure we know of all Karl's skeletons before the press does."

Tracy pursed her lips and shook her head. "Say what you want about Karl, but he is beyond approach."

Monty bit his lip and managed to keep a straight face. "I agree Karl is a good man, but everyone has something they wouldn't want getting out. Karl is no exception. He probably has something in his past he doesn't even want you to know about. Our job is to dig up the dirt before the press does it for us."

Monty maintained eye contact as Tracy uncrossed her legs and placed her hands primly over her bare knees.

"I'm not sure I understand what you're asking."

"Nothing out of the ordinary for a situation like this. I just need access to his home office. I'll need to go through and familiarize myself with his personal and professional lives before the CSMs, with any issues that may come up. It's—the PR department recommended it."

Tracy tilted her head, and the corners of her mouth turned down slightly, but she remained silent.

"Over the next few months," Monty continued, "Karl will be attacked from every angle. He'll need someone in his corner, someone prepared to address these attacks at the drop of a hat."

Tracy squinted and gave a small nod.

"Trust me, he's less likely to think he needs this than you are, so it's probably best we keep it between us."

She chewed on her bottom lip and tapped her fingers on her knees as she stared past Monty at a spot on the floor.

Finally, she said, "Okay, that makes sense. I'll do whatever I can to help Karl."

Monty reached over to her knees and covered her small hands with his. "I was hoping you'd say that."

CHAPTER 23
Now
October 17, 2030

"Yes, I'll hold."

It was ten a.m. the day after her excursion with Isabella, and so far, all Cheyenne had done was waste the better part of the morning on the phone. She paced around her kitchen as she was transferred to yet another department within the CSM headquarters. For such a supposedly well-oiled machine, it certainly had some squeaky wheels. Who didn't have a voice recognition answering service in this day and age?

She sat on a stool and rested her elbows on the kitchen island as she listened to yet another message about her phone call being recorded to improve customer service. She had an idea or two of how they could improve customer service, and it started with having someone who wasn't completely incompetent answering the phones.

Just when she was about to end the call, she heard her friend's voice. "Cheyenne?"

"Rebecca, finally! I thought I was going to have to promise them my firstborn child to be able to talk to you."

"Sorry, sweetie. It's been a busy week. Mr. Bradford has been in and out of several of the facilities, and everyone's on high alert."

"Who?"

"Just the boss man. So, what can I help you with?"

"Well, this is probably going to sound a little weird." All of a sudden, Cheyenne wasn't so sure of herself. "I don't know if this is even your area—"

"What is it, Cheyenne?"

"Um, well." She took a deep breath and dove in. "I have this friend, a surgeon. I haven't heard from him in a few weeks and—you know, this is stupid."

"Cheyenne." Rebecca's voice had lost the friendly tone. "I have work to do. Just tell me what you need."

"Sorry. It's just—I went by his place yesterday, and it looked like he hadn't been home since I last talked to him. He hasn't been to work in a couple of weeks, either. I was wondering if you could tell me if anything's changed. You know, career-wise."

"Ah, unrequited love." Clearly, she could make time for a little drama. Cheyenne heard a few clicks on a keyboard, and then Rebecca asked, "What's his provider number?"

"His provider number? Where would I find that?"

"It'd be on his medical license or a prescription pad. If you don't have access to either of those—"

"Wait, would that be the number I used to find Hamm the first time?" She reached for her TabScreen on the kitchen counter, and it came to life in response to her touch.

"Hamm as in Hamilton Walker?"

"Yes, Hamilton Walker." Cheyenne flipped through file after file, searching for the one that would contain Hamm's number. Then she stopped, registering Rebecca's question. "Wait. Why? Do you know him?"

"Only from your show. He is a dreamboat. I don't blame you a bit for trying to track him down."

"Yeah, well."

"I saw him come through on the CRP list. I only noticed it because I recognized his name from the segment. It was really good. One of your best so far."

"Thanks. So, you were saying something about a CRP?"

"Hey, what ever happened with those two adorable little boys, anyway? The segment ended kind of abruptly."

Cheyenne felt warmth in her cheeks as she struggled with her answer. "Everything's okay. I mean, it's complicated. The Reids needed a little time—"

"Henry even watched it with me, and that's saying a lot," Rebecca continued. "We kept saying how the Reids were people we would totally be friends with. So relatable."

"I'm glad, Rebecca."

"How did you find them, anyway?"

"Dumb luck, actually. I met Isabella in a restaurant where she worked. I started talking to her, thought she had an interesting story, and the rest is history."

"That's why you make the big bucks."

"Well, all the stuff that happened later was what really made the story." Cheyenne was nowhere near ready to have this conversation. "Like I said, dumb luck."

"Come on. Don't be so modest."

"Anyway." She began to pace again from one end of the kitchen to the other. "You said Hamm—Dr. Walker—was on some list?"

"Oh, yeah. We process the CRPs in this office. His started a couple of weeks ago, if I remember correctly. I'd have to go back through my email to tell you the exact date. Does that time frame seem about right?"

"Yeah, actually it does. What's a CRP?"

"Sorry." Rebecca laughed. "I forget everyone doesn't know this stuff. It stands for Career Renewal Package."

"Is that supposed to mean something to me?" Cheyenne stopped pacing.

"I guess not. The packages have been such a hot topic of conversation around the office for us underlings. You know: who was chosen this time and what they did to deserve it. It's the closest thing we have to celebrity gossip. I forgot other people don't really know about it."

"Okay." Cheyenne now sat with her chin resting in her hand, fingers tapping against the side of her face. "Sounds interesting."

"Yeah, well. It gets old after a while," Rebecca said. "The CRP program was supposedly intended to help with burnout—you know, to prevent another crash like in 2018—and then it became this prestigious thing. It's supposed to be quite an honor to be selected."

Her voice carried a bit of sarcasm, or was Cheyenne imagining that?

"Since they've been doing it, probably less than fifty physicians have been chosen for it."

Cheyenne furrowed her brow. Something just wasn't adding up. "Wouldn't it have come up in conversation? That he was going away for—how long is it, anyway?"

"About four weeks. From what I hear, though, the physicians aren't given a whole lot of notice beforehand. All the travel arrangements are made for them. Someone just shows up one day and gives them the good news. In four years, no one's ever turned it down."

"How are they supposed to just drop everything?"

"I don't know, but they do. Apparently, it's totally worth it. They take care of your work schedule and any other responsibilities. They notify your next of kin. All you have to do is hop in a vehicle and head to a resort for some rest and relaxation."

Next of kin. Hamm had no next of kin. Cheyenne was it for him, and even she had to admit it was a stretch to consider their relationship on that level. Not yet, at least.

Not ever, she amended.

"Where is the resort?" she asked.

"I don't know," Rebecca said. "I've never asked."

"Someone knows," Cheyenne said, determined now to find out more. After all, that was what she did for a living.

"Well, I hope you find what you're looking for. Let me know how else I can help." Rebecca sounded hopeful. "Maybe you could give me an assignment."

Cheyenne thought for a moment. "Actually, I think there is something you could do."

"What's that?"

"You said your office manages the CRPs. Could you send me a list of the doctors who have participated?"

"Well, I guess that shouldn't be too hard to put together."

Cheyenne heard the hesitation in her voice. "Maybe we could meet for lunch or something." She sweetened the deal. "I could even do a little interview with you to put on the show's website."

"That sounds fun. The girls will be so jealous."

"Then, it's settled. Can you meet later today?"

"Let me check." There was a moment of silence on the line, then Rebecca said, "Looks like I'm wide open."

"Great. Let's meet at that little deli on the corner of Hawkins and Delmont," Cheyenne said. "Twelve thirty okay with you?"

"Fine. See you then."

Cheyenne was smiling when she hung up the phone with Rebecca. She may have a chance of finding Hamm, after all. Her next phone call was to her cameraman.

"Ronnie? Pack up the tripod. I'm going to need you today."

"Really?" Ronnie sounded surprised and more than a little relieved. "Miss Rose, I was starting to think I was going to have to look for another job."

"Don't be ridiculous. I'm calling Roger right now. We'll be there to pick you up at noon. You'd better not make us wait for you."

"I won't, ma'am." Cheyenne heard the excitement in his voice and wondered if it was the first time in weeks for him, too. He must have thought he was going to lose his job because of her. She made a mental note to arrange for him to get a small raise once she was back at work.

In the meantime, she had no idea what the afternoon held for her. Regardless, she was determined not to step foot out of her apartment until she looked like a respectable journalist. She caught a glimpse of herself in the foyer mirror and had to laugh.

I might be here awhile, she thought as she headed to her bathroom to freshen up.

CHAPTER 24
Then
May 7, 2026

Aaron sat alone on his front porch with his third glass of bourbon and a career brochure. Only two weeks had passed since he returned from his CRP, but his life before the retreat felt like a distant memory. He had spent the last twelve days participating in an intense training course to prepare him for another reentrance examination, which he had completed the day prior. That day, Mr. Bradford had called Aaron into his office and told him he would need to look for another job. A nonsurgical one.

He opened the brochure and a sheet of paper fluttered out onto the floor. He swore under his breath and leaned over to pick it up. It wasn't until he had unfolded the page that he remembered Mr. Bradford dropping it in his rush to leave earlier that day. He blinked a couple of times to bring the words into focus. It was a memo labeled with the heading *CSM Protocols,* and it was sent from a generic email address within the CSM. The subject line said *Clearance Level 5.* Aaron glossed over the memo once, and then he read the body of the email again more closely.

The CSM Protocol initiative has been wildly successful thanks to the contribution of each region's department head.

Attached are two new protocols that should be distributed to your staff in the next week on a need-to-know basis. The confidentiality of the protocols is essential to their continued success. As before, the final documentation review and edit will be the responsibility of each department head.

Thank you for believing in the system and sharing my goal of providing better healthcare to the population as a whole. In a time of turmoil and change, we have not only maintained a high standard of medicine, but we have done so while decreasing spending and saving America's healthcare system from an impending crisis. As Thomas Jefferson is credited for saying, "It is incumbent on every generation to pay its own debts as it goes."

As always, this message is encoded for deletion after opening. Department heads should print one copy to keep in a secure location for reference.

Aaron had no idea what protocols the memo was referring to. He hadn't come across any in his day-to-day work, which meant they probably had something to do with administration. If that was the case, he was already bored. He dropped the paper onto the table beside him and picked up the brochure once more.

He idly flipped through the pamphlet now, occasionally sipping his bourbon. He was familiar with most of the career options for physicians, but apparently, the CSM management had come up with a few new ones. Postmortem Sample Retrieval. What the hell was that? Didn't matter. He wasn't going into any field where the patients couldn't talk back.

Aaron skimmed the rest of the brochure before abandoning it next to the memo. Whatever he was looking for, he hadn't found it. Not yet, anyway. He sat alone with his drink and thought about how his life was about to change. All he had ever done, all he had ever known, was surgery.

Just as his eyelids began to feel heavy, he heard the front door open.

"Hon? What're you doing out here? It's almost midnight." Elizabeth rubbed her eyes as she stepped into the harsh light of the single bulb on the porch ceiling. Her shoulder-length dark hair made her skin look almost translucent in the fluorescent glow.

"Just thinking."

"I woke up, and you were gone." Her voice had a slight whine to it. "I don't feel that great."

He set his drink down and reached out to her. She joined him on the rocking chair.

"Do you think we're going to be alright?" she asked, resting her head on his chest and shivering a little as a breeze ruffled the sleeve of her satin nightgown.

He pulled her closer. "It's going to be difficult."

She stiffened in his arms, then pulled back to look at him.

"Elizabeth, would you rather I lie to you? Tell you this is a good thing?"

"Of course not. I just—"

"Look on the bright side. What if I had knocked you up? At least it's just you and me we have to worry about."

She stood up as if scalded, tossing something onto the table as she did so. "Yeah." Her voice shook. "What a blessing." She went back to the door and stopped there, her hand resting protectively on her abdomen.

"Elizabeth, I didn't mean—"

"Never mind," she said and disappeared into the dark house.

He groaned and reached for his glass. Next to it was a long tube with a digital screen that hadn't been there before. He held it up to the light. It took him a moment to register what he was looking at, but once he did there was no misinterpreting the results.

It was one word. One word that changed everything.

Pregnant.

CHAPTER 25
Now
October 17, 2030

"I think we got some good footage, Rebecca," Cheyenne said. "People will be really interested to hear what goes on behind the scenes at the CSM Corporation. Your makeup was great. The bright colors will really pop on camera."

Rebecca beamed. "When can I see it?"

"We'll probably edit it over the weekend, so it should be uploaded to the website by Monday. I'll send you a link."

"This was really fun, Cheyenne." Rebecca wiped some crumbs off the table with her napkin. "Thank you so much. I can't wait to show my family. They don't believe I really know you."

"Thank *you*, Rebecca." Cheyenne patted her brief-case, which now held the manila folder Rebecca had brought. "I know it wasn't easy for you to get this, especially on such short notice."

She blushed. "It was nothing, really. I'm happy to help."

Cheyenne signed the credit card receipt and stood up, signaling the end of their lunch date. Ronnie and Rebecca followed suit.

"I'll be in touch." Cheyenne gave Rebecca a quick hug, and then she and Ronnie headed out to the car, where Roger was waiting for them.

"So, Cheyenne," Ronnie said. "What exactly is in that folder?"

"Not sure." Cheyenne opened her briefcase and pulled out the pages. She studied them for a minute and said, "Wow, this is way more than I was expecting."

"Catch me up. I'm dying over here."

"Sorry." Cheyenne glanced over at Ronnie. "No judgment zone?"

Ronnie just looked at her.

Cheyenne smiled. "Okay, okay." Of all the people at the studio, he was the only one she could say really knew her and cared about her no matter what. "I'm trying to find Hamm."

"I thought you would have given up on that prick by now."

"I did, but something made me change my mind." She told him about Hamm missing work and what she knew so far about the CRPs. "So, anyway, that's where he is. Now that I know—"

"You want closure."

Cheyenne pursed her lips and sighed. "I guess so."

Ronnie paused for a moment to think. "Okay, well, it's better than sitting on my ass at home." He gestured to the papers in Cheyenne's lap. "So, what do we have here?"

"It's a list of other doctors who have participated in this CRP program. Rebecca didn't know where the resort was. I figured one of them could tell me."

"Looks like a lot of people."

"Well, yes and no." She handed him one of the pages. "Rebecca not only gave me their names but their office addresses, as well as the dates they were in the CRP."

"Wow, she must be a really good friend."

"Something like that." Cheyenne avoided eye contact.

Ronnie cleared his throat. "That interview we just did. It's not going to make it to the website, is it?"

Cheyenne continued flipping through the papers, trying to ignore him. "Anyway, it looks like they've had forty-three participants. Forty-four if you count Hamm. Only five of them are within driving distance, though, if we wanted to—"

"If we wanted to drop in? See how they're doing?"

"It's probably a bad idea."

Ronnie squeezed her knee and settled back into his seat. "What the hell else are we going to do?"

Cheyenne smiled and felt the knot in her chest loosen ever so slightly. “Hey, it’s work, right?” She pressed the intercom button beside her. “Roger, next stop is 2342 Rosemont Drive.”

When the car stopped forty-five minutes later, Cheyenne looked out the window and saw they were in a parking lot. She had been engrossed in her work, thinking of questions to ask and bouncing ideas off Ronnie.

“Alright.” Cheyenne referred back to the list. “This is Dr. Patel. He’s from up north but has been practicing in the Southeast for about ten years. He was one of the first to participate in the CRP program.”

Ronnie opened the car door and started to step out, his camera in tow.

Cheyenne placed a hand on his shoulder. “Let’s leave that outside for now. He isn’t even expecting us.”

Cheyenne and Ronnie got out of the limo and walked to the entrance of the CSM office building. Everyone in the lobby, including the receptionist, looked at the front door as it chimed. Cheyenne felt conspicuous and out of place.

The patients looked like they were torn from the pages of *The Grapes of Wrath*. They stared at Cheyenne with blank faces and slack jaws. Almost everyone had the leathered skin of a fifty-year smoker. They wore ill-fitting, dirty clothes that reminded Cheyenne that the little North Carolina town’s main export, tobacco, had long since gone out of vogue.

Cheyenne had known towns like this existed, but she was surprised to find one in such close proximity to her plush studio and even plusher penthouse. She cursed her wardrobe choice for the day. She had worn a tailored, navy skirt suit and pumps to match. Her hair was pulled up into what she had thought was a simple bun, but now, compared to these people, she must look like she was going to some sort of awards ceremony. Even Ronnie, in his standard t-shirt and jeans, was wearing a designer these people had probably never heard of. She was glad her instinct had told her to leave the camera in the car.

Cheyenne took a deep breath and approached the receptionist's desk. "We're here to see Dr. Patel." The patients watched her in complete silence, and her voice echoed off the concrete and tile. She pulled her jacket tightly around her torso. She was in their territory now and had never felt like more of an outsider.

The woman peered down at the computer screen that was built into the countertop. "Patient ID?"

"Um, I don't have—" She started over. "My name is Cheyenne Rose. You may have heard—"

"Spell it."

"C-h-e-y—"

The woman swiped her finger a couple of times across the screen. "Don't got you down here, sweetheart. When was your appointment?"

"I don't have an appointment. I'm a reporter. I was in the area and had a few questions for the doctor." She was met with a blank stare. "I host a TV show, *Rose Colored Glasses*. Maybe you've seen it?"

"Only TV I got is the MedScreen, lady. Ain't nothing on there worth watching."

"I see. Well, I can wait. Could you just let Dr. Patel know I'm here? Cheyenne Rose," she repeated.

"Sure, I will. Go ahead and have a seat." The woman didn't budge.

Cheyenne stood at the desk a moment longer, then she and Ronnie obediently sat down in the lobby.

An hour and a half later, Cheyenne was thinking about leaving. She had written down every possible question she could think of to ask Dr. Patel. Then she had started poring over the list of CRP doctors again. A couple of the names seemed eerily familiar, but she just couldn't place them. Just as she started to put her tablet away, a woman's face filled the screen, replacing the file Cheyenne was looking at.

"Miss Rose? We missed you at home this morning."

Cheyenne looked around the lobby. No one even tried to hide the fact they were eavesdropping. She stood up and headed to an empty part of the room, pressing a small button behind her ear as she walked to take the care coordinator off the tablet's main speaker.

"I'm sorry, Valerie," she whispered. "I totally forgot. I went back to work this morning."

The woman peered past Cheyenne to examine her surroundings. "Is that where you are now?" Her voice was now transmitted through a small, implanted speaker in Cheyenne's right ear.

"Yes." She nodded. "Well, I'm on assignment. But working." She felt that was true enough.

"Okay. We're very happy to see that you've returned to work. Do you have your pills with you?"

"Yeah, they're right here." Cheyenne put down the tablet and poured the pills into her hand, then counted them out in groups of five. "Fifteen."

The woman looked to the right of the screen then back at Cheyenne. "Thank you, Miss Rose. That's the count I have, as well." She squinted, referring again to the right of the camera. "It says here your doctor would like to increase your dose."

"Really? This is the first I'm hearing of it."

"Based on your troubles over the past couple of weeks, he believes you would benefit from a higher dose of your antidepressant."

"I think I'm actually climbing out of it."

"Well, it can be fairly common to backslide. I believe your appointment is next Wednesday. You can discuss it with his assistant at that time. In the meantime, the new prescription will be ready for pickup this afternoon."

"Okay." Cheyenne didn't want to argue in the middle of the crowded lobby. She held out the hand with the pills in it. "What should I do with the rest of these?"

"Just set them aside for now. No need to throw them away. You can likely use them at a later date if your dose is decreased again."

"Okay." Cheyenne cupped her hand and dropped the pills back into their bottle. Just then, Ronnie stood up and motioned for her to join him.

"Is that all?" Cheyenne addressed the care coordinator.

"Yes, thank you."

Cheyenne closed the screen and joined Ronnie at the front desk, where the receptionist had beckoned him.

"Dr. Patel says he can't meet with you today. His schedule is already overbooked. If you leave your name and number, he can give you a call and maybe work something out."

Cheyenne's heart sank. "Sure, thanks." She wrote her name and phone number on a sheet of paper the receptionist provided then jotted a quick note.

Had a few questions re: the CRP. Shouldn't take too much of your time.

– CR.

"Alright. Like I said, he'll be in touch."

Cheyenne watched as the woman disappeared through a door labeled Patient Care Area—Authorized Personnel Only.

She looked at Ronnie. "Strike one."

"We've still got four more before we're out." He patted her shoulder, and they headed toward the exit.

Just before they stepped through the glass exit doors, Cheyenne heard the receptionist coming up behind her.

"Miss Rose? Wait." The woman was panting when she finally reached them. "Dr. Patel is taking a late lunch break. I handed him the note, and he said he could talk to you if you don't mind him eating at the same time. He only has about ten minutes.

"Sure, no problem." Cheyenne lifted an eyebrow at Ronnie as they turned and followed the woman across the lobby and through the restricted door.

The doctor's office was pristine. He stood up from his leather desk chair when they entered and remained standing as he greeted Cheyenne, then Ronnie. He was fit and well-dressed. His dark eyes were both intelligent and welcoming.

"Thank you, Regina." He nodded at the receptionist and then closed the door firmly, leaving her alone in the hallway.

"Please have a seat." His olive skin and black hair implied a Middle Eastern heritage, but there was no hint of an accent in his voice to suggest he was born overseas.

"Thank you so much for seeing us today," Cheyenne said. "I gather you're very busy."

"That's putting it mildly." There was humor in his voice, but his face remained unreadable. His food lay untouched on his desk.

"I'm sorry to interrupt you during your lunch break. We'll be brief. I'd like to ask you a few questions about the CRP you participated in a few years back."

He nodded slowly. "Regina mentioned something about that. Who are you?"

"Well, I'm a reporter. I don't know if you've heard of me. Cheyenne Rose?" He continued to look at her blankly. "*Rose Colored Glasses*?"

"I'm sorry, Miss Rose. I don't watch much television these days."

"It doesn't really matter." Cheyenne waved a dismissive hand in the air. "I was thinking of doing a show about the CRP program. Or, more likely, on some of the physicians who have experienced it. I'm just trying to put my feelers out and see if there's a story there."

"Well, my story is very boring, I'm sorry to say." He folded his hands and placed them on the desktop.

Cheyenne leaned forward and smiled at him, lowering her voice an octave. "I doubt that very much, Dr. Patel."

"Well, it's the truth. It's certainly not television-worthy." He pressed his palms down on the desk and stood up. "Now, if you'll excuse me."

Cheyenne remained sitting. She was not going to give up so easily. "Dr. Patel, I wasn't completely upfront with you."

The doctor's face was a mask, but she saw his jaw clenching and unclenching.

"I am a reporter," she continued, "but I'm not here for a story. The reason I'm here is because someone I'm very close to disappeared two weeks ago. It took me this long to find out he was chosen to be a participant in something called a CRP. I don't know anything more than that." She gazed up at him, pleading. "I'm just looking for some answers."

He sighed and slowly lowered himself back into his chair. "I was chosen for the program three years ago. Around that time, just before being chosen, I was engaged to a beautiful woman named Anna. She was diagnosed with a very serious condition called acute lymphocytic leukemia." He was matter-of-fact, but tears glistened in his eyes. "Her malignancy developed very quickly and, despite extremely aggressive treatment, she passed away within three months. My family tells me I was there when she died, but I remember nothing. I must have blocked it out."

"I'm so sorry to hear that." Cheyenne resisted an urge to reach out to him.

"Thank you." He stared off into space. "After her death, I was approached almost immediately by the CRP program and asked to be a participant. I think they recognized I needed some time away from my daily routine. Four weeks, to be exact."

"Interesting. I thought it was supposed to be an honor of sorts."

"I believe it is, but there are many, many candidates who qualify on their merit. As I'm sure you're aware, very few physicians are asked to participate. They have another way to narrow down the selection. I believe—at least, in my case—it was my need for the program. Not the other way around."

"Hmm."

"Might that ring true for your friend?"

"Maybe." Cheyenne nodded thoughtfully. "So, if I wanted to drop in, where is the CRP located?"

Dr. Patel smiled, a distant look in his eyes. "Wouldn't we all like to know?"

She blinked. "You don't know where you spent the better part of a month?"

"Isn't that strange? At the time, I wasn't too worried about it. I had access to everything I could possibly need. My family was updated regularly, and even though I wasn't supposed to contact them directly, I could get messages to them fairly easily. At the time, what I wanted most was to disappear."

"And I guess you did." Cheyenne shook her head. "Well, thanks again for your time."

She and Ronnie stood to go, and Dr. Patel followed suit.

He stood in the doorway of his office and shook hands with Ronnie, who then headed down the hall toward the exit. The doctor grasped Cheyenne's hand and shook it firmly, but he didn't let go. For the first time, the look in his eyes reflected an emotion Cheyenne could interpret, and it almost made her wish she hadn't come.

"Be careful, Miss Rose." He whispered the warning so quietly she almost didn't hear him. "I've only spoken about the CRP to one other person, and I deeply regretted it."

Cheyenne opened her mouth to ask why, but his eyes had returned to their blank stare, and she knew she would get nothing more from Dr. Patel. She nodded once, then she walked out the door and down the hallway after Ronnie.

CHAPTER 26
Then
May 25, 2026

Monty went over what he was going to say one last time as he pulled his Maserati convertible into Karl and Tracy's neighborhood. His plan of attack was flawless, as long as Tracy didn't get in the way. He had waited five years to put Karl in his place, and as he envisioned the evening in his mind, he felt more and more certain that tonight was finally going to be the night. With Karl out of the way, Monty would naturally be the person to step up and take over management of the CSMs.

Still, he couldn't ignore the bitter taste of stomach acid at the base of his throat, reminding him that this was Karl Buchner he was dealing with. The weasel always seemed to have something up his sleeve, and today appeared to be no exception. Karl had seemed a bit too eager for their meeting tonight. A bit too enthusiastic.

He tugged at his shirt collar, considered unbuttoning the top button, then thought better of it. He turned the air conditioning up to full blast instead.

Tracy answered the door in a modest white cocktail dress with little blue flowers. Her hair was swept back in a loose bun, and she wore small diamond stud earrings. She truly was playing the part of the sweet little housewife. The poor thing had no idea how her life was about to change, no idea the part she had played in bringing Karl down. Monty almost felt sorry for her. Almost.

"Mr. Montgomery, how good to see you." Her voice trilled like a Disney character's and was just a little too loud. "It's been entirely too long. Won't you come in?" She opened the door wide and gestured with a sweeping arm toward the living room.

With some effort, Monty refrained from rolling his eyes. "Thank you, Tracy. Always a pleasure." Then he added in a whisper, "Tone it down a bit, okay?"

"Karl will be down in just a moment. Please make yourself comfortable."

Monty headed into the living room and set his briefcase down on the coffee table, almost knocking a crystal ashtray off in the process. He lowered himself down in stages onto the delicate couch, and once he was sure it would hold his weight, removed a folder and began flipping through the papers inside.

The evidence.

The reason Karl would never become surgeon general.

* * * * *

Exactly one hour and three gin martinis after Karl had joined him in the living room, Monty sat before his stunned boss, waiting for him to say something. Anything. For once, Karl Buchner appeared to be speechless.

He had sat quietly and listened as Monty had produced page after page of evidence on the CSM's underground operations. While nothing was spelled out, Monty knew it was incriminating enough that Karl wouldn't risk letting the documents get leaked to the media. He had too much at stake.

Karl placed his hand in his pants pocket, fidgeting with whatever he found there for what seemed like an eternity before finally breaking the silence.

"So." He removed his hand from his pocket and picked up his glass from the coffee table. He took a long, slow sip. "What is it that you want from me?"

"I want you to step down from consideration for surgeon general."

Karl laughed, choking on his drink. After he regained his composure, he met Monty's gaze, wiping the tears from his watery eyes. "Why on earth would I do that?"

"If you don't, I'll take all this," Monty gestured to the papers stacked on the coffee table, "to the press."

"I'll have you arrested for treason." Karl's hand returned to his pocket.

"There's no way—"

"You don't have level-five clearance, Monty. Very few people do. There's a reason for that. Yes, there are things that happen within the walls of the CSM that are kept from the general public, much like the CIA or the FBI. It's an issue of safety." Karl's eyes flicked to Monty's right for a split-second.

Monty followed his gaze and noticed Tracy peeking around the corner. He gave her a look that he hoped said, *Get the hell out of here*. She winked at him, then disappeared behind the wall.

Unsettled, Monty turned his attention back to Karl. "I don't buy it, not for a second."

"You don't have to. It's not for sale, but I assure you, if you try to go public with this information, especially without any incriminating evidence against me, you will be destroyed, politically and every other way possible."

"I'm not scared of you, Buchner." Monty stood up, his knees knocking against the coffee table and sending their glasses toppling over. He bent over to recover the papers before they became soaked with gin and felt a hand on his back. Before he could turn around, Karl gave him a shove that sent him over the coffee table. He landed on his right shoulder with a sickening crack. He tried to lift his arm but couldn't. When he dared to look and saw that his shoulder joint had come out of its socket, he almost passed out.

The crystal ashtray lay on the floor directly in Monty's field of vision. He relaxed the fingers of his left hand from their grip around his injured shoulder, reached forward, and grabbed it, gritting his teeth at the searing pain that followed. Karl leaned over Monty now, his face framed by the chandelier's light directly behind his head. Monty took a deep breath and swung the ashtray backward toward Karl's head.

The ashtray connected with Karl's brow but not in the satisfying way Monty expected. Instead of a thud, he felt more of a scrape as Karl almost completely dodged his swing. Monty's arm fell limply to his side, the weight of the crystal all of a sudden too much for him.

"That's going to leave a mark." Karl's voice came from above. Blood dripped between his fingers as he pressed his hand to the right side of his forehead, where the ashtray had grazed him. A grotesque grin was plastered on his face.

In his other hand, he clutched a syringe like a knife, needle pointing downward and ready to thrust. He looked demented, maniacal, and for the first time, Monty wondered if he had underestimated the skinny, self-conscious man.

"Amnesopam. You wouldn't believe the lengths I went to in order to get this."

Karl lunged toward Monty. Monty tried to roll away from his assailant, but the excruciating pain from his shoulder stopped him midway through.

"Ahhh!" Monty clutched his shoulder once more, frozen in agony. He knew he needed to get to his feet if he had any chance of regaining control of the situation, but before he could catch his breath, he felt a hand grip his left shoulder firmly, a knee jab into his side, and a needle sink into his left thigh.

For a moment, he didn't notice a single effect of the medication. Then his senses started dropping one by one. First to go was his vision.

Tracy screamed, "Karl, what have you done?" It sounded as if she was right next to him.

Then, Monty's hearing went. He could feel Karl's weight on him, and he could smell the staleness of the Oriental rug as his face pressed deeper into it. The last thing he felt before losing all awareness was the sensation of fullness in his left thigh where the syringe and its needle were still anchored.

* * * * *

When Monty came to, he was handcuffed in the back of a Charlotte police car on Karl's street. In addition to the police car, there was an ambulance, a fire truck, and two other police cars. The door was open, and he could hear bits and pieces of a conversation between two nearby pedestrians.

"They think it was a psychotic break," one voice whispered.

"Does he have any history of—you know?"

"Not that I know of, but you never know what'll send someone over the edge."

"I heard he was obsessed with the guy's wife. Stalking her. Then he finally lost it and showed up at their house. Luckily, Dr. Buchner was home."

Wait. Were they talking about him? Saying he was obsessed with Tracy? Monty tried to step out of the police car to set them straight, whoever they were, but immediately lost his balance and went face-first onto the pavement.

"Well, hey there, Sleeping Beauty," one of the cops said, smiling down at Monty with hands on his hips. Two of the bigger guys roughly picked him up and tossed him back into the car. They paid no attention to Monty's wails as he landed on his dislocated shoulder. This time, a man stayed behind and stood guard just outside the car door.

Monty saw Karl and Tracy giving statements to the police up ahead. Karl had a large bandage across his forehead, and Tracy's eyes were red and puffy. Karl had a protective arm wrapped around her. Monty knew in that moment he was screwed. He couldn't remember how he had even gotten there, but he was on the wrong side of the police car for things to end well for him.

Tracy stood next to Karl, the perfect domestic partner, no doubt corroborating whatever bogus lie he had come up with to frame Monty. His only chance was to head them off at the pass. Tell his side of the story before their side was accepted as God's honest truth, but did he even know what his side of the story was?

He opened his mouth to tell the cop he'd like to give his statement, but the words didn't come. Noises, yes, but no words. He sounded like he had been to the dentist for a filling and then had gotten drunk. The officer looked at him warily then burst out laughing.

"Oh, you got ahold of something good, didn't you? Wanna tell me what it was? That's okay, we'll find out soon enough. I bet that drug screen's gonna light up like a Christmas tree." Then he yelled across the street to where several of his buddies had congregated. "Hey guys, come over here and listen to this shit!"

A couple of guys jogged over to where Monty and the police officer were. Fortunately, right at that moment, the officer who was talking to Karl and Tracy seemed to finish up. He jogged over to the police car in which Monty sat.

"Alright, Charlie, let's pack up. We need to get this one to the station so we can book him and get his statement."

"Good luck with that. I can't understand a word he's saying. Sounds like he needs to sleep it off."

"Well, anyway, let's get loaded up."

The police car drove silently down the residential street. No lights, no sirens. Monty leaned against the car door, his arms cuffed behind him, and looked out the window as they passed Karl's house. Karl stood in his front yard and waved as the police car cruised out of his neighborhood, the expression on his face one of complete arrogance.

This is not over, Monty thought, feeling a whole new level of hatred for Karl. *Not even close.*

CHAPTER 27
Now
October 17, 2030

Back in the car, Cheyenne couldn't stop thinking about Dr. Patel's warning. She was sure she hadn't imagined the fear in his eyes, but she couldn't make sense of it. What happened that had him so scared? Was he afraid for himself or for her?

The search for Hamm was becoming much more than a nice little diversion. What kind of place was he taken to? Was he in danger? And if so, did he even know it? And what was she thinking, getting herself involved?

She looked at Ronnie beside her. "What did you think of Dr. Patel?"

Ronnie settled back into his seat, crossing one ankle over the opposite knee and reaching his arm over the back of the seat. "I think he left out a lot of details."

"You're saying I should've probed more?"

"Nah, you did good to get what you did out of him. Some people just aren't talkers." He picked up the folder from where it lay between them and began to flip through the pages. "So, who's next?"

"Actually, I think we're done for today. I need to figure out a new game plan. I'll have Roger drop you off."

"Okay, but don't wait too long to call me next time or I may have a new job."

"Is that a threat?" Cheyenne knew he was all talk.

"Just sayin'. I got the wife and kids to think about."

"I know." *Believe me, I know*, Cheyenne thought. "It won't be too long," she promised as Roger pulled the limo up to the curb of Ronnie's apartment complex. "One, two days, tops."

“I’ll be waiting.” Ronnie headed up the sidewalk to his apartment building. His step was light and carefree.

Watching him, Cheyenne had a sick feeling in the pit of her stomach. What was she about to get them into?

After stopping at the pharmacy to pick up Cheyenne’s new prescription, Roger pulled the car into her parking garage. She said goodbye to Roger, told him she’d call soon, and got out of the car. He watched from the driver’s seat this time as she got safely into the elevator, then he pulled away.

Suddenly exhausted, Cheyenne leaned against the back wall of the elevator and closed her eyes. When the doors opened in front of her apartment door, she unlocked it and walked straight into the foyer without turning on the lights. She dropped her briefcase, keys, and pill bottle on the entryway table and headed toward the kitchen for a glass of wine.

A silhouette was barely visible against the light emanating from the window in the living room, but it stopped her in her tracks.

Cheyenne’s scalp tingled, and her heart pounded. She briefly thought of running, but the idea felt wrong somehow. Instead, she backed up and grabbed her keys without making a sound, positioning her can of Mace in her right hand. She took a couple deep breaths and flipped on the lights above the kitchen island, illuminating the person’s face.

He was someone she had never seen before, but he looked at her with a familiarity that made her skin crawl. He had piercing gray eyes that peered out from beneath two distinct, black eyebrows. His skin was thick and tan.

He smiled at her in greeting, and deep lines formed around his eyes and mouth. He was menacing beneath the hanging pendant lights; the shadows cast by his brows shielded his eyes and the top half of his cheeks from the light, exaggerating the sharp angles of his dark features.

“Miss Rose.”

The way he said Cheyenne’s name triggered something in her. “Have I—have we met?”

The man stood up, resting his hand on a pistol at his hip. Cheyenne bristled and took two steps backward.

"I'm sorry to have frightened you."

He spoke the words casually, as if the tension in the room had already dissipated, and this was all just a misunderstanding between friends.

"How did you get into my apartment?" She could barely hear her own voice over the pounding in her ears.

"Your landlord, Mr. Adams, was very cooperative once he understood the nature of my call." His hand remained on the gun.

Cheyenne became very conscious of the tiny hairs on the back of her neck and her arms standing at attention, desperately trying to tell her something was terribly wrong. Her mouth was dry, and she gave up trying to find the right words to answer him. She assumed he couldn't care less if she responded.

Sure enough, he took her silence as an invitation to continue. "I haven't been waiting long."

Oh, good, Cheyenne thought, dizzy and irrational. *I would hate to have put you out.*

"Shall we make ourselves comfortable in the living room?"

"I'm perfectly comfortable right here." She felt anger rising up in her. Who did he think he was, just letting himself into her apartment, acting like he owned the place? She didn't take her eyes off the man as she gestured for him to stay where he was, giving him a glimpse of the pepper spray in her hand.

Her mind felt equal parts sharp and fuzzy. She had a heightened sense of her surroundings and was sensitive to the man's smallest movements, but at the same time, she felt like she was talking and moving in slow motion.

"Very well. It has come to our attention that you are showing some interest in our CRP program."

Cheyenne's mind swarmed with questions. Who was the *our* this guy was talking about? And how had it come to their attention? Had Rebecca talked? Or Dr. Patel?

"While the work you do is certainly…entertaining, we believe this subject matter would be better handled by someone with a more professional background." His smile was wide, revealing two rows of gleaming white teeth embedded in glossy, pink gums.

Cheyenne's senses careened back into real time. "I'm sorry?"

"The CRP program has been kept confidential since its inception for good reason. We will not allow it to be sensationalized by a modern-day Jerry Springer."

And there it was.

Cheyenne felt a pressure build within her. She reached for the foyer table to steady herself. "I don't know who you think you are, coming into my house, making demands and veiled threats, but last time I checked, this is a free country." Her voice shook, and she tightened her grip on the can of Mace. "If there's something you're trying to hide about the CRP program, I can guarantee you I'm going to find out what it is, and if the American people need to know, you'd better believe I'm going to tell them, too."

She wanted to storm out to punctuate her point, but he was in her house. Instead, she walked briskly to the front door and opened it, then glared back at him. "Now, unless you're planning on kidnapping me or holding a gun to my head…"

He straightened his suit jacket around his hips. "Miss Rose, thank you for the hospitality. Someone will be in touch again soon. I think you'll find our position on this is nonnegotiable."

Cheyenne was silent, her hands trembling in anger and in response to the adrenaline coursing through her body. After he walked through the door, she closed it behind him and locked the deadbolt. Then she sank to the floor, her bravado instantly gone.

She considered calling someone, but could think of no one to call, no one she wanted to drag into this mess, anyway. Instead, she stood up and grabbed her prescription from the table. She made her way into the kitchen, and chased a pill with a couple of swigs straight from a bottle of Chardonnay. She then retrieved her briefcase and settled onto the couch, wine in hand, to do some research.

She didn't know who had sent the man or why they needed to keep the CRPs a secret, but she was more determined than ever to find out.

CHAPTER 28
Then
May 15, 2028

Aaron Isaacs woke suddenly from a deep sleep. It was how he started his day every morning for the last two years. One minute his mind was a blank slate, and the next, his thoughts raced so quickly through his head that he could almost see them vying for his attention. This morning, his thoughts settled on Andrew McClain.

These days, Aaron did what was asked of him at work and left at five o'clock on the dot. From five to eight, he could usually be found at one of the bars nearby, drinking and biding his time until he could put off going home no longer. He and Elizabeth would have dinner, the clinking of their silverware against their plates often the only sound, then they would go to bed. Once a month, she would remind him of her calendar, and he would do his duty, but that was all it was anymore. Then, two weeks later, almost like clockwork, he would find her in the bathroom staring vacantly at a pregnancy test.

The only things worse than the negative pregnancy tests were the miscarriages. Each baby was farther along than the last, making it that much more heartbreaking each time. Elizabeth's soft, dimpled, perfect body had shrunk until she seemed to be nothing more than skin stretched over bone. Sometimes, in the right light, it was as if you could see through her completely.

If going through the motions at home felt pointless, his work life felt even more so. He had seen so much death in the last two years, a disproportionate amount, in his opinion. He was starting to become numb to it. He now knew he couldn't save the world one patient at a time, so he rarely even bothered trying anymore. That starry-eyed Aaron was long gone, replaced with a disillusioned and sometimes downright mean version of himself.

But for some reason, Aaron could not stop thinking about his newest patient. Andrew McClain was placed on his service in the long-term care wing of the CSM just three days ago. As with most of Aaron's patients, it had already been decided that further aggressive measures would be futile. All he had left to do was get a hard copy of his advanced directive, which provided consent for organ donation, and pull the plug. Easy peasy. He could do it in his sleep. He didn't know why he was having such a hard time accepting the diagnosis.

He looked to his left, where Elizabeth was lying in bed, still asleep. She looked peaceful. Happy. He wondered if she was dreaming and if so, what about. Just then, she stirred. Aaron threw the covers back and jumped out of bed before she could open her eyes and see him watching her. Once he had safely made it to the bathroom, he poked his head through the doorway.

"Good morning. Sleep okay?"

She looked around the room with heavy eyelids and smiled. "Yes, I guess I did."

"I'm glad." Aaron hopped into the shower. After lathering up for a minute, he called out to Elizabeth. "Listen, I was thinking."

She padded into the bathroom. "Mmm-hmm?"

"We should go out tonight. What about that little place on the corner? The new one we keep meaning to try." He wiped the condensation off the shower door so he could see her reflection in the mirror.

"Sure, that sounds nice." She brushed her hair. "We can celebrate."

"Celebrate?" Oh God, had he missed their anniversary or something? No, that was—

"I'm thirteen weeks pregnant today." She turned toward him, leaning against the bathroom counter. "We made it to the second trimester."

"You're—you're what?" Thirteen weeks? That meant at least a couple of months since the last weepy episode on the toilet. A couple of months since she had reminded him of her fertile window. How had he missed that? Aaron knew he should be happy, but all he felt in that moment was a sense of dread. He didn't think he could survive another disappointment, and he knew Elizabeth couldn't.

He turned off the water and placed both hands on the glass. "Why didn't you tell me?"

"I wanted our pregnancy to be *good* news. Not something that would stress you out every minute of every day. So I waited this time." She flashed him a flirtatious smile. "It's been my little secret."

He smiled back, hoping she couldn't see how forced it was, and tried to sound casual. "You know, now that I think about it, you have been looking a little thick around the middle."

She turned sideways and frowned at her profile in the mirror, one hand on her flat belly. "I'm not even showing yet."

"You know I'm teasing." Aaron stepped out of the shower and put his arms around his wife from behind, letting his hands rest on her stomach. He closed his eyes, imagining her belly swollen beneath his palms, feeling those little twitches that would be his first physical contact with this baby, God willing.

She placed her hands over his and looked in the mirror. "I can't wait to start showing, actually. I feel like I've been pregnant for so long, and no one knows it but me."

"And now, me." Aaron kissed the side of her neck and gave her a slap on the rear before heading into the closet to get dressed. "So tonight, then? Dinner?"

"Sure. How about seven o'clock?"

"Sounds good. I'll probably have to meet you there. I think it's going to be a long day."

"I figured. I may just walk over. It's only about a mile from here."

"I don't know if that's a good idea, Elizabeth." He stepped out of the closet holding up two neckties. She pointed to the one in his right hand, and he began to tie it around his neck.

"I'll be fine, Aaron. Don't be such a worrywart. I'm pregnant; I'm not an invalid."

"I worry. It's what I do."

"I know, but there's no need to worry about me. Not now. Everything's going to be fine. I have a really good feeling this time."

Aaron didn't have to look at her to know she was grinning from ear to ear.

* * * * *

"Dr. Isaacs, you look like a Cheshire cat this morning!" his assistant, Betty, said as he strolled into work a few minutes late.

Aaron had wanted to keep the news to himself until it seemed more real, but he was having trouble wiping the smile from his face. He didn't say anything, just winked back at Betty and headed toward his office to start his day. The sooner he got started, the sooner he could get home to his family.

Family. Just thinking the word made his heart race, and he had to check himself.

He reached the door to his office and noticed it was slightly ajar. The only other person who had a key was Mr. Bradford. Or, as Aaron called him behind his back, the Grim Reaper. He supposed it was meant to be a show of respect that the CEO showed up every time they were about to pull the plug on a patient—maybe it was even required of him—but it just made the guy seem twisted and sick, like he enjoyed seeing people die.

Right now, he sat in Aaron's chair with his feet propped up on the desk. Aaron despised the meticulously dressed man, hated seeing him swagger around the hospital like he owned the place. Each time he came to visit the CSM, he made a comprehensive tour of the facility, barking orders and degrading the staff. Today would be no exception.

"Dr. Isaacs, good morning." His white teeth gleamed as he graced Aaron with a perfectly straight smile. "Fancy meeting you here."

"Yes. Why are you here, Daniel?" Aaron purposely used his first name to take him down a few notches. Piss him off. He did not want to make small talk with Bradford, not today of all days.

"I've been monitoring the documentation on our friend, Andrew McClain. It looks like we are nearing the end with him. Would you agree?"

"Actually, I've been thinking. I'd like to do a trial off sedation."

Bradford raised his eyebrows. "Has there been a change I should know about? Has he miraculously developed cortical brain activity?"

"No. I'd just like to make sure that's the case when we—"

"Not necessary." Bradford shook his head and stood up from Aaron's desk chair. "You know those medications don't alter brain wave patterns that much, at least not at the level used for vent sedation. Tomorrow is day thirty. Per the protocol, we will remove life support. There need be no further discussion on this point."

"Per the protocol, per the protocol. I am so sick of hearing you say that. Why hasn't anyone but you seen these damn protocols? I'm the man's treating physician, for God's sake."

Mr. Bradford looked calmly at Aaron. "The protocols don't concern you. All you need to know is they allow all patients to receive the same standard of healthcare across the continuum." He began to walk toward the door but turned around just before exiting. "Don't even think of going to the patient's family with this. The last thing they need right now is to be confused about his prognosis."

Aaron stared the other man down.

Bradford glanced around the office and then cleared his throat. "Are we clear, Dr. Isaacs?"

Aaron gave him a short nod and opened the door wide. The other man strode through it, not even bothering to say goodbye.

Aaron sat down to start his paperwork for the day, but he was so angry he could hardly see straight. There was no reason he couldn't do the trial on his own time between today and tomorrow. Bradford didn't need to know. He just needed to make sure no family members were planning on spending the night with Andrew so that he could do what needed to be done in privacy.

He got up from his desk to close his office door and noticed a camera crew outside Andrew's room. He could only imagine what was going on, but he didn't have time to go check it out, not if he was going to make it to dinner on time.

He sat back down and tried to focus. As he logged into his workstation, he felt a smile creeping back onto his face. He picked up the phone to call Elizabeth.

CHAPTER 29
Now
October 18, 2030

"I'm sorry. It appears that Rebecca Stephenson no longer works in the information security department." The man's voice on the other line sounded nervous and unsure. "Can I help you with something?" He was the third person Cheyenne had spoken to since trying to locate her friend, again. The evidence was certainly starting to pile up. It seemed that Rebecca was truly gone.

Cheyenne hesitated before answering. "No, thank you. I just had a specific question for her. I'm sorry to hear that she's been relocated. Do you know why?"

"I don't have access to that information. I can transfer you to the main office—"

"No, that won't be necessary," she said before he could put her on hold again. If she had to listen to any more elevator music, she was going to need a drink—even if it was only eight thirty in the morning. "I'm sure I'll be able to track her down." Even as she spoke the words, Cheyenne didn't believe them. Her temples began to pulse, and she felt beads of sweat forming on her face. She sat down at the kitchen counter and dropped her head into her hands just as the spots started to float across her vision. This was no coincidence. Rebecca's abrupt absence, her disappearance, had something to do with Cheyenne. There was no other feasible explanation.

She scratched *Call Rebecca* off her to-do list. Shaking her head, she added *Find Rebecca* to the bottom of it. She had made absolutely no progress since waking up at six thirty. It was the first time in over two weeks since the day of the surgery that she had woken up prior to nine without the assistance of an alarm clock. At least some things were returning to normal.

Her MedScreen switched on. “Pill count, please, Miss Rose.”

“Got the new bottle yesterday,” Cheyenne reminded her care coordinator. “So, twenty-nine pills.” She popped one into her mouth. “Twenty-eight.”

“Thanks. See you tomorrow morning.”

Cheyenne went back to the drawing board. She had tried to schedule appointments with three other doctors in the area who were involved in the CRP program, but she had gotten no cooperation. Now she stared at the last name on her list of local CRP alumni. Dr. Aaron Isaacs.

Born in the Northwest, Dr. Isaacs had come to the area fifteen years ago for residency, met his wife, and never left. He had set up a general surgery practice in a rural part of the state, which was bought by the CSM program five years ago.

When Cheyenne searched the online local news archives for the year in which he’d been to the CRP, she realized why his name sounded vaguely familiar. It appeared the doctor was involved in a controversial case involving a twelve-year-old boy with an abdominal tumor. He had removed the tumor without incident, according to the record, but the child had developed a deadly arrhythmia at the end of the surgery. Despite resuscitative efforts, the boy did not survive. His parents, who were understandably upset, filed a lawsuit, but the case never went to trial. The CSM settled with the family out of court. Shortly after, if the dates Rebecca provided were correct, Dr. Isaacs was granted a complete Career Renewal Package.

Was the CRP program meant to be punitive? She was given the distinct impression that being chosen to participate was something to be proud of. If it wasn’t, well, that changed everything, including the situation with Hamm.

Especially the situation with Hamm.

Cheyenne felt on the verge of a breakthrough, but her thoughts were like molasses coursing slowly through her brain. By the time they reached the forefront, she had forgotten their significance. Something connected the three doctors, something aside from their participation in the CRPs, but what was it?

Hamm was chosen immediately after the surgery in which Ridge had died. She knew nothing more because he hadn't spoken to her since.

Dr. Patel said that he was chosen after his fiancé died.

Dr. Isaacs was sent away on the heels of a medical malpractice lawsuit.

They had all experienced something tragic prior to being sent away. For two of them, it was a bad patient outcome. For Dr. Patel, on the other hand, it was losing a loved one. Something wasn't adding up. She knew she was missing something, and it was driving her crazy.

Cheyenne gave up trying to figure out the common thread and focused her attention once more on Dr. Isaacs. If she could talk to him, he might be able to shed light on what the CRP was truly meant to be.

The list Rebecca gave her had helped her track down the other doctors, but the location listed for Dr. Isaacs' office didn't appear to have been updated recently. What could that mean? Had he retired? Or maybe he was forced to quit practicing. How was she supposed to find him without a real address or phone number?

She tapped her computer screen and then spoke. "Search Dr. Aaron Isaacs, Center for Standardized Medicine, North Carolina."

"I'm sorry." Her computer spoke back to her. "There are no results matching the exact specifications of your search."

Cheyenne took a deep breath. How was there no record of this guy at all? It was like he didn't exist.

She tapped her fingernails on the granite, the rhythmic clicking sound a welcome distraction in the otherwise silent kitchen. It was starting to become pretty clear that someone didn't want this guy to be found. All traces of his professional life were erased. If he was alive, he had to be out there somewhere, and the harder he was to find, the more important it was becoming to Cheyenne that she track him down.

* * * * *

Cheyenne checked her reflection in the car's rearview mirror one last time before turning off the engine. This was her third and final stop for the day. She had located only a few families in the small town of Belmont who had the surname Isaacs. She knew there was no guarantee that Dr. Isaacs or his family had remained here after he stopped practicing, but this was her only lead.

Her hasty research had revealed that the double-wide trailer at the end of the long, gravel driveway was purchased by an Elizabeth Isaacs several years before. However, the post office had a different person on record as the occupant. Mackenzie Fowler worked two full-time jobs and had two school-age children who should be home right now. Mackenzie's shift at Burger King wouldn't be over until ten o'clock.

Cheyenne hardly recognized the person staring back at her in the rearview mirror. For once, her frizzy hair had come in handy, since her goal was to draw as little attention to herself as possible in the trailer park. She had pulled it up into a high ponytail, allowing the loose strands to frame her face. With the sun shining through the back of the car, it gave her the vague impression of viewing a solar eclipse. Her heavy makeup was already starting to make her skin feel greasy and dense in the heat of the summer day. She applied one more coat of blue eye shadow in an attempt to smooth out the creases already forming in the folds of her eyelids, but it only made things worse. Oh well, she looked the part. There was no denying that.

Cheyenne's phone rang in her lap, and she looked down to see that Isabella was calling. She pressed ignore and stared at Isabella's name on the screen until it finally disappeared. She knew Isabella was dying for an update, but Cheyenne didn't have any news—any good news, anyway—for her. For now, at least, it was safest to just keep her out of it.

She dropped her phone into the passenger's seat and then stepped out of the car onto the gravel driveway. A cloud of dust rose around her sneakers. She started to bend over and wipe them off but caught a glimpse of the path leading up to the door of the double-wide and decided not to waste her time. She reached into the back of the car for her bag of goodies and made her way toward the front of the house.

The door rattled beneath her knuckles with each knock. She heard rustling inside the house followed by hushed voices. Finally, the door swung inward, revealing a tiny kitchen with a stove, a microwave, and a sink along the far wall.

Cheyenne plastered a smile onto her face as she craned her neck around the door to get a look at the person who had opened it. "Hello?" she called in a strong Southern accent she had discarded years ago. "Anybody home?"

A forehead, partially covered with a limp piece of sandy-blond hair, poked out from around the door. It was about four feet off the ground and was followed by a pair of beady eyes and a freckled nose. "Who wants to know?"

The child spoke with such a heavy drawl that it took Cheyenne a few seconds to process what he had said.

"Well, hi there. What's your name, little guy?" Cheyenne sized him up and decided he couldn't be older than seven or eight. "Is your daddy home?"

"Name's Randy." The boy pursed his lips and placed his hands on his hips. "Who's ayskin'?"

"My name is Cheyenne Rose. I'm looking for Mr. Aaron Isaacs." She showed him her bag. "He won a raffle at the radio station, and he hasn't claimed his prize. We were just hoping to get it to him."

The boy let his guard down for a moment, and his facial expression turned into one of childlike curiosity. He let go of the door and reached for the bag Cheyenne held. "Cool. What is it?"

"Well, only Mr. Isaacs can open the prize." Cheyenne felt terrible for the lie. "Do you know him? Do you know where I could find him to give him his prize?"

The boy eyed her for a second longer then focused his energy on the bag in her hand. She could see his curiosity winning out over all the warnings he'd been given about strangers. Cheyenne held the bag close to her chest, allowed a minute or two longer for the boy's imagination to run wild, then said, "I suppose if someone were able to help me find him, then that person would deserve part of the prize, as well. Do you know anybody who might know where Mr. Isaacs is?"

The boy looked like he might explode, torn between his better judgment and the reward. Another child, a girl with the same blond hair and freckles, ventured out from behind the door. She was about five years old. Both of them stared at the bag, their bodies inching toward the threshold as if propelled by the sheer force of whatever was in the package.

The boy spoke up. "We ain't seen Uncle Aaron in near about two years. He used to come over near about ever' Saturday after he married Aunt 'Lizabeth, even though it took almost an hour to get here from the rich side of town. But my momma said he just about went plum crazy when—" He stopped himself. Even at his age, he seemed to know there was a line you didn't cross when it came to family secrets.

Cheyenne felt herself losing him. "That's a shame. I was really hoping I could get this Xbox Universe to him. I guess I'll just have to give it to the runner-up. Thanks, anyway." She turned around and started walking toward her car, taking her time and listening out for a change of heart from either child.

"Hey, lady. Wait up."

Cheyenne stopped and faced the boy.

"He lives over on Slater Street now, in the nuthouse. Ever since—"

The little girl beside him shoved him so hard that he fell sideways into the door frame.

Cheyenne could tell she would get no more information from the children, but it didn't matter. What Randy had given her was enough. She reached into her bag and pulled out the game console. The boy's eyes widened as she handed it to him.

"Thank you, Randy. I'm sure your uncle will be very happy to get his prize."

Randy smiled and stood up a little straighter. Cheyenne made her way back to her car. She drove away, the dust rising up in a cloud behind her.

As she neared the highway, she looked in the rearview mirror and saw the two children standing on the front stoop of the double-wide. The girl stood facing her brother, tiny arms waving above her head, ponytail flapping behind her as she lectured him. Randy clutched the Xbox.

Cheyenne felt a moment of solidarity with him. They had both gotten exactly what they wanted.

CHAPTER 30
Then
May 16, 2028

"Dr. Isaacs? Dr. Isaacs, are you asleep?"

"No, Sara. I'm awake." Aaron grunted and shifted in the uncomfortable, hospital armchair. As if he could fall sleep in this contraption. He yawned and made a mental note to request more comfortable furniture for the hospital rooms.

"Mmm-hmm." Andrew's nurse went about her hourly routine, checking IV drips and repositioning him in the hospital bed.

Aaron was relieved to discover Sara was working tonight. There weren't many people he trusted as much as her, and she had a reputation for being able to keep a secret.

"What time is it?"

"Two a.m."

It was only two? As a resident, he used to work thirty-hour shifts with no sleep whatsoever. He'd gotten soft in his old age. To be honest, the fact that he was there at all was a miracle. It was all he could do to part ways with Elizabeth after dinner, her heavy eyelids and wandering hands beckoning him to go home with her, to forget about whatever he needed to do at the hospital.

"Any activity from our patient?" he asked the nurse.

"Not yet." She fluffed the pillow beneath Andrew's head and straightened the thin blankets that covered him, like this was any other night in the hospital.

Five hours had passed since he'd turned off the drips. Aaron leaned forward. "Come on, Andrew," he whispered in his ear. "I need to see something from you tonight. Show me something." He watched Andrew for a full minute, seeing no response. He fell back in his chair, crossed his hands over his belly, and closed his eyes. He would just rest for a minute or two and then check on Andrew again.

What felt like only a few minutes later, Aaron opened his eyes and pulled out his phone to check the display. Four a.m. Damn it, he'd done it again.

He sat up in the chair and rubbed his eyes. He looked over at Andrew's quiet, still body. Aaron felt like his patient was on death row, and he was anxiously awaiting the phone call that would pardon him at the last minute. There would be no phone call, no generous judge ready to set him free, just Aaron and only a few hours left to see if Andrew would live or die.

Aaron stood up and moved to Andrew's bedside. "Hey, Andrew. It's Dr. Isaacs. Can you move your hand for me?" He reached out and touched his patient's hand. "Come on. I know you're in there."

He backed away from Andrew and headed toward the door. "I'm going to go grab some coffee. You want anything?" He waited, got no response, and then headed toward the cafeteria.

When Aaron returned to the room, he was already feeling more energized. He hadn't had his first sip of coffee yet, but just inhaling the scent perked him up. Andrew was just as Aaron had left him: eyes closed, head at a forty-five degree angle, arms by his sides, hands flat with fingers splayed open—

But not both of them. The fingers on his left hand were fanned out, but his right hand looked like it had tried to form a fist and gave up. It wasn't that way when Aaron had left the room fifteen minutes prior. *It's probably nothing*, he told himself. *Don't get too excited just yet.*

Coffee in hand, Aaron made his way back to the armchair. From where he sat, he had a view of Andrew's bed as well as the door out to the hallway. It was only four thirty. He had a couple of hours before people would start to wonder what he was up to, but two hours was not a lot of time, not when talking about days—no, weeks—worth of sedatives. What he needed was a way to reverse the effect of the medications more quickly.

He eyed the bags that had infused medications into Andrew's veins just hours ago. They now hung dormant on the IV pole, casting an eerie shadow on the hospital room floor. Midazolam. Fentanyl. Tube feeds.

Antidotes existed for both the fentanyl and the midazolam, but like any medication, he would have to enter an electronic order to make them accessible. That would create a trail, and since he wasn't even supposed to be here—

"Code Blue, room 123. Code Blue, room 123." The distress call came over the loudspeaker, disrupting his thoughts.

Aaron jumped up from the armchair, spilling his coffee on his scrub pants but not feeling the wet heat. His heart raced in response to the adrenaline now coursing through him. He was like Pavlov's dog, and the Code Blue was his bell.

He ran down the hallway to room 123. A group of people had already congregated around the door. A crash cart sat just outside the room.

Dr. Isaacs pushed his way through the crowd and quickly assessed the situation. The pulse oximeter was not picking up the woman's oxygen saturations, and he could tell from her blue lips and shallow breathing that it wasn't due to a problem with the equipment. On the cardiac monitor, the patient's heart raced at over 150 beats per minute.

"Is that sinus rhythm?"

"SVT."

"Give adenosine, six milligrams, STAT."

Someone tore the breakaway flap that normally kept the crash cart locked, located the adenosine, and passed it to the patient's nurse. She drew up the medication in a syringe.

"Six milligrams of adenosine going in."

"Where's respiratory? We need to bag her and get an ABG. Rhythm?" The language of medicine, so familiar and universal, coaxed Aaron into his own kind of rhythm.

"SVT at one-twenty. One-thirty. One-forty." The nurse narrated as the heart rate climbed back up to its previous level.

"Give another adenosine. Twelve milligrams, STAT."

Three long seconds passed as the medication was administered, and the patient's heart stopped temporarily in response.

"Sinus, ninety-four."

"BP?"

"One-oh-six over fifty-seven."

"Alright, let's hang a liter of normal saline."

"Here's your ABG, Dr. Isaacs."

He reached out to grab the paper, took a quick look at the results and made eye contact with the respiratory therapist who had handed it to him. "We need to intubate."

Dr. Isaacs made his way to the head of the bed, ordered the required medications for induction, then slid the endotracheal tube through the slippery, V-shape of the woman's vocal cords and into her lungs.

The whole ordeal had lasted less than five minutes, and now it was over. The chaos of the code came to an abrupt cessation as quickly as it had begun. The patient was stabilized. The excitement was over.

Dr. Isaacs waited a moment, taking in the scene in front of him. He gave the patient's nurse a few final orders that would facilitate her transfer back to the intensive care unit of the CSM. Then he turned to go, passing the open crash cart on his way out.

He stopped and looked around at the dozen or so people who were nearby. None of them were paying any attention to him. He knew exactly where the naloxone and flumazenil were kept—in the third drawer and toward the back. It would take him all of two seconds to grab them. He squatted down as if examining the outside of the cart and located the two vials.

The next thing he knew, he was walking briskly toward Andrew's room with the antidotes—and the answer, he hoped—in his pants pocket.

* * * * *

The nurse's station outside of Andrew's room was mercifully deserted, giving Aaron enough time to check the supply room for a couple of syringes, needles, and alcohol swabs. Once he had stocked up, he slipped into Andrew's room once more, this time, closing the door behind him.

Andrew lay so still that Aaron wondered how he could expect anyone to imagine there was life behind those eyelids. The only movement was in his chest as the ventilator forced air into his lungs. Otherwise, he was a warm body full of organs someone else could put to good use. Bradford knew it. The nurses knew it. Hell, Aaron knew it, too.

He drew up five times the normal dose of flumazenil, the antidote for the midazolam infusion. He then attached the syringe to the IV port and emptied the entire contents of the syringe into Andrew's system. He watched the monitor as the heart rate increased to a hundred and twenty beats per minute. It was an expected physiologic response to taking anyone with an intact brainstem off a benzodiazepine cold turkey. Aaron watched Andrew's face closely for any sign of an emotional response to the obvious physical stress he was experiencing. Beads of sweat began to form on his forehead, but Andrew's face remained relaxed and calm.

There was still enough flumazenil in the vial to give the same dose two or three more times, but Aaron didn't see the point. The dose had clearly been sufficient judging by the stress it had caused Andrew's body; it just hadn't had the effect Aaron was hoping for. He toyed with the other vial in his pocket, the naloxone, and tried to decide whether it was even worth the effort.

He went back and forth a few times in his mind. First, if he reversed the fentanyl and Andrew was able to feel pain, then it would be excruciating for him regardless of whether he had retained any cortical brain function. Second, and perhaps even more of a deterrent than the pain he would cause, was the fact that Aaron didn't have any more ideas for how to help his patient. If the naloxone didn't work, then Andrew's case was considered hopeless and he would die later today. It was nothing Aaron hadn't been through before with numerous other patients, but somehow this time felt different. More personal.

Aaron realized he was probably transferring his feelings about his own life to Andrew's situation. Yes, others were lost along the way, but he *needed* this baby to make it. Therefore, he needed Andrew to make it. Even though he could recognize it was irrational, he still couldn't seem to let go. Not yet.

He drew up more than enough naloxone to reverse the fentanyl in Andrew's system, and before he could talk himself out of it, he emptied the syringe into his arm.

Aaron clenched his jaw and both fists as he waited for the naloxone to take effect. He stared, unblinking, at Andrew's face. At first, it seemed as if the antidote had made no difference whatsoever. Then, as if a switch had flipped, Andrew's back arched off the hospital bed, and he bit down on his endotracheal tube hard enough to completely obstruct the flow of oxygen into his lungs. His eyes shot open, exhibiting unmistakable pain and terror. His gaze found and locked on to Dr. Isaacs, making perfect, sustained eye contact.

The monitors began beeping uncontrollably. Andrew's heart rate was a hundred and eighty, his oxygen levels were plummeting, and the ventilator was unable to push air past the barricade of Andrew's clamped teeth. Aaron knew he only had a few seconds before there would be a crowd of people in the room responding to the alarms. He shoved the empty vial into his pants pocket and hooked Andrew back up to the Fentanyl drip. As the clear liquid began to drip into his arm, Andrew visibly relaxed, and his heart rate began to drop back down. His jaw relaxed its grip on the breathing tube, and the ventilator began its rhythm once more.

Just as Aaron had taken his seat in the armchair next to the hospital bed, Sara charged in. Her eyes settled on the patient, then the monitors, then Aaron. She let out a deep breath.

"Sara, you look like you've seen a ghost," he said, forcing a smile.

"What was going on in here, Dr. Isaacs? I just about had a heart attack."

"The pulse-ox slipped off his finger. You know how sensitive those alarms can be."

Sara cocked her head to the side. "It looked like he was in some sort of heart arrhythmia, too, but obviously, that's not the case." She gestured to the monitor, where the telemetry strip was ticking away in sinus rhythm at seventy beats per minute.

"Probably just artifact," Aaron said. "He did have some muscle twitches when I picked his arm up to replace the pulse-ox."

"I'm just glad you were in here, Dr. Isaacs."

Aaron nodded and grinned. "Me, too, Sara."

"I'm assuming no luck with your experiment?"

He looked at her evenly and without emotion, trying to choose his words carefully. "I'll be talking with Mr. Bradford this morning about Mr. McClain's care. In the meantime, the plan remains the same. Keep him comfortable and stable."

"That's what I figured." Sara stared down at Andrew for a few seconds before stepping away from the bed, wiping her eyes. "I just feel so bad for his fiancé. One day she's planning on spending the rest of her life with the love of her life, and the next—"

"I know, Sara." Aaron stood up and handed her a box of tissues from the bedside table. He placed his hand on her lower back and ushered her to the doorway. "I'll sit with him a little longer if you want to do the rest of your rounds."

"Thanks, Dr. Isaacs." The nurse looked up at Aaron, eyes still glistening. "I wish you stayed over every night."

Aaron closed the door behind Sara and stood with his back against it. He stared at Andrew lying unresponsive in bed. Had he imagined it all?

Nope. Definitely not.

He checked his watch. Six o'clock. Only about an hour until he could meet with Bradford. He settled into the armchair and closed his eyes, finally giving in to the sleep he had been fighting all night.

* * * * *

Aaron looked at his reflection in the mirror above the tiny call room sink then turned on the faucet, wetting his face and then his hair to smooth down the occasional unruly curl. He used some of the crusty mouthwash that had sat on the edge of the sink for as long as he could remember.

In ten minutes, he would be meeting with Andrew's family to tell them the good news. Earlier that morning, he had updated Mr. Bradford, and just as he had expected, he was cautiously optimistic.

"It's reasonable to hold off on plans to remove supportive care for the time being," Bradford had said, "but the young man still has a long recovery ahead of him, even if everything goes perfectly. We all know things rarely go perfectly in medicine."

Aaron, of all people, hadn't needed that reminder.

Satisfied with his appearance, he opened the door into the hallway and headed toward the family meeting room, where everyone would be waiting to hear from him.

He tried to picture Andrew's fiancé. Would she cry and insist on giving him a hug? Or maybe she would listen stoically, knowing they were still looking at a long, hard recovery. And what about Andrew's parents? He felt sure they would break down.

Aaron couldn't suppress his smile as he opened the door to the meeting room. When he found it empty, he checked his watch: one o'clock on the dot. He went to the nearest nursing station and located the nurse manager.

"Geena, where is the family for room 109? We were supposed to meet at one o'clock to discuss goals of care. I don't see anyone. Am I in the right place?"

Her face was confused at first, then surprised, then horrified. "Dr. Isaacs, didn't anyone tell you? Today was his day. Day thirty. They withdrew care about an hour ago."

"That can't be right." Aaron's voice echoed in the hallway, but he didn't lower it. "They wouldn't have withdrawn care without me there. I spoke with Mr. Bradford; there was a change." He shook his head and placed both hands on the counter. "We were going to give it time, gather more information."

"Mr. Bradford is the one who gave the go-ahead." The woman's voice was small, and she spoke slowly as her eyes darted from Aaron's face to her computer screen. "Since you were unavailable."

Aaron braced himself on the counter, staring at his hands as the veins bulged and his knuckles grew white. He felt a strange mixture of fury and sadness, the two reactions fighting to see which rose to the surface. He looked up and made eye contact with Geena. The fear in her eyes told him which emotion won out.

"Where is he?"

Silently, she pointed in the direction of Andrew's room.

Aaron looked down the hallway and for the first time, noticed the crowd outside room 109. He had met Andrew's parents only one time. He saw them now, aged ten years in the last month, standing off to the side. His mother cried inconsolably, and his father stood impotently beside her, hand on her lower back. Their lives, their marriage, would never be the same. It affected people like nothing else, losing a child. In all his experience with death over his career, Aaron had never met a parent that wouldn't have gladly traded places with their dying child. It was innate. Instinctive.

Tears welled up in Aaron's eyes as he watched the grief take hold of Mrs. McClain's tiny shoulders, then Mr. McClain's more substantial ones. The two seemed to visibly shrink under the weight of it.

Aaron turned back to Geena, who stared up at him, silent and full of despair.

"I'll be in my office. Please let Mr. Bradford know I'd like to speak with him."

Something was going to change between them today, and it was going to be big.

CHAPTER 31
Now
October 18, 2030

Slater Street was a five-hundred-foot stretch of asphalt that was bisected by Elm Street, the four-lane road that meandered through the entirety of the small town. On one end of the street, there was a large apartment building complex. On the other, Cheyenne saw a sign for the Slater Street Long-Term Structured Residence. She slowly pulled her car into the gravel parking lot and cut the power.

She took a sip of water followed by a few deep breaths to clear her head. All day she had felt like she'd been in a fog, and she wasn't sure why. Maybe it was getting back into the swing of things, or maybe it was the lack of alcohol over the last few days. Either way, she wasn't feeling like herself at all. She was tempted to go home for the day, prepare a proper list of questions for Dr. Isaacs, and come back later. There was no reason to think he wouldn't still be there tomorrow. He had been here for two years according to Randy. What was one more day?

Cheyenne looked down once more at her phone. It was like a hot potato in her hand, demanding her attention. Isabella's voicemail still played in her head. "Just wondering if you'd found anything…been thinking about you a lot…driving myself crazy with the possibilities…"

Cheyenne ran a brush through her hair and did her best to reassemble it into a neat bun. She dug a tissue out of her purse and, after getting most of her makeup off, reapplied a light coat of mascara and lip gloss. Satisfied with her makeover, she got out of her car, closed the car door behind her, and headed toward the one-story bungalow.

The group home was in desperate need of an update. Its light green vinyl siding was faded on the left side of the house, where there were no trees to block the harsh sunlight during the day. There were two windows, one on either side of the front door, the paint on their shutters peeling and cracked.

She rapped lightly on the front door and took a step back to wait. She leaned over to peek into one of the windows, but the blinds were closed.

Did I knock hard enough? She jumped at the sound of a twig breaking and turned around just in time to see a raccoon disappear around the side of the house. She took a few deep breaths to slow her heart.

Is it too soon to knock again? She practiced her smile and whispered her prepared greeting under her breath. She shifted her weight from one foot to the other and checked her watch.

Will I seem impatient if I use the doorbell now? She hadn't heard any voices or footsteps. It was starting to look like no one was even home.

Cheyenne had just decided to leave and was backing away from the door when she thought she heard a voice call out. It sounded so distant that she wasn't sure. Then she heard a second voice that sounded as if it were just on the other side of the door.

"Got it." The words sounded like they were spoken under water.

A few moments later, a man opened the door. He stared down at her, his face blank and his bottom lip hanging loosely. Pools of saliva collected in the corners of his mouth, and Cheyenne couldn't help but swallow her own spit in response to the sight of it. Thankfully, before the drool began to make its way down either side of his chin, the man brought his bottom lip flush with the top. She saw his Adam's apple move slowly up and then down again. Then, as if that act had taken all the effort in the world, he opened his mouth and his lip once more succumbed to the forces of gravity.

After they had thoroughly sized each other up, Cheyenne said, "My name is Cheyenne Rose. I'm looking for—"

"Well, hi there. It's not often we get visitors!" Cheyenne heard the vivacious, friendly voice before she saw the equally vibrant woman to which the voice belonged. "Richard, honey, you can go ahead and get back to your puzzle. Thanks for answering the door."

Once Richard had backed cautiously away from the front door and out of Cheyenne's line of sight, the woman turned back to her. Everything about her was loud: her clothes, her makeup, her bleached blond hair. Her voice.

"My name's Veronica. Welcome to Slater Street! How can I help you? You here to visit one of our residents?" She dragged out each vowel so that each one seemed to have two or three syllables all to itself. Her speech was slow and carefully constructed, but each sentence followed the one before it with hardly a pause for breath, making it hard to know when to interject.

"I think so," Cheyenne said tentatively, hoping the woman would continue to be as loquacious as she seemed at first pass.

"Well, come on in, darling! We love visitors. We don't get 'em a lot, but we sure do love it when we do." Veronica put an arm around Cheyenne's shoulders. She squeezed tightly as she propelled her into the cozy living room. Cheyenne felt as if she had been transported back a hundred years as she took in the room's décor and old-fashioned lighting fixtures.

"Now, why did you say you were visiting? I always ask questions and then don't stick around for the answer. It drives my husband berserk!"

"I'm just trying to get more involved, you know, in the community." Cheyenne said the first thing that came to mind, hoping the woman wouldn't see straight through her.

"Oh, well that's wonderful. We don't get a whole lot of attention way out here." Veronica gestured around the house, looking slightly embarrassed. A young girl in white scrubs peaked around the corner, but she ducked her head back behind the door frame as soon as Cheyenne made eye contact. Veronica followed her gaze.

"Hilda, come say hi to our guest." Her singsong voice echoed across the small kitchen. She turned back to Cheyenne and said in a stage whisper, "We got Hilda from overseas."

Cheyenne took a deep breath then dove right in. "I'd love to meet some of the residents, spend some time with them. I'm sure it can get boring around here for them."

Veronica nodded. "Oh, honey, that's the understatement of the century." She giggled. "Let me introduce you around."

Veronica had made her way through the kitchen and into a living room before Cheyenne realized that she was supposed to follow her. When she caught up, Veronica was still speaking. "We've always got about six folks staying here, but only three of them are permanent residents: Richard, who you've already had the pleasure of meeting. He prefers to go by his first name. Say hi, Richard." She addressed the blank-faced man who had answered the door. He waved absently, not looking up from his puzzle.

"You married?" Veronica glanced back at Cheyenne but kept walking.

Unbidden, his face appeared in Cheyenne's memory, his crooked smile so lifelike she felt like she could reach out and touch it. It stopped her in her tracks, and she leaned on the wall. Veronica had noticed Cheyenne was no longer behind her and stopped. She stood, waiting for an answer.

"I was engaged. It...didn't work out."

"Shame. You're such a pretty girl." Veronica shook her head and started walking again. "There's Miss Francis." Veronica gestured to a woman just ahead of them. "Her last name's too hard to pronounce—Polish, I think—so I just call her Miss Francis." The woman sat in a chair with a book. Her lips moved as she read, and as Cheyenne closed in, she realized the woman wasn't reading to herself. Miss Francis was just repeating the same phrase over and over again.

"I'm sorry you had to see that. I'm sorry you had to see that. I'm sorry you—"

"Miss Francis," Veronica interrupted her, putting her hand gently on Francis' arm. "We have a guest. Can you say hello?"

The woman froze, gazing up at Cheyenne with a frightened look on her face. She grabbed both of Cheyenne's hands in her own and squeezed hard. She spoke slowly and deliberately. "I'm sorry you had to see that." Then her face crumpled, and she began to cry. Cheyenne withdrew her hands and took a couple steps back from the woman. She looked at Veronica with wide eyes.

"She'll be okay," Veronica assured her. "This is a hard time of year for her."

There was one more person in the large living area. He sat in front of a player piano, facing away from Cheyenne and Veronica as they approached. He held his hands limply in the air, moving them in time to the music like a conductor. He sang along to the music, whispering the lyrics so softly that Cheyenne had to strain to convince herself he was singing at all.

"After the ball is over
After the break of morn
After the dancers' leaving
After the stars are gone
Many a heart is aching
If you could read them all
Many the hopes that have vanished
After the ball."

Cheyenne followed Veronica around the edge of the couch until they faced the man. He stared straight ahead at the piano, as if determined not to acknowledge their presence. Cheyenne studied him. He was lean but muscular, like a former marine. His jawline was defined, and his eyes were sunken deep into their sockets. He turned his head toward Cheyenne, and when their eyes met, a chill ran through her.

Before a new song began, Veronica spoke. "This is Mr. Isaacs—no, *Dr*. Isaacs," she corrected herself. "He's our other long-term resident. Been here two years. Haven't you, Dr. Isaacs?"

Veronica didn't seem to expect a response from him. She had already turned to lead Cheyenne away when he released what sounded like a low growl from the back of his throat. She jumped almost imperceptibly then turned back around. "Dr. Isaacs, that is no way to treat our guest. This is—" She turned to Cheyenne. "Now, what did you say your name was, doll?"

"Cheyenne. Cheyenne Rose."

The man's eyes revealed a moment of clarity. He took her in and nodded, making eye contact for the second time. Then he said two words that, in the same moment, chilled her and brought a heat from her very center.

"Andrew McClain."

CHAPTER 32
Now
October 21, 2030

Cheyenne squinted under the harsh lights of the studio. Her plan to put all the recent drama behind her and focus on her work was not going so well. This was her third day back at work since her visit to the group home, and despite her desire to forget about that day, it seemed to be burned into her memory. She couldn't remember where she'd put her keys that morning, but she could remember everything about meeting Aaron Isaacs.

On top of everything else going on, she was pretty sure she was coming down with something. Her skin was flushed and the letters on the prompter swam in front of her eyes, evading her. She was trying to wing it, but no one seemed to be very happy with the results.

"Welcome back to *Rose Colored Glasses*." She tried again. "I'm Cheyenne Rose, and I'm here with—here with—"

"Gerald Lake," her guest said, placing both hands in his lap and lifting his eyebrows. "Of Lake's Cakes," he reminded her.

"Yes, of course. Gerald, you have designed wedding cakes for a seemingly endless list of Hollywood royalty." Her armpits were slimy, and she knew her smile looked forced. "Thank you so much for being here. Tell us more about—what it is that you do."

"Cut!" her producer yelled from somewhere behind the lights and the teleprompter. "Why don't we take five, Cheyenne? We can start setting up for tomorrow's taping, and you can get your act together."

Normally, Cheyenne would have fired back with a quick retort, but she knew he was right. She did need to get her act together. She looked around the studio, but no one would make eye contact with her. So she just nodded, stood up, and made her way to her dressing room, holding onto the wall for support. She walked right past her door the first time, not realizing it until she looked around and recognized none of the artwork on the hallway walls. The vertigo that had started a couple days ago was getting worse, which made it difficult to walk a straight line, much less turn around. Just as she thought she had finally made it to the door of her dressing suite, she swung wide and banged the toes of her left foot on the door frame.

As she stood bent at the waist and nursing her throbbing toes, she heard a group of people walk by her in the hallway. She wondered briefly if they had seen her run into the wall, and then she heard the hushed whispers and knew they had. She cursed under her breath, blinking back hot tears.

Still rubbing her foot, she stepped into her dressing room and closed the door. She took a deep breath and sank down onto her small but elegant sofa, gripping the armrest with both hands until she made contact with the seat cushions. It was her favorite seat in the whole suite—entirely white, its back and arms forming one continuous, curving piece—and the amount of makeup they had put on her that morning to cover the dark circles and worry lines seemed enough to ruin it with one misplaced cheek. There would be no napping for her, not today.

Directly in front of her was the coffee table, which had a glass top and iron legs. Its understated quality had made it the perfect accent for her otherwise ultra-feminine décor. She scooted forward onto her knees in front of the table and pressed the side of her face to the glass, enjoying the way the cool, smooth surface cleared her head.

As she kneeled there, arms at her sides and face plastered to the coffee table, she looked around the right side of the room. The walls were covered with various framed awards she had received in the past couple of years, many of which she had already forgotten about. There was also a bookshelf on which trophies and other keepsakes were displayed. Opposite the couch, directly in front of her and just out of her current field of vision, was a TV. Switching cheeks, she saw more of the same on the left side. The only difference here was a set of double doors separating the sitting area from her actual dressing room.

Cheyenne lifted her head up and sat back on her thighs, taking a few deep breaths. A small piece of paper caught her eye. She picked it up and saw it was a pamphlet advertising something called Healing Hearts. The slogan, emblazoned across the top of the brochure, read *Healing Hearts and Minds One Day at a Time*. Cheyenne huffed. She was going to have to have another talk with the security team about letting random people with fliers into the studio. It was a little unnerving, to be honest. One of them could be a stalker or something.

She opened the pamphlet and read the first line. "Alcoholism is a disease with no cure."

Cheyenne tossed the flier away from her as suddenly as if it had burst into flames. She stared at it lying there on the floor as tears burned her eyes, and she felt a sudden hollowness in her chest. This was not a random pamphlet. She stood and paced the short length of the sitting room.

Was that what all her coworkers were thinking? That she was walking around the studio drunk all the time? Sure, she was known to have the occasional glass of wine or cocktail at work, but it had always been discretely in her dressing room. Plus, she had really stuck to her guns lately. She hadn't had a drop of alcohol since finally coming back to work after her two-and-a-half-week hiatus.

Her face burned, and her hands shook uncontrollably. She felt lightheaded and started to sit down, but immediately stood up again. She was too wired to sit. How would she ever be able to face everyone now, knowing what they thought of her? Knowing they had probably discussed it behind her back?

Just as she contemplated opening the fridge for a drink, her TV screen came to life.

"Miss Rose?"

She grabbed a bottle of water from the counter and sat down on the couch facing the TV. "Yes, I'm here. What time is it?"

"Nine thirty. I tried your house, but when I didn't get an answer, I just assumed you'd be here."

"Good assumption."

"Still getting used to it." Valerie smiled. "We decided to keep your time the same until we're sure there won't be any more schedule changes."

Cheyenne forced a laugh. "Makes sense. Twenty-six." After counting the pills out for her care coordinator, she popped one into her mouth and chased it with a sip of water.

"How have you been?"

"Fine. I think I'm getting sick, but otherwise, no issues."

"Any side effects to the higher dose of your sertraline?"

"Like what?"

The woman tilted her head. "Dizziness, confusion, memory loss."

"Now that you mention it, all of the above."

The care coordinator took a few notes then made eye contact again. "Have you mentioned these side effects to your doctor's assistant?"

"Haven't seen him yet."

"Oh. Well, please do mention it to him next time you see him. He will be happy to know that the medication appears to be at an effective dose."

"If this is what an effective dose feels like—"

"The good news is that if the symptoms are related to the medication, they should pass. Just keep taking the pills as they're prescribed. Before long, you won't even notice anything is awry."

After Valerie disappeared from the screen, Cheyenne stood up again, still too wound up to be still. She opened and closed her water bottle, fighting the urge to replace it with something a little stronger. She sure had picked a terrible time to quit drinking. It seemed like things were getting worse, not better.

Cheyenne fingered her watch. She had activated the tiny recording device embedded inside when she was at the group home. This had allowed her to replay her convers-ation, if you could call it that, with Aaron Isaacs over and over again. When he had spoken Andrew's name out of the blue, the memories had all come swarming back suddenly and without mercy.

The morning of the accident, Cheyenne had woken up three minutes before her alarm clock went off. She had just gotten out of the shower and was drying off when she heard her phone ring. She padded into the bedroom, wrapping the towel around her as she went, and found her phone in the covers. She tried to answer but was met with silence on the other end. She shrugged and tossed the phone back onto her unmade bed. Probably a wrong number.

She turned to go back into the bathroom as the phone started back up. She let it ring several times before picking it up again, trying to ignore the sudden ominous feeling in the pit of her stomach.

"Hello?"

"May I speak with Ms. Cheyenne Rose?" The voice was hesitant, almost apologetic.

Cheyenne's irrational feeling of dread was quickly replaced by one of annoyance. Who cold-called at this time of morning? She had enough trouble getting to work on time as it was. "This is she. May I ask who's calling?" She cradled the phone between her left ear and shoulder as she pulled up her pantyhose and made a mental checklist of what she still needed to do before leaving the apartment.

"Do you know an Andrew McClain?"

"He's my fiancé." The man had her attention now. "Why? What is this about?"

"You were listed as his emergency contact. He was in an accident this morning."

Cheyenne's head straightened, and she almost dropped the phone. She sat down on the edge of the bed, gripping the phone now with both hands. Her heart pounded and her palms felt sweaty and cold.

"What kind of accident? Is everything okay? Is he okay?"

"Ms. Rose, he's been stabilized and is en route to the Monroe CSM. I suggest you meet him there."

Her thoughts scattered, leaving her brain empty of everything but an overwhelming sense of dread. "It's bad, isn't it? Oh, God, tell me he's going to live. Tell me."

"I'm sorry, ma'am. I don't know anything more."

Cheyenne was inexplicably freezing. She sat in her towel on the edge of the bed, still holding the disconnected phone to her left ear with both hands and shivering uncontrollably, her skin prickling with goose bumps. Her mind raced, but she couldn't grab hold of a single thought for more than a moment. An unseen gag blocked her throat, and she began to gasp for air. The center of her chest began to burn, the sensation expanding until every inch of her body felt the pain. She didn't know how long she sat like that, struggling for air and shaking, but as quickly as the attack had come on, she snapped out of it. She was needed at the hospital.

Once she reached the Monroe CSM, Cheyenne was led into a tiny ICU room. Instead of four walls, the room had three walls and a large glass partition, allowing anyone at the nurse's station to see what was going on in the room at all times, which, from what Cheyenne could tell, was a whole lot of nothing.

Andrew, so boisterous and cheerful in life, looked thin and pale beneath the fluorescent lighting. A tube snaked down his throat, held in place by what seemed to be an unnecessary amount of clear tape. His chest rose and fell in time with the waveform on the machine by his bedside. Each breath was a calculated volume, length, and frequency.

A second monitor gave a continuous report of Andrew's heart rate, oxygen levels, and blood pressure. Every few seconds an alarm went off, which hardly seemed to garner any attention from the five or so nurses assigned to the unit.

Cheyenne sat in a chair next to Andrew's bed and pulled her feet up into the seat beside her. She fought the panic that threatened to return. Andrew needed her to be calm. The cold, sterile room wrapped its frigid arms around her. Her world, so perfect just a few hours ago, suddenly made no sense to her. The nurse had told her the person lying in that hospital bed was Andrew, but without the ID bracelet, she wouldn't have even recognized her own fiancé.

On the left, his eye socket appeared to be crushed and was so swollen Cheyenne couldn't even tell if he still had his eye. Above his brow, his hair was matted to his head with what she could only imagine was dried blood. His left arm was immobilized in a sling, and his whole bottom half was in a cast suspended from a large pulley system at the foot of the bed.

"Andrew? It's me, Cheyenne." They had told her he may be able to hear her if she talked to him. It couldn't hurt. "I'm here. You're okay. You're going to be okay, sweetie." She stopped, almost expecting a response from him. He absolutely hated it when she called him sweetie. She waited a few seconds for a sign that he was in there, that he had heard her. When there was none, she continued.

"I know you weren't excited about my work dinner this weekend, but this is a little bit much, even for you." She attempted a laugh, but it degenerated into a sob. She doubled over and let herself cry for the first time. It wouldn't be the last.

She leaned forward to grab Andrew's hand, and her nostrils were assaulted by a metallic mixture of antiseptic and blood, two competing scents that somehow went hand-in-hand with the hospital—familiar but unwelcome.

When the tears finally stopped coming, Cheyenne continued to talk. She talked about work, about their friends, about making plans for the weekend. It all felt so inconsequential, so trivial, but still, she talked. The quiet was so much worse. Finally, Andrew's nurse came in to let her know that visiting hours were over.

That night was the first of many sleepless nights spent worrying and expecting the worst, and it was the night she had come up with her first idea for a story, the story that ultimately propelled her into the spotlight.

So much of that time was a blur, but she remembered Dr. Isaacs now. He had taken care of Andrew for the last few days before his death. That must have been why his name had seemed familiar to her. She had only met him one time, but in that single encounter, she was able to tell a lot about the doctor. He was intelligent. He was dedicated to his patients. Most importantly, he was an extraordinarily caring man.

So, what in the hell had happened to him?

The man she had met a few days ago could not have been more different from the Aaron Isaacs she remembered. After the initial shock of hearing Andrew's name had worn off, Cheyenne had tried to talk to the doctor. He obviously recognized her and even connected her to Andrew, but when she asked him questions, it was like he shut down. He had stared at her as if looking through her, silent except for the occasional nonsensical phrase. It had taken all the strength she had not to grab him by the shoulders and shake the information out of him.

Veronica had eventually placed a hand on Cheyenne's shoulder and squeezed firmly, putting an end to the barrage. "Dr. Isaacs has had a long day. I think you should go now." The woman who was so friendly moments before now reminded Cheyenne of a mother bear protecting her cub. Cheyenne knew there was no arguing with her. It hadn't mattered, not really. This man couldn't tell her anything she needed to know.

"Some days are better than others," Veronica had said, backing down slightly. "I could call you. Could you come back another time?"

Cheyenne had nodded and given the woman a tight-lipped smile. "That would be nice."

She wasn't going to hold her breath for that phone call.

During her drive home that night, Cheyenne decided that she was going back to work. Not this pretend investigative work that was just an elaborate cover for trying to track down Hamm. Real, honest-to-God, eight-to-five, nose-to-the-grindstone work, and she was going to do it sober.

But now, as she sat in her dressing room feeling alone and judged, she couldn't help but second-guess her decision. She pressed play on her watch to listen to her conversation with Dr. Isaacs for the hundredth time, hoping for answers she was starting to fear she would never get.

CHAPTER 33
Then
May 16, 2028

"Dr. Isaacs. Sleep well?"

Aaron looked up from his computer screen to see Daniel Bradford leering at him from the office doorway. He turned his desk chair away from his monitor and toward his boss.

"We need to talk." He motioned toward the only other chair in his small office.

"Don't mind if I do," the other man said. "Been quite a morning." As he lowered himself into the chair, he let out a long sigh.

"I asked you to delay the withdrawal for Andrew. You gave me every indication that you would. What the hell happened?"

"Aaron, it's common for physicians to get too attached to their patients in situations like these, especially when there's family involved. I could see you were losing your objectivity. I did what needed to be done."

"There was nothing subjective about my findings last night. You even agreed that Andrew had a shot."

"He had a shot at living another miserable few months or, God forbid, years. He would've gotten bedsores, recurrent infections, and would have ultimately had the same fate." He crossed his left ankle over his right knee.

"You don't know that. You didn't see him this morning; I did. He looked straight at me. He was in there."

"I may not have been in there with you this morning, but I know that Andrew McClain was worth more dead than alive." Bradford picked at a hangnail. "That's all I need to know."

A chill traveled down Aaron's throat and settled in his chest. "What did you just say?"

Bradford leaned forward and stared at Aaron with cold, detached eyes. "Don't be naïve, Dr. Isaacs. How much do you think a full recovery for someone like Andrew would have cost?" He barely gave Aaron time to process the question before answering it himself. "Upwards of three million dollars, and that's being conservative."

"We're talking about a person's life here."

"Oh, come on, Aaron. You can't come to work in this place day after day and not have an idea of what's going on behind the scenes. Save the innocent act for someone else."

Aaron's mouth went dry. What Bradford was alluding to, he was a part of it, whether he knew what was happening or not. *Oh God, what have I done?*

Aaron studied the man across from him, whose placid face revealed nothing. He told himself what Bradford had said couldn't be true. There was no way they would make a decision about whether someone lived or died based on a cost-benefit analysis. Regardless, whatever was going on, whatever Bradford was up to, Aaron wanted no part of it. He and Elizabeth were bringing a son or daughter into this world. The thought that someone would ever treat his child's life as a business decision made him want to pack up his family and move to some remote part of the world where no one had even heard of a CSM.

"I quit." His voice was quiet, but the power of those words filled his chest, and he sat a little taller in his chair.

Bradford's gaze remained focused on Aaron. "I'm sorry, but that's not an option."

"Bullshit. I'm not working for you for one more second. If this is supposed to be some kind of joke, it's sick. I'm sure as hell not staying around to find out. I'll leave it to the police to decide."

"The police?" Bradford's humorless laugh sent tingles up Aaron's spine. "Dr. Isaacs, I recommend you choose your next words very carefully. I would hate for your wife or your unborn child to suffer for something you said in the heat of the moment."

Aaron didn't know how Bradford had learned about Elizabeth's pregnancy, but he didn't care. Blind with fury, he stood up and rushed Bradford, grabbing him by the throat with both hands. Even as Bradford gasped for air, his hand traveled down to his belt and pressed a button on his phone. Moments later, Aaron heard three loud chimes followed by an announcement overhead.

"This facility is conducting a mandatory fire drill. All staff members should proceed to their designated safety area. I repeat, this is only a drill."

Aaron's office door swung open automatically, and Bradford's eyes taunted him as he released his grip, hands trembling.

"You just made things much easier for me," he whispered. "You should have finished me off when you had the chance." He stood up and rested his hand on the door of Aaron's office for a moment before joining the crowd of people filing down the hallway.

Stunned, Aaron stared after Bradford for a moment then closed his office door. He had some things to figure out, and he suspected he didn't have much time. He knew he had no way to prove his allegations about Andrew's death. Besides, who would he even go to? It sounded like everyone was in on this "business plan" except him.

He caught a glimpse of his reflection in his computer screen. "Log in," he said, and the screen lit up. He pressed his palm to the surface. Once he was in the program, he searched for Andrew's account. There had to be something to indicate Andrew's true medical condition prior to his death, that he had a chance—however small— at recovery. All he needed was for one person to have made a mistake and included some piece of information that would support his theory. He scanned the lab values and radiology reports then moved on to the physician documentation. Just as he was pulling up Andrew's History and Physical from the day he was admitted, the system logged him out. He cursed under his breath then placed his palm once more on the monitor.

"You do not have the clearance to access this information," the computer-generated voice said.

Aaron stood up too quickly, his thighs banging on the underside of his desk and almost toppling the computer off the opposite side. He had no idea how deep this conspiracy went, but it was starting to look like some very powerful people were involved. People that had a lot to lose.

He needed to get out of this place. He reached for his white coat, ID, and wallet and started to head to the exit, but was met at the door by two security guards.

Aaron recognized one of them as the man he spoke to every morning on his way in to work. Aaron put his hand on the doorknob and willed him to move out of the way.

"I'm real sorry, Dr. Isaacs. Orders are we've got to escort you home. Mr. Bradford explained what happened." He glanced at the floor. "He's not going to press charges. He said you've been going through a lot lately, and you're going to be taking some time off. He just wanted to make sure you got home safe."

Aaron eyed the guard and nodded slowly. The man avoided eye contact. What had Bradford really told them? And what were their orders once the three of them left the building? Unfortunately, there was only one way out of his office, and there were two hulking security guards in front of it. Now was not the time to make a scene.

Aaron sighed, suddenly exhausted. "Thanks, Tim. I just need to collect a few things. Meet you outside?"

Tim shook his head once, still refusing to look at him.

Aaron stood looking at him for a moment longer, the gravity of the situation finally setting in. "What if I just—" He stopped short when he saw the larger man reach for his gun holster.

"Alright, alright, I'm coming." Aaron put his hands in the air in a gesture of surrender.

As Aaron left the building, flanked by the two security guards, he had the distinct feeling he was walking the plank. He just had no idea what waited for him on the other end.

CHAPTER 34
Now
October 22, 2030

The morning after her botched interview with Gerald Lake, Cheyenne woke up on the floor of the hallway in her apartment. She sat up and rubbed a sore spot on her right hip, wondering how she had gotten there. The last thing she remembered was crawling into bed the night before.

The hallway was windowless, but she could see down the hall into the kitchen, where the sunlight harshly announced its presence. She stood up too quickly, immediately regretting it as she fell against the wall. She stayed there for a second, waiting to regain her balance. When she finally felt like the room had stilled, she made her way into the kitchen.

She leaned against the island as her coffee brewed, trying to put the pieces of the night together. No matter how hard she tried, she couldn't remember getting up. She couldn't remember having any dreams, either. She must've been dead to the world. Had she ever sleep-walked before? Too bad she couldn't ask Hamm.

Or Andrew.

A blinking red light in the foyer caught her attention. At least she'd had the wherewithal to set her security system. She wasted no time getting it installed after her unexpected visitor had weaseled his way into her apartment just a few days ago. What good was having a deadbolt if your landlord had the key to your apartment? She had given the asshole a piece of her mind, but still felt the need to add that extra layer of security. She shuddered involuntarily.

The phone startled her when it rang. It seemed louder and more insistent than she recalled it being in the past. She lowered herself onto a stool and rubbed her temples.

"Answer." She spoke into the air. Then, after hearing the click, she said, "Hello?"

"Hello?" The voice that floated through the kitchen was not one that Cheyenne recognized. "Miss Rose?"

What was that accent? She couldn't quite place it. "May I ask who's calling?" At that moment, the coffee maker beeped, and she rushed to the counter, where the coffee pot sat.

"Miss Rose, this is Hilda." There was a pause. "From Slater Street. I'm sorry to call your personal line. You left your card."

Cheyenne braced herself on the counter with one hand as she poured a half-cup of steaming coffee with the other, stopping when she almost splashed herself. "Oh, yes." She remembered seeing the shy girl at the home, the one Veronica had said was from overseas. "What can I do for you, Hilda?"

"Well." She cleared her throat. "It's not really my place, but…"

There was a long silence. Finally, Cheyenne asked, "Hilda? Are you still there?"

"Yes, sorry, Miss Rose. I'm here. I'm calling because—it's just that—Dr. Isaacs, he has been asking for you." The girl's words rushed out now, one following the other like dominoes. "He's very insistent. He's—" There was a short release of breath. "He's not been himself since you came."

Cheyenne picked up her phone now, glancing around her kitchen. For some reason, even though she knew she was alone in the apartment, it felt like the right thing to do. Her voice was low when she spoke again. "What exactly has he said?"

"He says lots of things. Nothing that makes much sense. Miss Veronica can't get him to take his meds, not since that day you came." Hilda's speech slowed again, like she was choosing her words very carefully. "He keeps saying that name, Andrew McClain. He insists on talking to you, but Miss Veronica won't—"

"Why are you calling me? What do you think I can do?"

The girl sighed. "I don't know. Probably nothing. Miss Veronica said she is going to have to give him the injection if he doesn't start taking his meds soon."

"Injection?" Cheyenne sat back down and took a sip of coffee.

"It's for times like these. I've seen it. It's not good." She was whispering now. "The last time he got it, he didn't eat or drink for a week. She had to take him to the hospital for an IV."

Cheyenne could tell Hilda cared for these people. She felt her desperation through the phone as poignantly as if the girl were standing there in front of her. It must have taken a lot for the girl to call her. Then Cheyenne pictured Dr. Isaacs, bright-eyed and chattering. She couldn't resist hearing what he had to say, even if it did just end up being the mutterings of a crazy person.

"I'll be there in an hour." The words had left her mouth and met Hilda's ear before Cheyenne was even sure she'd said them aloud.

"Oh, thank you, Miss Rose," the girl said, her voice already a bit lighter. "I'll be waiting."

Cheyenne slowly removed the phone from her ear and stared at it for a moment before placing it on the counter. She took her time finishing her coffee, hoping it would help her wake up. When she could procrastinate no longer, she sent a message to her boss and Ronnie, letting them know she was going to be a couple of hours late.

She worried that she was overestimating the amount of clout she had at the studio, especially with all the recent drama, but she knew that nothing, even the threat of losing her job, would keep her from visiting Dr. Isaacs today. She cautiously made her way down the hall to the bathroom, the whole time leaning against the wall for support.

* * * * *

Roger had seemed skeptical when Cheyenne asked him to head in the opposite direction of the studio. Now, as they pulled into the small gravel clearing in front of the Slater Street residence, he was starting to look just plain worried.

"I'll be done in no time," she assured him. "Needed to follow up on a lead. It's for a story I haven't pitched to the producers yet."

He didn't look convinced, but he also didn't ask her any follow-up questions. Cheyenne was grateful for that small blessing.

"Be right back," she called over her shoulder, already taking small, shuffling steps toward the house's front stoop. Just as she reached out to brace herself on the front door, it opened, and Hilda practically catapulted out of the house.

"Miss Rose, thank God you're here." She was breathless with excitement or agitation, Cheyenne couldn't tell which. "Miss Veronica went on an errand. She shouldn't be back for twenty or thirty minutes." The girl tugged at Cheyenne's arm, dragging her into the house.

"What's going on? Is Dr. Isaacs alright?"

Cheyenne walked faster but pulled her arm away from Hilda, unsettled by the girl's bizarre behavior. She had seemed so much more reserved over the phone. Now Cheyenne didn't know what to think.

When Cheyenne stepped into the house, it took a moment for her eyes to adjust to the relative darkness. She stood still, bracing herself against the wall. After a few moments, the dining room table slowly came into focus straight ahead of her and to the right. She took a few more steps into the house and saw that the table was covered with stacks of loose-leaf paper. Each piece of paper was covered from top to bottom with small, cramped letters in black ink. Occasionally, there was a large blot where too much pressure had resulted in the ink bleeding onto the page.

Dr. Isaacs sat at the far end of the table, pen in hand, watching her intently. His eyes had a spark that she hadn't noticed at their previous meeting, almost a wild animal quality. Cheyenne found herself glancing behind her to map out an escape route, should one become necessary.

"Cheyenne." His voice saying her name sent chills up and down her spine. "Cheyenne Rose."

"Yes. That's me." Her voice was shaky, and for some reason, she felt herself fighting back tears.

"And Andrew," he whispered.

"How did you remember us?"

"I remember. Even though they want me to forget, and *I* want to forget." He shook his head. "I just remember."

Cheyenne took a step toward him, forgetting her fear. "Who wants you to forget?"

"Them." He began pointing at the ceiling, the walls, the television set. "Them. Them. All of them." He became more and more agitated until Cheyenne had backed all the way against the far wall, and Hilda had pulled a liquid-filled syringe out of her pocket.

"Aaron." Hilda's voice was soothing and calm. She held up the syringe. "Aaron, it's okay. Please sit down."

He looked at her, his eyes unseeing, but something inside him responded to her voice. He sat down, picked up his pen, and began writing again.

"They give me the little green pills, but they don't help me forget. They just screw up my thoughts so I can't tell up from down, but I always remember."

He shook his head back and forth as if trying to rid the thoughts from his mind. "Think of the day that Andrew McClain died, they said. Think of it. Now forget it. Forget it. Take these pills. Have a nice day. Always so polite. So professional. Take the pills. Forget Andrew. Don't forget the pills. Have a nice life." He began to lose control again, his words overlapping one another until they were unintelligible, inseparable from the ones before or after.

He stopped suddenly and dropped his head in his hands. His shoulders shook. The room was silent except for his occasional sob. When he finally looked up at Cheyenne, his eyes full of despair, tears were streaming down his cheeks.

"I remember *everything*."

CHAPTER 35
Then
May 16, 2028

Aaron considered gunning his decade-old Toyota Corolla through the yellow traffic light, but he glanced in his rear-view mirror at the security vehicle that was escorting him home and slowed to a stop just past the white line. No need to further upset anyone. Elizabeth was already going to be mortified when he told her about the last eighteen hours. Unauthorized patient experimentation, medication theft, aggravated assault. No need to add a car chase to his growing list of misdemeanors.

When the light turned green, he coasted through the intersection and toward his neighborhood. For the first time in recent memory, he noticed a speed limit sign. Had it always been thirty-five through here? Even at forty miles per hour, it felt like he was driving his car through quicksand. His arms tingled, and his foot twitched over the gas pedal, but every time he lowered it, the car seemed to lurch forward. He turned on the air conditioning and aimed the vent at the heat emanating from his face.

Aaron squinted at the road and massaged his forehead, feeling the oil beneath his fingertips. The more he thought about Mr. Bradford's words, the more he was convinced he had misinterpreted them. There were checks and balances just to take a piss nowadays, not to mention the hoops he had to jump through to actually care for a patient. There was no way a conspiracy of that magnitude could be going on right under everyone's noses.

He became aware of a car horn honking. Looking up, he saw he was at a four-way stop and had activated his right turn signal. He was about a half a mile from his house with no memory of how he'd gotten there. He ignored the chill that ran up his spine and made the turn. After pulling into his driveway, he stepped out of the Corolla and saluted the security officers as they continued driving down the street. He watched their taillights until they took a left at the next stop sign and disappeared from sight.

He walked toward the house. It was the moment of truth. He made his way to the front porch and tried the knob, finding it unlocked.

"Elizabeth," he called out as he entered the foyer. "Elizabeth, I'm home."

No answer. He made his way to the kitchen for a glass of water. As he stood in front of the refrigerator holding a tumbler beneath the narrow stream of water, he scanned the kitchen. He saw a pile of unopened mail on the counter and an abandoned cup of coffee on the kitchen table next to a carton of half-and-half. Aaron rolled his eyes. Elizabeth could be so forgetful. He reached over to grab the creamer and tossed it into the trash can.

"Another one bites the dust," he said to no one in particular.

He took his water and made his way up the stairs to look for Elizabeth. He was very aware of his heart beating in his chest. He dreaded having this conversation and began to think of ways he could put it off for a little while.

He smiled when he heard the running water. It was one of her favorite things to do, sit in the tub and read magazines until her fingers were all pruny and the water was lukewarm.

He rapped on the door then poked his head in. "Hey, Elizabeth, I'm—"

The bath stood on claw feet in the far corner of the bathroom. Water cascaded over the sides and splashed, pink and murky, onto the white tile. Elizabeth's dark curls hung over the side. Only her forehead and knees were visible above the water.

He made it to the bathtub in two large strides and stepped, fully clothed, into the rust-colored water. He put his arms underneath hers and heaved her body up out of the water. She slumped against him, almost knocking him over before he regained his footing and sat down on the edge of the tub. The water and her body were the same temperature. He knew before he pressed his fingers to her neck, there would be no pulse.

He sat with his arms wrapped around her, her back to his chest, as her body grew heavy and cold. He felt detached, like he was watching this happen to someone else. The water was still trickling from the tub, each drop echoing off the bathroom tile.

"Liz. Liz. Liz." At some point, he realized it was his voice chanting her name in time with the water. He noticed his hands folded over her abdomen and watched as one raised up to turn off the faucet. His clothes were soaked through with the dingy water, and with that small movement, he began to shiver.

Silent and purposeful, he reached down to open the drain and stepped out of the bathtub. He struggled to drag Elizabeth's body with him. He laid her down on the hard tile floor and sat next to her, wishing he had a pillow to put underneath her head. There was no more bleeding. She had bled out before he stepped foot in the house.

It took him a moment to realize that the bleeding hadn't originated from her womb, as he had assumed. She had two long, deep cuts that ran halfway down the length of both forearms, approximating the path of her radial arteries.

Elizabeth was afraid of knives. Couldn't stand the sight of blood.

The significance of this stole the breath from his lungs. He propped himself up with arms that grew weaker under the weight of his torso, gasping for air that refused to come. He was close to losing consciousness before his body relaxed enough to let his lungs fill with oxygen. He lay on the cold tile, drinking in the air, his mind now blank.

When his phone rang, he didn't have to look at the screen to know who was calling.

CHAPTER 36
Now
October 22, 2030

Cheyenne stared down at Dr. Isaacs' slumped shoulders as his shaking gradually subsided and his sobs became less frequent. She searched Hilda's face but only saw a baffled look that she knew mirrored her own. When Dr. Isaacs had finally calmed down, Cheyenne asked to speak with him privately.

Hilda fidgeted with the hem of her white scrub top. "Miss Veronica will be back before long. I don't think she would be happy that I called you. I can give you fifteen minutes at the most."

"Fine. Fifteen minutes." Cheyenne sat down across from Dr. Isaacs. "I'll come find you when we're done."

"Okay," she said, chewing on her bottom lip as she backed toward the door. "I'll be right around the corner if you need anything. Just call out."

"Thank you, Hilda."

Once she and Dr. Isaacs were alone and staring across the table at one another, Cheyenne was at a loss as to how to proceed. She knew better than to barrage him with questions like last time. However, there was a certain clarity to his eyes now that wasn't there a few days ago. Cheyenne bit her lip and studied him, searching his face for some sort of explanation. As she watched, he leaned back in his chair and crossed an ankle over his knee, resting his left arm against a neighboring chair back. *What exactly was going on here?*

"Tell me what happened."

He looked toward the door through which Hilda had just exited the room. Cheyenne followed his gaze and noticed it was slightly ajar. She reached a foot out and nudged it closed.

He relaxed into his chair. "Why did you come here, and what do you know already?" His voice was calm, business-like. He sounded nothing like the Aaron Isaacs she had met less than a week ago.

Cheyenne swallowed. "Not much. I know about the CRP. I know that doctors seem to get sent to one after something bad happens." She struggled to maintain eye contact. He was staring at her as if could see her soul.

Dr. Isaacs nodded. "I think they thought I knew more than I did." He uncrossed his legs and leaned forward. "I didn't know anything, not at first. I never would've stood for it." He shook his head and stared down at his hands. They were pressed down on the tabletop, but Cheyenne could still see them trembling.

Cheyenne wanted to ask who *they* were, but she fought back the urge. She didn't want to do anything to interrupt his lucidity. It seemed to have come out of nowhere, and she had no idea how long it would last.

"They offered me this trip. Called it a Career Renewal Package. I was to participate in a research project, do a little CME—continuing medical education—and the rest of the time, I was told I could just enjoy myself, and I did. I should have known it was too good to be true."

"What do you mean?" So far, his story lined up with Dr. Patel's. That was a good sign. However, unlike Dr. Patel, Dr. Isaacs seemed ready to talk.

"The purpose, from what I put together later, was to achieve some sort of huge cover-up. Exactly who's involved, how high it goes up the chain, I'm not sure. They hid their intentions well; they were pros. In an entire month, I only had three sessions with them. I was told it was for a research project, but I know now that mind control was the primary purpose of the CRP."

Mind control? Cheyenne felt her heart sink. She had let herself believe that Aaron would help her find answers, but he was obviously still delusional. What had she really expected from him, anyway? Everything he told her would have to be confirmed with research and actual proof.

If she could just come out of this meeting with a lead or two, she would consider that a win. She pressed the tiny button on the side of her watch to record their conversation, just in case.

Seemingly oblivious to Cheyenne's disappointment, Aaron continued. "They were trying to erase specific memories I had of treating certain patients, patients whose care had somehow been compromised. You see, most of the time, the system worked flawlessly. Patients were prepped in the OR, the surgeons did the procedures they were told to do, and everyone went about their merry way. But occasionally, there were questions."

Cheyenne felt the beginning of a tension headache and rubbed the back of her neck. "What kinds of questions?"

"Normal questions, questions about whether a certain surgery or procedure was necessary or whether a treatment could potentially benefit a specific patient. Doctors were used to being closer to the decision-making process, see." He was becoming more animated now, his hands gesticulating wildly as he talked, punctuating his sentences. "When we were delegated to becoming surgery monkeys, well, let's just say some took it better than others. Some people actually liked it." He waved a dismissive hand in the air. "Hell, I liked it at first, too."

Cheyenne thought about Hamm. He had said the CSM program let him do what he loved without bothering with all the paperwork. So maybe there was another nugget of truth from Dr. Isaacs.

"So, you asked the wrong question?"

"Yes."

"Which was?"

He shook his head and clenched his jaw. "I don't remember."

"You don't remember?" Cheyenne resisted the urge to shake him. She was so close.

"All I know is I must have made enough of a stink that I became viewed as a liability."

"Therefore, the CRP."

"Exactly, and the memory erasure. But for some reason, there were complications. The procedure, it basically uses laser surgery to target specific memories. I know this because they tried it again on me later, but it didn't work. That's when they started giving me the green pills to make me forget, but we'll get to that."

She stifled a sigh and glanced at the door. Had it been fifteen minutes?

"I think it was relatively new technology at the time, and maybe they were still getting it right. In my case, in addition to the targeted memories, they managed to zap my memory of the fine motor skills I had spent years developing during medical school and residency. Of course, I had no idea at first that it was because of the treatments. I had no idea they had even done anything to me."

"Okay. So, what happened?"

"I was no longer able to operate."

"Why would that be?"

Dr. Isaacs shrugged. "I still don't completely understand it. It was the most bizarre thing. One day I could do anything I wanted with my fingers, my hands, and the next…" He swallowed. "It was like someone had just sliced out the part of my brain that had anything to do with my surgical skills. They put me through several reentrance examinations, and each time I would just fumble around like I'd never even held a scalpel before. Then I'd play golf or tennis, and it was like nothing had happened. It was as if those guys had targeted the spot of my brain where I stored my memories of the OR."

Cheyenne found herself letting go of her reservations and enjoying the conversation, enjoying her all-access pass into his bizarre world. She was so absorbed in what he was saying she didn't notice Hilda's timid knock, not until Aaron stopped talking and eyed the door.

"Miss Cheyenne? I'm sorry, but I must ask you to go. Miss Veronica will be back any minute."

Cheyenne looked back at Aaron and was surprised at his sudden transformation. The man, who just a moment before was engaged and conversational, now stared blankly at a spot just past her on the wall. She could feel a sudden tension and sensed he was avoiding her gaze.

She studied him a moment longer, then she nodded at Hilda and stood up slowly from the table. She took a moment to get her balance as the blood rushed from her head, then she walked around the table and bent down to Aaron's level, holding onto the back of his chair for support. "I'll be back," she said. "We can finish our conversation."

He didn't acknowledge her except to allow the drool that had collected in his bottom lip to spill over onto the table. She looked at the table, then back at him, and tilted her head slightly. She said nothing more, just followed Hilda out of the room.

"I'm sorry to cut your conversation short. I'm sure it was very nice for him to chat with someone. He doesn't get visitors often."

"It was remarkable. To be inside the mind of someone—"

"I know what you mean. His delusions have remained quite consistent. Most patients' do. It's fascinating."

"What has he told you?" They were outside on the porch now.

"Just that the reason he lost his job was because his surgical abilities were erased." She lifted an eyebrow. "With a laser."

Cheyenne nodded. It was hard to keep a straight face as Hilda said it so matter-of-factly.

"And that he began to work in a long-term care facility after that," Hilda said. "Eventually, he was taken out of the workforce altogether—that part I know is true. I imagine his illness became too difficult for him to hide."

"Yes," Cheyenne said. "That must have been when he was Andrew's doctor."

"Who?"

"My fiancé. He recognized me last time because he was my fiancé's doctor. It's been a couple years."

Hilda nodded. "Yes, that would be about right. He's been with us for going on two years."

Cheyenne made a mental note to do some research on Dr. Isaacs' career change. Surely something like that would be accompanied by a lot of documentation.

"I was pretty amazed he remembered me after so long. We only met face-to-face once."

"I'm not surprised. Dr. Isaacs seems to have a photographic memory, at least where people are concerned. He never forgets a face."

Something had nagged at Cheyenne since she'd left Aaron. She only spent a few minutes with him earlier that week, but something was different about him today, something important, and she couldn't leave until she understood why.

She grabbed Hilda by both arms. "I need to ask Dr. Isaacs one more question. It can't wait."

"But Miss Veronica—"

"Do what you have to do. Just keep her away for five more minutes." Cheyenne didn't wait around for Hilda's answer. She was already headed back into the house.

CHAPTER 37

Aaron looked up, startled, as Cheyenne stormed back into the room. He hadn't moved from his seat at the table where she had left him.

"You said they gave you green pills. What did those pills do to you?"

"Aside from putting me in a complete fog and making it so I couldn't walk a straight line?" He shook his head. "You get used to that part. You become 'tolerant'." He stared off into space for a long moment before answering. "Long-term, they made me forget, made me stop caring."

She shook her head. "I want to believe you, Aaron, but it just doesn't add up. If you knew all of this was going on, why didn't you try to do something to stop it? Why in the hell did you keep taking those pills?"

A darkness settled over Aaron. His face lost all its vigor, and his body sagged underneath an invisible weight.

He looked at Cheyenne with eyes deep and penetrating, eyes that told her more about his loss and hopelessness than he would ever find the words for.

She knew in that moment she had more in common with Aaron Isaacs than she ever cared to. He was a broken man, just like she was broken before Andrew entered her life. Just like she was broken now.

"Surely I don't have to explain it to you, of all people." He clenched his jaw, barely moving his mouth as he spoke. Cheyenne had to strain to hear him. "When there's no reason to get up in the morning, there's certainly no reason to fight for what you believe in. There's nothing *to* believe in. You want to know why I took the pills?"

She didn't, not anymore, but she couldn't speak the words to stop him from telling her. She sunk down into the chair next to him.

"After the CRP, I did what I was told for a few years. Something felt off, sure, but I wasn't interested in ruffling any feathers. I had a wife to think about, and we were trying to start a family.

"I was reassigned to a nonsurgical job within the CSM system—the long-term care facility where Andrew ended up. I minded my own business for the most part. Didn't ask too many questions. But people—healthy people—kept dying. At first, I chalked it up to bad luck, bad disease, bad genes. Then it became…" He paused as if searching for the right word. "It became not *uncommon*. I could no longer ignore the feeling there was more going on behind the scenes than I was aware of."

Cheyenne felt tears sting her eyes. She dreaded where his story was taking her, but she couldn't bring herself to stand up and walk away.

"When Andrew was first transferred to me after he was stabilized, I was told that his prognosis was poor. He had an intact brain stem, so he wasn't technically brain-dead, but he would never have any meaningful quality of life. Add to that his multiple orthopedic injuries, which no doubt caused him a lot of pain, and the existence of his advanced directive stating very clearly that he did not want to be kept alive on life support. It was a no-brainer. We needed to withdraw care, allow him to die with dignity, but for some reason, I felt obligated to confirm what I was told about his condition before proceeding. I spoke to my superior and asked for permission to reduce his sedation and reassess his ability to come off the ventilator."

"And?" Cheyenne's nails were digging into her palms. She wanted to run as far as she could away from this man, but she was captive in her own body, helpless to do anything but hear him out.

"I was told that his situation was hopeless. All the necessary trials and diagnostic tests had already been performed to confirm it. We were just waiting on family to okay pulling the plug."

"That was me," she whispered.

"That was you," he said. "Honestly, I had no reason to doubt what I was told. Your fiancé was in bad shape. No one who saw him would question that." He almost stopped there, but after a moment's hesitation, he continued. "For some reason, I did. The night before Andrew died, I visited him. Mr. Bradford, my boss at the time, was initially skeptical. He discouraged me from getting my hopes up—or yours. I can only say that what I witnessed that night was very promising."

Cheyenne squeezed her eyes shut, tears spilling over and pouring down her face as she listened to Dr. Isaacs talk. She felt a weight on her chest that made it hard for her to breathe. She didn't want to swallow, cough, or blink for fear she might miss what the doctor said next, even though she already knew how the story ended.

"After hearing the good news about Andrew, even Mr. Bradford seemed enthusiastic. He requested I be present for a family meeting that afternoon to discuss my findings with Andrew's loved ones—with you—and I was ecstatic. When I arrived at the conference room that day, it was deserted. I started to feel that something was terribly wrong. I spoke with the charge nurse, who told me that Andrew's life support was discontinued earlier that morning, and his body had already been wheeled away for organ donation.

"I saw his parents in the hallway, holding each other, looking lost. You were there, too, with a camera crew. A nurse came up to you and handed you a bag of Andrew's stuff, called you by name. I only met you the one time, but I never forget a name."

"Dr. Isaacs, what are you saying?"

He shook his head once then was perfectly still. "I don't know anything for sure, Cheyenne." His voice had become flat, emotionless, as if he were reading someone else's story from a teleprompter.

"Yes, you do know. Andrew had a chance at recovering. That's what you're saying, right? They lied to me." There was no way to process what he was saying. No way to hear that and not go crazy herself. It was everything she could do not to grab him by the shoulders and shake him as hard as she could. "I killed my own fiancé."

His eyes were glassy and focused on something Cheyenne couldn't see. "The rest of that day was the worst of my life. I only remember bits and pieces, the worst parts."

The worst day of your *life?* Somehow she doubted it could top hers. "What happened?"

The look Aaron gave her was detached, despondent. She met his gaze and felt herself being sucked into his world, into the hopelessness that radiated from his eyes.

He shook his head. "They tried to do it again," he said. "Tried to erase my memory of that day, but I did everything I could to fight it. I thought of television shows, books I'd read, old friends from elementary school. Everything but what they wanted me to think about. I wish I hadn't. I wish I didn't remember anything, didn't know anything.

"They started medicating me after a day or two of observation, once they realized how much I remembered. They thought I was a threat. So they put me here, and Dr. Buchner visited me personally once a month for six months to give me an injection." Isaacs simulated six slow stabs of a needle into his right thigh. "I didn't fight it, didn't care at that point."

Cheyenne thought of the man in her apartment. What lengths were these people willing to go to?

"Then he finally realized I had no desire to fight it, no desire to be in my right mind. That's when they started just giving me the pills. Said they'd know if I wasn't taking them. I haven't missed a day taking them ever since. Not until a few days ago, anyway, when you tracked me down."

"So what's different now?"

"You."

"Me?"

"I knew when you showed up a few days ago it couldn't just be a random coincidence, and I knew if you went through the trouble of finding me, you wouldn't just let this go. Not like I did. Someone needs to follow through on this until the bitter end. I think you will."

Cheyenne knew it was way too late to walk away. She nodded. "If it kills me."

As if out of nowhere, sharp footsteps echoed down the wood floor in the hallway. Aaron leaned forward and whispered something urgently into Cheyenne's ear. She wasn't sure she had heard him correctly, but there was no time to ask for clarification. He was just leaning back into his seat when Veronica rounded the corner into the room.

Immediately, Aaron's shoulders slumped, and his lower jaw went slack. He stared at a spot on the table just in front of Cheyenne's folded hands then lifted his head up, again surprising her with the sudden change in his eyes.

"They're all out to get us. It's only a matter of time. Look around you." Aaron gestured wildly around the room, to unseen bugs hidden in the ceiling and the walls. "You're not safe, either." He poked at the air in her direction. "Not here."

"Miss Rose," Veronica said through clenched teeth. "What a pleasant surprise." She stared at Cheyenne with a mixture of contempt and suspicion as she closed the space between herself and Aaron. She gripped his upper arm and helped him up from his chair. "I'll need you to leave now. It appears you've upset Dr. Isaacs. As you can see, our patients are very fragile."

Cheyenne stood and gripped the chair back as a crippling wave of nausea washed over her. She met Veronica's gaze, and the woman's eyes were hard. She was no longer the welcoming southern belle Cheyenne had met a few days ago.

"Of course. I apologize. I was just in the area." Cheyenne held out a hand to shake, but Veronica just stared at it, both hands still clutching Aaron tightly. "Shall I call first next time?"

"I'll call you."

Cheyenne made her way to the front door. She looked around for Hilda, but the girl was nowhere in sight. Cheyenne paused with her hand on the knob and turned around, but the entryway was empty. She let herself out, focusing on the gravel path as she made her way toward the car, where Roger was waiting. She was still thinking about the last thing Aaron had said to her before he'd resumed his schizophrenic act. It made no sense to her now, but she had a feeling it would become very important, very soon.

"The protocols. Get your hands on the protocols."

CHAPTER 38
Then
May 16, 2028

Aaron felt an angry heat rising from his skin as he tried to process what had happened, what Elizabeth must have gone through. He answered the call.

"You psychopath." Saliva flew from his mouth as if he were a rabid animal, but he barely noticed. "I'll find you, and I'll kill you," he screamed into the phone.

"Hello, Dr. Isaacs. I see you've made it home safely."

Aaron stood up from the tile floor of the bathroom, gripping the phone so hard his hand ached. "If you think for one second I won't go to the police—"

"You won't. Trust me."

Aaron released a bitter laugh that degenerated into a sob. "What more can you possibly do to me? You have no leverage. Not anymore."

"Threats aren't the only way to control someone's behavior, Dr. Isaacs."

For a fleeting moment, Aaron felt unsure of himself. *What did he mean by that?* He looked down at his wife's pale, swollen body and felt a sudden urgency. Once more, he was a sitting duck. For what, he didn't exactly know, but he knew he needed to get out of this house.

The blood that ran through Aaron's veins was scalding hot and full of adrenaline. He wished he could stay with Elizabeth until the police came, but there wasn't time for that. He leaned down, brushed a stray piece of ebony hair from her forehead, and kissed her goodbye. He closed the bathroom door softly behind him and headed to his bedroom.

Aaron needed to keep talking, needed to keep Bradford on the phone. “How long has this disgusting practice been going on, anyway?” He rifled through his dresser drawers, tossing a change of clothes and a few other essentials into a bag. “How long have you been sacrificing patients to benefit the bottom line?”

He dug around in his underwear drawer until he felt the cold metal of his revolver. He placed the gun and a box of bullets into his duffel bag. When he straightened up, he noticed the bedroom windows offered a perfect view of the abandoned house across the street. He shuddered. Had someone been watching them?

“Don’t be so naïve, Aaron. Doctors and hospitals would no longer be accessible to the average consumer if we hadn’t found a way to make healthcare financially sustainable. Are you familiar with the theory of utilitarianism? We sacrifice one for the good of many.”

As Aaron headed back downstairs, each step he took seemed to echo throughout the house. A layer of sweat had collected on his skin and he worried he might lose his grip on the railing. “How do you pick the one?” He tried to drown out the noise of his steps. “And who decides what sacrifice is necessary, how many people must be helped before saving their lives are worth ending another? Sounds like a slippery slope, Mr. Bradford, but it’s not really about ethics, is it? It’s about money.” Aaron threw his front door open and squinted into the blinding afternoon sun.

“You certainly pose some interesting questions,” Bradford said, his voice sounding closer now, “but it really doesn’t matter. My orders come straight from the top.”

Aaron lifted the phone away from his ear and stared at it, confused. He turned his head in the direction of Bradford’s voice but was a second too late. He saw a blurry shape approaching him, then he felt a sharp pain as something jabbed through his pants and into his upper leg. At first, he felt nothing but a throbbing discomfort in his thigh. It didn’t take long before his legs gave out from under him, and he crumpled to the ground. His gaze followed the hand that held the empty syringe until he was looking up at the face of Daniel Bradford himself.

"As I said before, you won't be speaking to the police." He replaced the cap of the syringe and tossed it into the bag hanging on his shoulder. "You will never speak about this. To anyone. Ever again."

Aaron's vision blurred, and his arms went numb. His hearing sounded like he was inside a tunnel.

Bradford stared down at Aaron lying helpless on the front porch. He placed a foot firmly over his sternum and dug in his heel. "What a shame you had to make this so difficult for yourself. You could've done even more for our cause than you already have."

Under the crushing weight digging into his chest, Aaron couldn't speak. A blinding light replaced Bradford's face as the pain became too much. He breathed a sigh of relief when he felt his consciousness begin to fade away.

CHAPTER 39
Now
October 22, 2030

As Roger pulled the car out of the gravel parking lot and onto the road to head back to the studio, Cheyenne tried to slow her heart rate with some deep breaths. She crossed her ankles, then uncrossed them, then pulled one leg up underneath her. Nothing felt comfortable. She tried to corral her thoughts, but they all swarmed around in her head, just out of reach.

She needed to speak with someone, someone that could talk some sense into her before she did something crazy. Problem was, she was running out of options. Hamm would have been her go-to at one point. Isabella was out, at least for right now, and Rebecca—well, Rebecca was MIA since their last conversation a week ago. She hadn't even answered the cell phone she had promised never left her side.

Cheyenne felt another wave of nausea and dropped her head into her hands. Saliva began to build up in her mouth, and she had to swallow several times before the moment passed.

Taking a deep breath, she pulled out her makeup bag to freshen up before getting to the studio. She tried to distract herself, rifling through the case looking for a neutral lip gloss, but her mind kept coming back to Rebecca. What had the operator said when she'd called last week? Something about how she was no longer with the CSM headquarters. Was she fired because of what she'd done for Cheyenne?

Cheyenne gave in and lowered the screen from the car ceiling to initiate yet another phone call to Rebecca's cell. She didn't have high hopes but needed to feel like she was doing something.

Rebecca answered on the first ring.

"Rebecca?" Cheyenne clutched her makeup bag in her lap and spoke into the screen's speaker. "I'm so glad you answered! I called your work last week, and they said you were gone."

"Cheyenne? Is that you?" Rebecca spoke in a hushed voice.

"What's going on? Where are you?"

"They took me off the phones. I'm in the basement now, organizing files all day."

"What? Why?" She had pulled out a tube of mascara and now held it suspended in midair.

"Cheyenne, I can't really talk right now. Can we just meet up later? I'll come to you."

Cheyenne fought the urge to ask Rebecca a million questions. "Okay, sure, but, Rebecca?" There was silence, so Cheyenne continued. "Have you heard anyone talking about some sort of protocols? Supposedly they have something to do with the CSMs, and I think they might be relevant to my research."

"Protocols? No, I don't think so."

"That's okay, I'd still like to—"

"Listen, Cheyenne," she whispered. Her voice had an urgency Cheyenne didn't remember from before. "I'll see what I can find out about the protocols, but I need this to be over after tonight."

Cheyenne froze. "Is something—?"

"Just tell me where to meet you."

"Okay, Rebecca. Let's see." She tried to sound calm and reassuring. "How about the 506 Diner? Six o'clock. It's right down the street from my place, and it shouldn't be crowded at that time of day."

"It's okay. The more people, the better. See you then." Rebecca hung up the phone before Cheyenne could respond. Rebecca's tone had definitely changed since they last spoke. If that conversation had cost Rebecca her job, Cheyenne could hardly blame her for being a little standoffish.

Cheyenne looked around, trying to get her bearings. Roger was taking the back roads. It was a good call, because the highway could be really crowded at that time of morning.

It was drizzling and overcast. The white Honda Accord directly behind them had on its windshield wipers and headlights. There was one other vehicle on the road a few car lengths behind the Accord. Cheyenne almost didn't notice it at all, but there was something about the way the car blended with its surroundings that drew it to her attention. It was a dark sedan, she wasn't even sure what make, and the driver was a barely visible silhouette rising up above the steering wheel. The headlights were off, making the car virtually disappear whenever they drove into the shadows of the trees on the wooded two-lane road.

She kept her eyes on the car for a few minutes. No matter whether they sped up or slowed down, the car maintained the same amount of space between itself and the Accord in front of it. When the white car finally turned off onto a side road, the sedan made no move to close the distance separating it from Cheyenne's car.

After watching the car for ten minutes with nothing happening, Cheyenne decided she was being paranoid. She turned back to her screen still hanging from the ceiling. She logged into her work email, but after going through a few generic memos, her mind began to wander. She returned to her home page and typed "CSM + protocol" into the search function. There were hardly any hits, and as she began to click through them, she couldn't shake the feeling they all seemed a little whitewashed. Most of the results were stories from years ago, and the protocols were to determine when and where new CSMs would be opened.

Valerie's face took over the screen. "Good morning, Miss Rose."

"Good morning." Cheyenne tried to hide her annoyance at the interruption. "How are you?"

"I'm well, thank you." Valerie smiled. "More importantly, how are you feeling? Still having some difficulties?"

"I'm still getting lightheaded, so it's hard to walk without falling over unless I really take my time, and my concentration is pretty much shot."

"I'm sorry to hear that. I want you to know that I did discuss your case with Dr. Millwood. He is aware of the symptoms you are having and will have his assistant address them with you next week at your appointment. In the meantime, he encourages you to continue taking the current dose of your sertraline."

"Fine." Cheyenne dug the pill bottle out of her purse and poured the green capsules into her hand. Were they always green? No, she was sure they were pink before, before the new prescription.

As she stared down at her palm, beads of sweat sprouting on her forehead, she had to laugh at herself. First the car and now this? Aaron's suspicious tendencies must have rubbed off on her.

"Fourteen," she said, popping one of the pills into her mouth.

"Thank you, Miss Rose. I'll see you tomorrow morning."

Valerie disappeared from the monitor, and Cheyenne folded up the screen. She sat perfectly still for a moment longer, trying to rationalize with herself. She then spit the pill into her hand. After eyeing it for a moment, she rolled down the window and tossed it to the side of the road.

A few minutes later, they turned into the TV station parking lot. The black sedan continued straight down the highway, not even slowing down at the entrance to the lot. Cheyenne smiled to herself, shaking her head. When did she become so paranoid?

She got out of the car and stopped at Roger's door. He rolled the window down, and she handed him a twenty. "Thanks for your help today. Grab yourself a coffee or something."

He shook his head. "Miss Rose, that's not necessary. You pay me more than enough."

"I insist." She shoved the bill at him. "I really appreciate you driving me all over the map, no questions asked. I don't know what I would've done without you today. I certainly couldn't have driven myself, not with the way I've been feeling."

He took the twenty with obvious reservation. "You take care of yourself, Miss Rose."

"Can you be back here at five thirty? I have an important meeting at six."

"No problem. See you then."

Cheyenne headed into the studio to face her almost certainly irate boss. She hoped she would end up with a big story to offer him as an olive branch, but at this point, she would settle for having a good excuse for her tardiness.

So far, she had neither.

* * * * *

Cheyenne exited the studio at five thirty on the dot, hoping to beat Rebecca to the diner and get a quiet booth in the back of the restaurant. Roger was waiting for her in the parking lot. She made a beeline for the backseat without stopping to talk with him and didn't notice the phone lying in the seat next to her until it began to ring. She studied it for a moment then picked it up gingerly. It rang several more times before she finally answered it.

"Hello?"

"Miss Rose? Don't hang up. My name is Buck. Dr. Isaacs asked me to contact you." His voice was quiet and had a nasal quality, and Cheyenne plugged her left ear with her finger to block out any extraneous noise. She had the vague sensation she had heard this voice before but couldn't place it. She had a million questions racing through her head, but she couldn't seem to verbalize any of them.

He continued, “I understand you have some questions about the CRP program. I believe I can help you.”

“How did you get—”

“That phone you’re holding, I dropped it off with your driver. Nice guy.”

“But—”

“I don’t have much time to talk,” he said. “I’m afraid this may not be as secure a line as I had hoped.”

“Wait, I don’t understand. You’re saying you think your phone has been bugged?”

“Maybe, maybe not. I can explain later. There are some things you should know about the CRP, things they want kept secret. You wouldn’t believe me if I told you. I need to show you.”

“Show me? How are you going to do that?”

“I know where the CRP operates. I can bring you there.”

“I thought no one knew where the CRPs were.”

“So do they, and it’s vitally important it stays that way.” The man went silent. Cheyenne thought he had hung up, even pulled the phone away from her ear to check, then heard his next instructions. “After tonight, I’m going underground.”

“But—”

“At the corner of Elm and Mayview, there’s an old, deserted playground. Meet me at the very back tonight at nine thirty. Come alone, and don’t say anything to anyone. Not your driver, not anyone. No one is safe.”

Before she could ask him anything more, he ended the call.

Cheyenne lowered the partition between the backseat and the driver’s compartment. “Roger? How did this phone get back here?” She held it up between her thumb and pointer finger for him to see.

“Oh yeah, I almost forgot about that.” Roger looked at her in the rearview mirror. “Some guy in a black car drove up right after you went inside. Said you left it at the home.”

Cheyenne nodded slowly. “Did he say anything else?”

“No, not really.” Roger turned around and frowned at her. “Everything okay, Miss Rose?”

She smiled, despite feeling her heart start to race.

"Of course, Roger. Everything's great." She dropped the phone into her purse. "Let's get going."

CHAPTER 40

Cheyenne walked into the 506 Diner ten minutes early and scanned the restaurant for vacant tables. The place was already packed.

She weaved through the restaurant and placed her purse down on a dirty table with a thud. She sank down into a chair just as a waitress approached to clean it.

"I hope it's okay I sat down."

"I didn't see anything." The waitress picked up the check, stacked the remaining plates in her left hand, and swiped the table a few times with a dingy cloth. "I'm Bonnie. Need a menu?"

"Yes, thanks."

Once she was alone, Cheyenne traced the wood markings in the table with her finger and replayed her bizarre day in her head.

"Sorry I'm late."

Cheyenne clutched her chest and jerked her head around as Rebecca's voice broke into her thoughts.

"God, Rebecca, you scared me." She gestured to the chair next to her. "You're not late. I'm early."

Rebecca sank down into the chair and glanced around the table, both arms wrapped around her oversize purse. "I can't stay long."

"Thanks for coming. You don't think anyone followed you here, do you?"

"No." Rebecca's face clouded over. "Not that I could tell."

"Menus. Silverware." Bonnie set the items down in the center of the table. "Can I get you ladies anything to drink?"

“White wine. House is fine,” Rebecca said, not taking her eyes off Cheyenne as she placed her order.

“Water,” Cheyenne said. As hard as it had been, she hadn’t had a sip of alcohol since coming across that brochure in her dressing room. Not that quitting seemed to be helping anything.

Rebecca picked up Cheyenne’s phone from the table and turned it around in her hand. “Nice phone.”

“Uh, thanks.” Cheyenne set her menu to the side. “So, did you find out anything about the—”

“What is it, a SmartScreen 3? No, it must be a 4.” Rebecca nodded at Cheyenne as she spoke. She laid the phone off to the side then pulled a manila folder out of her bag, clutching it tightly.

“Thanks.” Cheyenne reached out for the folder. As she flipped through the papers, about twenty in all, Bonnie returned with their drinks. She sat them down and left without speaking.

Cheyenne looked up and noticed Rebecca examining her SmartScreen again. She cocked her head to the side. “Are you thinking about getting a new phone?”

“Maybe. If I can afford it,” Rebecca said. She pulled a pen out of her bag and wrote on a napkin then slid it toward Cheyenne.

Cheyenne glanced at the napkin. She read and reread the message a couple of times before looking back up at Rebecca. “Well, feel free to play around with mine all you want. I need to go to the ladies’ room. Be right back.” She stood, slid her chair back so that the legs scraped on the wood floor, and left the table. Rebecca followed close behind.

Once they were out of earshot of the table, Rebecca said, “I came across something today when I was looking for those protocols you mentioned. It’s the original proposal for the MedScreens, from almost eight years ago. Most of it details how the program is to be carried out, nothing we don’t know already, but look here at the bottom.” She pointed to the last paragraph. It was separated from the rest of the document by several spaces.

If the above proposal is passed in Congress, our care coordinators will not only have the ability to interact with patients via the two-way system, but will also be able to continuously monitor patients using a technology referred to as "patient-blinded one-way monitoring." The patient will have the freedom to go about his or her usual daily activities, and our care coordinators will be able to monitor and intervene only if necessary. The estimated net savings in healthcare dollars exceed the tens of billions in the next five years alone. Patient lives saved are projected to reach one million in five years.

Cheyenne looked in the direction of their table, where her phone looked like a bomb ready to explode. "You think they're monitoring everything I do and say?"

"All I know for sure is what I just showed you, but it sure seems possible." Rebecca ran her fingers through her hair. "Especially if you're giving them a reason to."

Cheyenne thought back to the last few weeks, the places she'd gone and the conversations she'd had. If someone were monitoring her, they had really gotten an earful. It would certainly explain that man showing up in her apartment a few days ago, and maybe even the car she had noticed this morning.

If they were trying to hide something, and it was really starting to look like they were, it must be something she hadn't stumbled upon yet. She supposed it made sense for them to keep following her and to only perform damage control if and when the time came, but how much longer could she really count on them keeping their distance? And was she willing to put Rebecca and Aaron at risk in the meantime?

"So you think they know I'm here right now? With you?"

"I'm sure they do." Rebecca crossed her arms over her chest and scanned the dining room again.

"Rebecca." Cheyenne took the woman by the shoulders and looked her in the eyes. "These guys, the ones who wrote those protocols, they're keeping some big secrets. Bigger than this." She waved the paper in her hand. "I haven't figured out what those secrets are yet, or even who the major players are, but I'm close, and they must know it." She let go of Rebecca. "I don't think they would have any problem with getting rid of someone—anyone—who threatened their position."

Rebecca's voice trembled when she finally spoke. "Cheyenne, you're scaring me."

Cheyenne gave her a knowing look. "You should be scared."

* * * * *

Cheyenne had Roger take her directly home from the restaurant. She sat in the back seat, staring straight ahead. She thought back to Rebecca's parting words. Cheyenne had to admit that she was scared, too.

Now, she was faced with a decision. Did she go through with the meeting tonight or follow her better judgment? On the one hand, it was her best chance to get answers about the CRPs, answers that she had never thought she would have access to. On the other, there was no way to know it wasn't some sort of a trap. She had no way of validating the man's story that he was friends with Aaron unless…

She stared at her phone. Should she even try to call the group home after her conversation with Veronica earlier that morning?

She decided to try Isabella first. Maybe she would be the voice of reason that Cheyenne needed to hear. As the phone rang, she thought about what she should say. What she *could* say. When the call went to voicemail, she decided not to risk leaving a message.

It was a quarter past seven when Roger pulled into her parking garage. Cheyenne took the elevator up to her apartment and sat down at her kitchen table with the folder Rebecca had given her. She had over an hour to decide whether she was going to meet Buck or not. She hoped she would get some sort of clarity between now and then.

Cheyenne held the folder without opening it. She couldn't shake the feeling that she was being watched. She glanced into the corner of the foyer at the blinking red light of the camera that had seemed so reassuring earlier that morning. She took out her phone and deactivated the camera but felt no relief.

Her chest tightened, and her breathing became more rapid. She stood up from the counter, her stool scraping and ultimately crashing onto the tile floor behind her. The sound of wood splintering barely registered with her as she grabbed a plastic bag and began to storm through the apartment, collecting her electronics. Once she had gathered all her portable devices, she tied the bag tight and placed it on the kitchen counter. She stared at it for just a moment before shaking her head. She opened a cabinet below the counter and tucked the bag behind her mixer, then closed the door.

Cheyenne tossed a kitchen towel into the air a few times before it caught on the camera and blocked the lens. After enjoying a moment of calm, her eyes locked on the small TV in the corner of her kitchen. She grabbed an armful of bath towels and made her way around the condo, covering each TV screen.

She had just come back into the kitchen and noticed the broken stool when she heard a faint ringing. Maybe it was Isabella. Deciding against using her hands-free system to answer the call—she already felt too exposed—Cheyenne opened the cabinet, dropped to her knees, and dug past her appliances as the phone continued to ring. She grabbed the bag and tore it open, digging through it until she found her phone.

She pressed the answer button mid-ring. Before she could say hello, she heard a frantic voice on the other line.

"Miss Rose? Miss Rose, are you there? It's Hilda."

"Yes, I'm here." Cheyenne tried to make her voice sound calm, willing Hilda to do the same.

"I'm sorry to call so late, but I thought you would want to know—" Hilda took a deep breath then let out a sob.

Cheyenne sat up straighter in her chair. "What is it, Hilda? Slow down and tell me."

"It's Dr. Isaacs. He did it. He talked about it all these months, and he finally did it."

"Did what, Hilda?"

"He killed himself. I found him hanging in his room just a few minutes ago. Miss Veronica's in there now." The girl barely got the words out before her voice degenerated into sobs. "I don't know why I called you. I just—I just felt like you would want to know."

Cheyenne got up from the table and paced the length of the kitchen. "Why do you think he would kill himself? Why now?"

"Why does anybody do it?"

Cheyenne couldn't accept that. The Aaron Isaacs she had met acted like someone who finally had something to live for. It made no sense to her that he would choose to end his life now. "Was anyone home?"

"Miss Veronica was taking some of the folks to dinner, but Dr. Isaacs didn't want to go. He was acting really paranoid, talking about someone tracking him, trying to shut him up."

"He said that?"

"Yeah, but that was nothing unusual for him. I told Miss Veronica I'd stay home with him. I had gone out back for a few minutes to water the garden, but—" She let out a sob. "When I walked in, I knew right away something was wrong."

"Oh, my God, Hilda." Cheyenne shook her head in disbelief. "Did he leave a note?"

"I—I'm not sure. I can look when I go back in."

"Hilda, this is very important. Has Veronica called 9-1-1 yet? Or the medical examiner?"

"Um, I think so, but no one's in there yet besides her." Her sobs were dying down now, and she was starting to breathe more regularly. "She usually likes to spend some alone time with the patients before everyone comes in."

Cheyenne felt very sad for Veronica and Hilda in that moment, sad they had a usual routine for situations like this.

"Good, Hilda. That's perfect. Do you think you can do me a favor before they come?"

"What is it?"

"Could you—" Cheyenne closed her eyes, rested her elbows on her kitchen counter, and dropped her head in her hands. "Could you take a few pictures and send them to me?"

"What? Why?"

"Hilda, I know how it must sound, especially coming from me, but I promise I would never publicize them. I just need to see it for myself. You know, to believe it."

"Miss Rose, I don't know how I—"

"Hilda, please. It's important."

She sighed. "I'll see what I can do, but I can't make any promises."

"I understand. Thanks." Cheyenne hung up. Something wasn't sitting right with her about Aaron's death. She couldn't bring herself to think of it as a suicide. Not yet.

She had no idea why she'd asked Hilda to send pictures, no idea what she expected to see in them. Maybe she just needed closure.

She had seen Dr. Isaacs' true state of mind. When they talked alone, he seemed coherent and purposeful. He certainly hadn't struck her as a man who would kill himself, that was for sure, but what was his motivation for hiding that part of himself from others? Was he afraid of something or someone? And if so, was that why he had ended up dead tonight?

Her phone alerted her to a new message. Her arm felt heavy as she reached for it, as if her hand were no longer a part of her body.

She glanced at the pictures Hilda sent, three in all, then quickly looked away. She had only seen one other hanging victim in her life, as part of a story, and she had never been able to forget it. She squeezed her eyes shut, but the images of Aaron remained in her mind, taunting her, drawing her attention to every gory detail: the swollen face, the blood pooling in the feet, the ligature mark around the neck.

Her eyes snapped open, and she looked at her phone again.

Within seconds, she had grabbed her keys and her phone and was headed to her car. She needed to see this for herself. She just hoped she wasn't too late.

CHAPTER 41
Then
May 17, 2028

"Let's start from the beginning, shall we, Mr. Bradford?"

"Call me Daniel."

Karl focused his gaze on the man sitting across from him, ignoring the other two men in the room. They were just here to bear witness and to assist with containing the problem if needed, just in case he and Bradford couldn't come to an understanding today.

"Okay, Daniel." The name slid heavily off Karl's tongue. He was in no mood for Daniel's bullshit today. "Exactly what happened yesterday?"

Daniel raised an eyebrow. "He knew too much. That's what happened."

"How did he come about knowing too much?" He spoke slowly, as if talking to a child.

Daniel shook his head. "No idea. He got it in his head that guy, Andrew, could be saved." He craned his neck to look at the two burly men seated behind him. "Look, why am I here, anyway?"

Karl took a deep breath and picked up a paperweight from the edge of his desk as he felt himself slowly losing control. "Sacrificing an important member of the medical CSM team is a big deal. It is a last resort. We're here to talk about why it was necessary and what we can do to avoid it in the future."

Daniel nodded and picked at something in his teeth. "It was the only option. Maybe I could have been a little more vigilant about him before, but by the time I noticed his...

divergence, it was too late. I would think you'd allow me a little leeway, considering…"

Karl stood up and placed his hands on the desk, daring him to continue. "Considering what, Daniel?"

A look of apprehension passed over the other man's face for a moment, then it was gone. His eyes flashed. "Considering you wouldn't be here if it weren't for me, Karl."

"That's what you think? You think you're so special, that there aren't hundreds of other black market creeps out there willing to sell their souls for a buck or two? You think I couldn't replace your ass tomorrow?"

"It was my idea, my plan. You know it never would've dawned on you, and even if it did, you never would have had the connections to pull it off."

A calm settled over Karl. He smiled, sat back down in his desk chair, and crossed his ankle over his knee. "You're right, Daniel. You're absolutely right. I needed you."

Daniel stood up, a smirk on his face. "Then are we done here?"

"I needed you." Karl ignored him. "But I don't need you anymore."

The smirk disappeared. "What are you saying, Karl? You can't—there's no way—"

Karl subtly nodded at the men seated in the back of the room, and they stood. They approached Daniel on either side and hooked their arms through his. He struggled, but they each outweighed him by at least fifty pounds.

"There is no way you can do this without me. My clients, they're loyal, they trust me!"

"Money is an amazing negotiator. Without our middle man, I'm sure your clients and I can come to an agreement that is to both our liking."

Karl nodded toward the double doors leading out of his main office and into the private sitting room. The two men carried Daniel out, his feet not even touching the floor as he resisted.

"It didn't have to come to this, you know," Karl called out as the doors swung closed behind them. Then he closed his eyes and took a deep, cleansing breath.

Karl hummed to himself, his hand floating in the air in time to the music, and listened as Daniel protested, his voice rising an octave. He heard the struggle and then a gasp, followed shortly by the thud of dead weight hitting the floor.

He smiled.

CHAPTER 42
Now
October 22, 2030

Cheyenne's car skidded to a stop a few feet in front of the white line as the blurry red traffic lights swung in the wind. She hadn't seen another car in miles, but she seemed to be hitting every stoplight. She tapped her fingers on the wheel and leaned forward to watch the light for the cross street through the misty windshield. She glanced down at her phone in the passenger seat. She started to pick it up, but there was no need. The pictures Hilda sent were still burned in her mind.

The lighting was terrible, and the angle looked like Hilda had taken them with her phone halfway in her pocket, but Cheyenne had seen enough. Aaron's body was already cut down and laid over a white sheet on his twin-size bed. His eyes stared upward, and his arms hung unnaturally off the sides of the mattress. In the background, she could see the overhead fan partially torn out of its place in the ceiling.

He had used a belt. It was looped tightly around his neck in the first two pictures. By the third picture, whoever was in the room with Hilda had removed it. What remained was the deep maroon ligature mark cutting straight across Aaron's neck like a tattoo, an emblem. A warning.

Why did that feel so wrong? It was different, somehow, than the other hanging victim she'd seen. She couldn't put her finger on why, but it had made her drive all the way out to the home. Unfortunately, the ambulance carrying Aaron's body, along with any answers Cheyenne had hoped for, was pulling out of the gravel parking lot just as she arrived. The trip wasn't a total waste, however. The note

Hilda had tucked into Cheyenne's palm had provided her with the last little push she needed to meet with Buck.

If she wasn't too late.

A driver laid on his horn behind her. Cheyenne's heart leapt in her chest, and she jerked her head up in time to see the light above her turning yellow. She pressed her foot down on the gas, and the car behind her barely squeezed through before the light changed to red again.

The clock on her phone said 9:32 as she turned down the dilapidated road in the dark. Her headlights only seemed to reach a few feet in front of her car before the beams vanished in the fog. Her wipers swept back and forth, squeaking against the barely wet glass.

The area to which Buck had directed her looked like it had been deserted years ago. Thick tree branches reached out into the road, blocking her view and occasionally interlocking with branches from the other side. She took slow, deep breaths and tried to remind herself that Aaron had known this guy, Buck. Trusted him.

Just when Cheyenne had decided the playground must have been torn down, she saw a swing set and jungle gym straight ahead. The road dead-ended at a parking lot. Cheyenne pulled into a spot and stared straight ahead, wondering for the millionth time what she was doing here. Especially without anyone knowing where she was.

She pulled Aaron's note out of her pocket, the one Hilda had found in his room. It was wrinkled and moist, and the ink was smearing, but the message in large, scrawling handwriting could not be clearer.

Cheyenne,
I'm sorry I couldn't help you finish what you started.
You can trust Buck.

Aaron

With Aaron dead, she was the only person who could follow this through to the end, and it was looking more and more like Hamm was in real trouble. She would never be able to forgive herself if something happened to him and she could have prevented it. She hoped there was still time.

She looked at her clock again. It was 9:35. She started to dig the flip phone out of her purse to see if there was a way to contact Buck when a pair of headlights appeared in her rearview mirror.

Her stomach dropped, and her head pounded. She gripped the steering wheel as she tried to collect herself. *Come on, Cheyenne. It's no different than any other interview.* She shook her head a couple times to clear it then tucked her purse and phone underneath her seat. Almost as an afterthought, she opened the glove compartment and studied the tiny revolver hidden there for a moment before grabbing it and shoving it into the waistband of her jeans. She took one last look at her reflection in the rearview mirror, smoothed her hair down, and stepped out into the drizzling rain.

The car did not appear to be slowing down. It headed straight for her, the blinding headlights making it impossible for her to see anything else. She panicked for a few seconds then made a run for the front of her car to take cover. At the last second, the car swerved left then took a hard right and skidded to a stop perpendicular to Cheyenne's car, inches from where she had just been standing.

The back car door opened, and Cheyenne heard a crunching sound as someone got out, his heels digging into the gravel with each step. Then she heard a voice.

"Cheyenne Rose. It's so good to finally meet you." It was the man from the phone call.

Cheyenne squinted in the direction of Buck's voice and started to walk toward the car. The mist settled on her bare shoulders, chilling her. "I can't see shit past those headlights." She let out a nervous laugh.

"Oh, my apologies."

Cheyenne heard two raps on the roof of the car, then everything went black. It took several seconds for her eyes to adjust to the relative darkness, but as they did, she took in the man whose voice she knew as Buck.

He was about five feet six inches tall and wore a black suit that fit his thin frame loosely. Once again, she had the sense that she knew him from somewhere, but she still couldn't quite place him.

As she squinted into the dark, she thought she could make out a scar on the right side of his forehead. Something felt like it was about to click, but the sound of more feet hitting the ground broke her concentration. Two bulky men in suits headed toward her.

"Care to join me for a drive?" Buck asked.

She eyed the two men. "Why don't we just talk here?"

He smiled, but his eyes seemed to stare right through her. "Actually, I'd prefer we drive."

Cheyenne backed toward her driver's side door, still trying to put the pieces together. Before she could reach the handle, the two men had flanked her on either side. One patted her down, quickly finding and disposing of her revolver, while the other held her arms tightly against her body.

"What the hell is going on here?" Cheyenne had a burst of adrenaline, and anger took over her fear. She looked at the man to her right. "Let me go before I—"

"Before you what?" Buck asked.

"My producers, friends, *everyone* knows where I am. They'll be looking for me if I don't check in."

"Somehow I doubt this meeting has been sanctioned by your producers, Miss Rose." He turned toward the car. "All the more reason to get moving."

The men led her the rest of the way to the car, one holding her wrists loosely together behind her back while the other opened the trunk. Inside was a roll of duct tape, some rope, and a couple of old rags stained with blood. Someone was here before. Was it Hamm? And if so, was he even alive?

Cheyenne tried to back away from the trunk, but the solid man behind her might as well have been a brick wall. Instead, she used what little leverage he had allowed in her wrists and reached toward him. She dug her nails into his groin as hard as she could, trying to startle him enough to make him let her go.

His yelp of pain made her think she had succeeded, but seconds later he had twisted her arms behind her so hard that her knees gave out. He pinned her to the ground with his foot, the wet gravel and sand digging into her left cheek as she felt the unmistakable warmth of fresh blood.

"Try that again, bitch," he said for only her to hear.

The other man arrived with the tape and rope, and they made quick work of tying her up, taking her fingernails and any other potential weapon out of the equation. They picked her up and dropped her into the trunk as if she weighed nothing.

Knowing that no one would hear her way out there, she didn't bother trying to scream. That was the whole point of the location Buck had chosen. She cursed her own ambition. Her stupidity.

As the car pulled out of the gravel lot, pebbles clanging against the body of the car, Cheyenne's heart sank. She was right to be suspicious. Aaron hadn't committed suicide; she was sure of that now. The knowledge hit her too late to be of any use. If Aaron had hung himself, the belt would have left a mark straight up the angle of his jaw. Instead, the ligature mark had traveled straight back. Someone had been holding the belt there, pulling it tight around his neck.

And if Aaron hadn't killed himself, then he hadn't left that note for her, either.

She wasn't any closer to understanding what was being covered up, or why, but she knew without a doubt that it was even bigger than she had originally thought.

It was worth killing for.

CHAPTER 43

Cheyenne gritted her teeth and tried to use her legs to brace herself in the car's trunk. There was nothing else to keep her from being tossed around as the car bounced down the rough side roads. Each time her head or shoulders slammed into the side of the car, pain shot through her like electricity and threatened to make her pass out. If she gave in to it, she worried she wouldn't wake up again.

She practiced slow, even breaths, but she still felt as though her air supply was dwindling. Did that happen? Could someone suffocate in a trunk? Her eyes searched the darkness for a crack where air could possibly get in, but everything was pitch black. Her heart pounded in her chest, and saliva built up in her mouth faster than she could swallow it. She felt around blindly with her feet, but every time she thought she was getting close to finding a taillight to kick out, the car took a sharp turn or hit a pothole, and she lost her bearings again.

She had no idea whether they were going north, south, east or west. All she knew was she wouldn't have long to act when they took her out of the trunk if she hoped to escape. They hadn't taken her keys from her front pocket, which meant she had a can of pepper spray as a weapon. *If* they were stupid enough to untie her. She would have to convince them that wasn't too much of a risk.

The car came to an abrupt stop, and Cheyenne's body slammed into the front wall of the trunk so hard it knocked the breath out of her. Car doors slammed and footsteps approached.

Her shoulders ached, and her arms had started to fall asleep. She repositioned herself on her chest and knees to relieve some of the pressure, but the stale, metallic odor emanating from the blood stain on the carpet made her stomach turn, and she had to roll back over. She heard voices getting closer, and the clumsy fingers of her right hand searched blindly for her watch's record button.

The trunk popped open, and she squinted, trying to see past the searching beam of a flashlight that was shining into her face. She froze, all her plans for escape having suddenly left her.

"Did you enjoy your ride?" The light lowered, and as Buck's face came into view, Cheyenne realized why he had looked so familiar. The man standing over her and sneering looked so unlike the congenial man she had seen in news briefs and television interviews. She could hardly believe it was him, but the scar was unmistakable. It rose like an extension of his right eyebrow, reaching almost to his hairline.

"It's...you?" She struggled to get into a seated position without the use of her arms. "Karl Buchner?"

"In the flesh."

He smiled down at her, and Cheyenne shrunk away from him involuntarily.

She remembered it like it was yesterday, the day he had gotten that scar. The headlines that had followed in the next couple of weeks floated around in her head: *Trusted Partner Attacks Karl Buchner*; *Long History of Previously Undisclosed Mental Illness*; *Montgomery to Receive Care in a Top-Ranked Psychiatric Facility*. The story seemed eerily familiar. The weight in her stomach grew heavier and made it hard for her to breathe.

She remembered thinking Karl was so gracious afterward, expressing nothing but concern for his longtime colleague. He had made it his personal mission to ensure Mr. Montgomery got the best inpatient psychiatric treatment and had even overseen the initiation of that treatment himself. As far as Cheyenne knew, Alexander Montgomery was still rotting away in a psychiatric facility somewhere, and Karl had cinched his own selection as surgeon general later that year.

If he could do that to his own colleague, was there anything he wouldn't do?

He motioned to his bodyguards, and they stepped forward. Each of them grabbed an arm and ignoring her halfhearted efforts at pulling free, they dragged her out of the trunk.

One of the men went to move the car as the other patted her down once more. He found her car keys and put them in his pants pocket. Cheyenne tensed up when he ran a hand down her arm, but he barely acknowledged the old-fashioned watch other than to give a quick chuckle.

"Time for an upgrade," he said under his breath. He then moved behind her and pulled her arms together until she arched her back in pain.

"Welcome." Karl swept both arms dramatically outward, gesturing to the buildings around them.

She took in her surroundings. Even though it was dark, there were enough light posts scattered throughout the compound that she could appreciate the majesty of it all. Seven sprawling buildings bordered the courtyard in which she stood. Within the courtyard were two tennis courts, a lap pool, and a volleyball court, along with what looked like a golf course at the outer edge of it all. The landscaping was meticulous, without a single dead flower or blade of grass in sight.

Karl searched her face as if looking for a sign of recognition. She racked her brain for the significance of what he was showing her but came up short. It was beautiful, serene, certainly not somewhere she would resist going. What was she missing?

"This is the CRP, isn't it? Where does the money come from for something like this?"

"Medicine is big business, or haven't you heard?" Karl smiled, his face twisting in the light of the flashlight. "At least, my version of it is. Part of running a business is making sure your employees are well taken care of."

Cheyenne felt a chill run down her spine as she stood gazing out at the resort, feeling Karl's eyes glued to her. So this was it, the CRP where Aaron, Hamm, and countless others were taken once they were recognized as liabilities.

She hung her head, wincing as the sudden movement caused the bodyguard to tighten his grip on her arms. No one even knew she was missing, much less where to start looking, and once Karl was finished with her, there would be no evidence she was ever here, except—

"Inside," Karl said.

The bodyguard began to propel her forward, each movement causing a hot pain to shoot through her shoulders and bringing tears to her eyes.

Cheyenne fought back her rising panic and let the man lead her inside.

CHAPTER 44
Then
May 19, 2028

"Are there any leads in Mr. Bradford's disappearance?"

Karl squinted toward the voice as camera flashes went off from all directions. Tracy, her eyes bloodshot and swollen, stood beside him on the stage.

"No leads, but we have our best men working on it." He reached out to Tracy and squeezed her arm. "He wasn't just an excellent colleague. He was family."

"Is he believed to be dead, then, Dr. Buchner?"

Karl's breath caught in his chest, and he felt sweat beading on his forehead. He mentally kicked himself for the slip. Casting his eyes downward, he said, "We know that in any missing person case, the first twenty-four to forty-eight hours are crucial. We have not given up hope, but I'm afraid we also must be realistic."

More flashes, more voices.

"Do you know of anyone who wanted him dead?"

"What?" Karl looked up. "No. That's ridiculous. Why would anyone want him dead?"

"Is there any insider information he may have had—"

"That's enough questions for today." Karl held his hand up to stop the barrage. "My wife and I are requesting privacy during this difficult time."

The barrage of questions continued as Karl led Tracy off the stage, his arm wrapped protectively around her waist. She covered her face, and her shoulders shook. Out of the corner of his eye, Karl saw a movement followed by a bright flash, and he smiled inwardly. It was a perfect picture of the grieving couple.

Once they had rounded the corner and were out of sight of any prying eyes, Karl stopped and turned Tracy to face him. He put his arms around her.

"I'll do everything I can to find him."

"Be honest." She gazed up at him, searching his eyes. "He's not coming back, is he?"

Karl blinked.

"I've never asked you questions about your work. About how Daniel plays in. About what happened with Monty. I've always trusted you to make the right decisions for me, for us." Her hands rested on either side of his chest, and she leaned into him. "Don't lie to me."

"No, Tracy." He felt as if a weight had lifted. "He's not coming back."

She nodded once, ran her tongue over her teeth, and took a step backward, away from him. "I'm sure whatever he did—I'm sure you were justified."

"I'm not really at liberty to—"

"You're going to need help, now that he's gone." It was as if she was talking to herself, now.

"Well, the first thing—"

"Whatever it is, I want in."

CHAPTER 45
Now
October 22, 2030

"Is this really necessary?" Cheyenne hoped Karl hadn't noticed the tremor in her voice. She strained against the cold metal bracelets that pinned her arms and legs to the leather chair, and she peered up at the hollow, white sphere suspended above her head. She heard a loud click, then a blinding light slammed into her vision and erased everything else. She squeezed her eyes shut and turned her face downward, but the light continued to blaze against the cover of her eyelids.

"Everything I do is necessary, Cheyenne."

Karl's voice was closer now, and Cheyenne felt the wet heat of his breath in her ear. She fought off a wave of nausea.

"Why did you bring me here?"

"Isn't it obvious? You were getting too close."

"Too close to what?"

She dared to open her eyes and had to blink several times. Karl slowly came into focus. He leaned back against a rail that encircled her chair, which sat on a raised platform. Beyond the rail, an expansive research laboratory was in full operation. People in white lab coats milled about, moving from one workstation to another, seemingly oblivious to her presence.

"There have only been a few dozen people before you who have threatened my vision." He gazed past her, contemplative. "The key is to take care of the threat before it becomes anything more than that."

Karl pushed up from the railing and brushed his hands together, then he walked down a set of stairs that led him to a panel of computer screens on the main laboratory floor. For the first time, Cheyenne noticed an attractive woman sitting in front of the control panel. Karl strode over to her, grabbed a handful of blond hair, and planted a forceful kiss on her lips. Cheyenne's first instinct was to defend her. But instead of pushing Karl away, the woman pulled him closer. When they finally broke apart, Karl glanced around the lab.

"Everyone clear out," he said into a microphone, his voice echoing over a loudspeaker. The researchers filed through the exit without so much as a glance toward Karl. Then he looked down at the woman. "You too, babe."

She started to protest but stopped when she saw his fists clench. She stood up and gave him another lingering kiss, his hands groping her backside, before she sauntered past him to the exit.

Cheyenne watched her leave, and the hot discomfort in her stomach became impossible to ignore. "How am I a threat? I have no idea what's going on here." She attempted a laugh, but it came out as nothing more than a puff of air. "Trust me, I wish I did."

"We'll just have to see about that." Karl pressed a few buttons on the screen in front of him. The sphere lowered until it surrounded Cheyenne's head on three sides and she could only see directly in front of her. When he spoke again, his voice was devoid of all emotion. "State your name."

"State my—?" Her voice cut off as a surge of energy coursed through her body. She bent at the waist as much as the metal bands would allow, trying to absorb the shock. "What the hell?"

"I'm asking the questions, here." He was calm, his face now trained back on the computer screens. "State your name."

"Cheyenne," she said quickly. "Cheyenne Rose."

"Good, and how do you know—sorry, how *did* you know—Dr. Isaacs?"

"I met him—I was volunteering and got assigned to Slater—ahh!" Another jolt stopped her mid-sentence. She examined her skin directly underneath the metal bands. It was already pink and raw.

"The truth."

Cheyenne's head was heavy as she raised it and gazed down at Karl. He met her eyes.

"I'll know, Cheyenne. Recalling a memory utilizes a very different part of the brain than fabricating one."

"I went looking for him. I was trying to get more information about the CRPs, trying to find Hamilton."

"Mmm-hmm." Karl touched the screen in a few more places. "How did you get his name?"

"I just—I did some research." Cheyenne didn't like where this was going.

"Does the name Rebecca Stephenson ring a bell?"

"Yes, it does sound familiar." She felt a warmth rise up her neck, and she cleared her throat. "We went to school together if I'm not mistaken." The shock was more powerful this time, numbing her entire body and making her ears ring. Cheyenne had difficulty relaxing her muscles again after it had passed.

"Try again."

"We reconnected more recently. I knew she worked for the CSMs, and I tried to get some information out of her but—"

Karl activated another shock, and Cheyenne flinched, her eyes shut tight.

"Yes?" He held his finger menacingly over the screen.

"I gave her no choice." Cheyenne stared down at her lap. "This has nothing to do with her."

"Oh, well then. I wish I'd known that before—" Karl waved a dismissive hand in the air. "Never mind, it's in the past now."

Cheyenne's mouth went dry. "What did you do to her?"

"*I* ask the questions." His eyes darkened, and the fingers of his left hand curled into a tight fist. "Do not forget that."

Twenty minutes and several more electric shocks later, Cheyenne sat slumped in the leather chair, her chin bobbing just above her chest as she struggled to lift her head. "When are you going to believe me? That's all I know." She let out a long, deep breath. "I've told you everything."

Karl now sat next to the control panel, legs crossed and leaning back so far that the desk chair threatened to topple over with him. He nodded slowly. "I believe you. I'm a little surprised and disappointed, frankly, but I believe you."

"What did I miss?"

"Only the big picture, Cheyenne. The reason all of this even exists." He gestured around the room. Cheyenne could hear the pride in his voice, see it in the way he sat a little straighter in his chair, puffing out his chest.

"So, tell me what you'd like me to know. Tell me how you have succeeded where so many others failed."

"Well, since you asked." Karl dug in his jacket pocket and pulled out a partially smoked cigar. He was painfully slow in lighting it and took a leisurely draw before continuing. "I simply approached the situation—the challenge—as I would approach any business venture. Unlike most of my predecessors, I had a medical background. I was able to understand the challenges facing both sides. In the end, it all comes down to a simple issue of dollars and cents."

"Someone whose life was at stake might beg to differ."

"That's the eternal dilemma, isn't it?" Karl planted both feet on the floor and moved to the edge of his seat, elbows resting on his knees. "No one wants to accept it, but the fact is that there is a finite amount of money with which to pay for medical care. The obvious solution, and a very unpopular one, was to somehow ration healthcare. Limit spending. The period right after the crash was a very dark time for America. There were debates over who had the right to decide which patients received which procedures. It became reminiscent of the Civil Rights Movement, and it reopened wounds for many people."

Cheyenne tried to sit up straighter in her chair, but the burns on her wrists rubbed harshly against the metal bands, and she went limp from the pain. "I remember," she said.

"Then the Centers for Standardized Medicine were introduced. The program was just another attempt at limiting spending, this time by giving the government the final say instead of the insurance companies. It was designed to be a standardized way of rationing. Patients were identified only by their patient number. No demographic information was linked to their account in any way, shape or form."

"The program was a huge success."

"Yes, and no. Yes, the program paid for itself, but we needed it to do more than break even. The country was almost bankrupt at that point. We needed something to add money to the pot, not just keep from taking any more out."

"Enter Karl Buchner and the infamous MedScreens."

There was a glazed-over look in his eyes as he seemed to relive his glory days. "Most people already had access to tablets or laptops, anyway. The technology was there. It was just a matter of applying it, and for that small percentage of patients to whom we had to supply a MedScreen, the cost-benefit analysis was a no-brainer."

"But that's not the whole story, is it, Dr. Buchner?"

"How astute of you." He gave her a tight smile. "No, it's not the whole story. I already told you that it all came back to simple economics, right?"

"Right."

"Well, we were still just coming up with ways to spend the money in our pot more efficiently."

"That was a problem?"

"Not a problem in itself, no. What made it problematic was that we were ignoring the other half of the issue."

“Which was?”

He looked at her as if the answer was obvious. “How to get a bigger pot of money. That’s where patients like your little friend, Ridge, came in.”

CHAPTER 46

Cheyenne stiffened at the mention of Ridge's name. Just when she thought she was getting somewhere, Karl threw her another curveball. How could an innocent boy possibly have anything to do with this whole conspiracy?

Karl seemed to delight in her confusion. He gave her a smug grin. "Instead of telling you what I mean, why don't I just show you?"

Cheyenne couldn't find her voice to answer, so she just waited.

Karl rubbed his hands together then began to tap the screens in front of him once more. He fanned his arms out to enlarge the view until it spanned all nine monitors of the panel. He pressed a button, and the monitors rotated in unison until they faced her.

He pressed play, and on the screen, she saw the inside of an operating room. The surgeon, although covered almost from head to toe in a surgical hat, mask, and sterile gown, seemed oddly familiar. When he spoke, she recognized his voice immediately.

"Hamm," she whispered. She lifted her hand to reach out to the screen, forgetting her restraints for a moment until her raw skin scraped against the cold metal. She winced.

The video continued. Hamilton's hands searched Ridge's tiny body for the precious, life-saving kidney. Cheyenne saw the ambience in the operating room change as if it were something tangible, saw Hamilton's body tense and his movements become more frantic.

She gripped her armrests, afraid to blink as the horror of that day unfolded in front of her eyes. All the questions she had for Hamm were answered as she watched his emotions transition from confusion to anger to despair. As he ignored the orders he was given and tried desperately to save Ridge's life.

Her nose burned as she fought back tears. She saw him realize a moment too late that he was being drugged. Saw him fall to the ground and his body get dragged out of the surgical suite. Saw a new doctor come in to take his place, finish the job he had started.

The endotracheal tube was removed from Ridge's mouth, and the boy's pulse rate slowed on the monitor until his heart beat for the last time. Cheyenne could no longer stop the tears from streaming down her face as she watched Ridge's lifeless body get wheeled out of the operating room only minutes after Hamilton.

"So? What do you think?" Karl searched her face for a reaction.

She stared back at him, at a loss for words. Finally, she shook her head. "I have no idea how that video explains anything."

Karl sighed. "I had hoped this would help tie everything together for you."

"Well, it doesn't. What I just saw, it doesn't make any sense to me, whatsoever."

"Ridge's parents thought his appendectomy was paid for by the *government*." He used exaggerated finger quotes as he spat the word. "It wasn't. No, Ridge paid for his own surgery and more."

She pressed her lips together. "I still don't get it."

"We provided him with a life-saving intervention; he provided us with a kidney." He paused and cocked his head to the side. When she didn't respond, he continued. "Do you have any idea what a kidney goes for these days?"

Cheyenne stared at him. "No, that's not possible." She shook her head so forcefully she felt a wave of vertigo. "Organ donation is completely voluntary in the United States."

"Precisely. Which is why I've had to look elsewhere for financial support." He seemed to revel in the look of shock that came over her face.

"That's illegal." Cheyenne's eyes flashed. She was thinking of Andrew now, and her body strained against the shackles. "How can you justify this?"

"It's quite simple: I don't have to. Everything is done outside the national donor registry. Otherwise, well, there's no way we could have stayed under the radar."

He stood up and walked around to the computer screens, tapping them a few more times. He displayed a document on the screen closest to Cheyenne. It was a menu of sorts, but instead of entrées, it listed organs, and the prices were much more substantial.

"After a very fortuitous meeting with a like-minded entrepreneur, introduced to me by my beautiful wife, I was able to identify a previously untapped demand. That was only the first step. As you know, demand has never been the limiting factor when it comes to organ donation. We needed to increase the supply. Where better to find healthy organs than healthy patients?"

He said it so matter-of-factly that it took a moment for Cheyenne to process his words. She studied his face. "You didn't—"

"Truth be told, it started with harvesting tissue from dead bodies." Karl waved his hands as he spoke, so relaxed he might as well have been talking about the weather. "You would be surprised at how many uses one can find for cadaver tissue. Then, I recognized an untapped resource with much greater financial worth—the living donor."

"You can't take someone's organ without their consent, and most people aren't going to consent to having an organ removed for a perfect stranger." Cheyenne felt like she was stating the obvious and had the uncomfortable sensation that she was still missing the big picture.

Karl sighed theatrically. "Have you ever heard the story of *The Little Red Hen*?" At Cheyenne's blank look, he continued, "It's a fable about a little red hen who decides to plant a grain of wheat, harvest it, mill it into flour, and ultimately make a loaf of bread out of the flour. Each step of the way, she asks for help from the other barnyard animals, but they all decline. Then, when the bread comes out of the oven, all of the other animals want to help her eat it."

"And?"

"She doesn't let them, of course! They haven't earned it." His eyes flashed, and the tendons in his forearms twitched as he gripped the railing directly in front of her chair. "Don't you see? Americans are no better than the animals in that story. Everyone wants access to healthcare, but no one wants to pay for it. Where do they think the money comes from? From the sky? From a money tree?"

She was silent.

"The money *was* coming from the government," he said in answer to his own question, "and the government finally ran out. But that didn't stop people from getting sick, did it? It didn't change their expectations, either. Not in the least.

"If someone needs a surgery to save their life, then we'll perform the surgery, regardless of their ability to pay. It's the American way. Now, as payment, they may end up donating a kidney, or part of their liver, or something else they're not using. Tit for tat. It's only fair."

"There has to be a better—"

"Why do you think that everyone who came before me—*brilliant* financial minds, the best of the best—all failed at reforming healthcare in America? Because Americans expect to receive more than they're willing to pay for. That is not a problem that can be fixed, not without a little creative thinking."

"That's what you call it? Creative thinking?" Her body tensed again, and she barely avoided reopening the burn wounds on her wrists. "I call it illegal. Unethical. Disgusting."

"Well, there's some people in very high places that couldn't care less about what you call it. How else do you think I've managed this long without being exposed? It always comes down to money. Always. The sooner you learn that, the better off you'll be."

"So what happens now? You have to know I'm not just going to forget this conversation."

He laughed a deep, guttural laugh that echoed off the walls of the cavernous room.

"That, my dear, is precisely what you're going to do."

CHAPTER 47

Cheyenne eyed the contraption directly above her as Karl's words echoed in her head. Aaron's outrageous claims of having his memory erased came barreling back into her consciousness. It was starting to seem like nothing was unlikely anymore.

"How on earth have you convinced so many people to go along with this twisted plan? I can't imagine most doctors share your perspective."

"Doesn't matter." Karl pushed away from the railing and began to circle the platform, hands behind his back. "You've heard the phrase 'the left hand doesn't know what the right hand is doing'? We created so much bureaucracy and red tape that it's virtually impossible for a healthcare worker to verify any part of a patient's medical history. Why would they need to? Everything they have to know is right there in the electronic medical record." He approached her chair and stared into her eyes until she looked away. "Ask me," he whispered, leaning down in front of her and placing a clammy hand over hers. "I know you want to."

She felt like she would be sick as the magnitude of his confession began to sink in. There was no doubt in her mind that he didn't plan to let her out alive. She was going to die in this chair, and his secret would die with her. Just like it had multiple times before.

"You doctor the charts to say whatever you need, whenever you need." It was not a question. She had never been more certain of anything in her life.

Karl's eyes sparkled as he straightened up and towered over her. "As in the case of Ridge Reid, Dr. Walker was told to harvest a kidney, but the documentation reflected a run-of-the-mill appendectomy. Foolproof."

"Until Hendrix needed a kidney."

"I have to admit, that situation did raise some interesting quality control issues. No one knew the boy was already missing a kidney until that moment in the operating room. All in all, I think it was handled rather brilliantly."

Cheyenne flexed her wrists and searing pain shot up her arms and into her neck. Tears sprang to her eyes. "Can you loosen these for a few minutes? I'm dying here."

Karl took her in for a long moment then eyed the bands. He turned his back to her and made a locking and unlocking motion toward a mirror. A moment later, there was a loud, mechanical click, and the chair began to make a whirring noise. The sphere returned to its original place suspended above the chair, and the bands slowly separated until Cheyenne could get her arms free, then her legs.

She stepped out of the chair and misjudged the distance to the floor, almost falling face-first onto the platform. When she had righted herself, she said, "You can at least have the decency to tell me what Andrew had to do with any of this. He doesn't seem to fit into your neat little box. He didn't live."

Karl turned back around to face her. "Nothing gets past you. What a stellar reporter you must be."

"Just answer the question." She could see nothing but Karl's silhouette against the harsh lights of the lab.

"This whole thing has been a progression. None of it was anything I anticipated or planned. Whether you believe that or not, it's the truth. As I mentioned, we started with harvesting tissue from corpses, then we realized the incredible potential and moved to living donors. Soon, it became obvious to me how much more money we were leaving on the table. These patrons were willing to pay exorbitant amounts of money for organs such as the heart and lungs—organs one can simply not survive without—but the donors had to be chosen very carefully. They were people who were healthy but had suffered an unfortunate event, usually a trauma, that would leave them with a long, expensive recovery." He smiled again, this time to himself. "We both save money and make money. The idea was all mine, and I am the one who carried it out. Only a few trusted individuals are even aware of that protocol."

Cheyenne felt a wave of heat just below the surface of her skin. She gritted her teeth in a futile attempt to calm herself. Before she realized what she was doing, she lunged at Karl. She dug her fingernails into his eye sockets, hearing a horrified scream and reveling in it for just a moment before his thugs came out of nowhere and pulled her away from him.

Karl appeared blurry through her tears. She blinked over and over again, but the tears just came back, making it impossible for her to see the damage she had done. She clenched and unclenched her fists, enjoying the satisfying squish of a sticky, warm liquid she could only assume was blood.

After a moment, he said, "I may have underestimated you a bit, Miss Rose. Rest assured, it will not happen again."

She took a moment to get herself together. When she spoke, her voice shook with anger. "So, why did you really do it, Karl? It wasn't for the good of the country, to improve healthcare for Americans, like you say." She shook her head. "No, I know people like you. You're a narcissist without anything to brag about. You always thought you should be getting attention, praise." She strained against the guards, but they held her back. "But you were just average, boring, and ugly." She mustered all the hatred she had in her. "Weak."

"You have no idea what you're talking about." His smugness returned.

"You thought when you got an impressive job, made it onto TV, that would do it, but you still felt too small. Then you lucked out and some poor woman actually agreed to marry you. Surely that was enough."

Seeming to ignore her tirade, he strolled over to a desk next to the control station and opened the top drawer. A moment later, he pulled out a small handgun and aimed it at Cheyenne. "I suggest you stop talking. I would hate for you to miss my next trick."

Cheyenne didn't think he would shoot, but she didn't want to risk it. She sat back down in the chair, arms still gripped tightly by the two guards. She didn't think she had the energy for any more surprises. "What trick?"

Instead of answering her, he spoke to the guards. "You keep her here. I'll be right back." He made sure the safety was on before placing his gun in the waistband of his slacks, then he left the room through a back door Cheyenne had not noticed before.

He returned a moment later with Hamilton Walker.

CHAPTER 48

Cheyenne drank Hamilton in from her vantage point on the platform as Karl led him into the lab through the back door. He was no different than she remembered, tall with a quiet confidence. His graying hair was a little longer than she was used to, but his ice blue eyes were exactly the same, cutting straight through to her center and making her feel completely powerless. Then he saw her and grinned.

"Is that Cheyenne Rose? The reporter?"

"Yes, it's me, Hamm." Her body tingled, and her heart fluttered, just like the first time she had ever seen him. She had assumed the worst, had assumed he was dead, and now here he was standing before her. It seemed too good to be true. "I'm so glad to see you."

The smile melted from Hamm's face, and he glanced to his left at Karl. Then Hamm leaned down and whispered something in Karl's ear. The other man nodded and placed a reassuring hand on Hamm's back.

Something was wrong. "What's going on here? What did he tell you?" Cheyenne tried to stand up, but the two men restraining her tightened their grips, keeping her in her seat.

"Why is she—" He once more looked to Karl.

"It's…for her safety."

Hamm nodded, satisfied. He then looked back at Cheyenne. "I'm sorry, have we met?" His face reflected a mild embarrassment at having forgotten her but nothing more.

A vice grip tightened around her chest. "Hamm, quit joking around."

"How do you—" He took a hesitant step toward her. "Only my close friends call me Hamm."

She studied his eyes for a moment longer, seeing no recognition there. She took a shaky breath. "Do you remember Ridge and Hendrix?"

He had made it to the steps of the platform now and stood looking up at her. He visibly relaxed and nodded his head. "Oh, sure. I remember them." His smile broadened, his dimples on full display. "That's how we know each other, then, through the Reids. How're my little guys doing, anyway?"

Cheyenne's breath caught in her throat. How were they *doing*? She caught a glimpse of Karl standing behind Hamm, quietly observing the scene as it unfolded. The look of pride on his face infuriated her.

"Are they getting nervous about the surgery?" Hamm asked.

"They already had the surgery, Hamm. On September twenty-ninth." *Don't make me say it.*

Hamm cocked his head to the side. "But I was—I couldn't have—"

Cheyenne looked away.

"What happened?" He had made his way up the stairs and knelt before her so she could no longer avoid his eyes. Deep pools of worry now replaced his carefree baby blues.

You know what happened, she thought. *Don't make me say it.* She closed her eyes and shook her head.

He leaned back and let out a breath that sounded like a laugh, but when Cheyenne opened her eyes and took in his face, she saw no humor there.

"Tell me."

Cheyenne took a deep breath before plunging in. "Don't you remember? You performed the surgery. Hendrix is doing fine, but Ridge—Ridge didn't—"

"That's enough," Karl interrupted. "Dr. Walker, I brought you here to demonstrate for Miss Rose the amazing work we're doing, not for you to catch up on mutual acquaintances." He shot a look at Cheyenne, who still remained in the leather chair flanked by his assistants. He gave them a meaningful look then jerked his head to the left. The men twisted Cheyenne's arms further behind her back and forced her to a standing position, then they led her to the left side of the platform. Karl gestured to the now-empty chair. "Dr. Walker, if you would be so kind."

Hamm stood up, glancing at Karl then taking another long look at Cheyenne. She could see him trying to put things together. She stared back, reaching out to him through her eyes, willing him to remember her. He blinked once, then he climbed into the seat she had just vacated.

"Alright, Doctor," he called out to Karl. "Ready whenever you are."

Karl pressed a button, and the hollow device began to lower from the ceiling until it surrounded Hamm's head, obstructing his view.

Cheyenne opened her mouth to warn him, but before she could get the words out, one of her captors reached around her head and covered her mouth. He dug in his pocket with his free hand and located a handkerchief, which he stuffed down her throat. She couldn't breathe, and a fire rose in her chest. She lunged forward and gagged, bringing the handkerchief up just enough to clear her airway. Before she could dislodge the gag any further, the man secured her mouth with a long piece of duct tape, which he then wrapped around the back of her neck.

She watched in helpless silence as Karl pressed another button, and the bands tightened over Hamm's arms and legs.

"Take a look," Karl said as he repositioned the monitors to face Cheyenne. "This contraption is what's known as a functional MRI. These pictures are real-time views of Dr. Walker's brain."

Cheyenne could see two images of Hamm's brain, one of each of the computer screens. The first appeared as if someone had taken a knife and cut his head open from top to bottom and she was looking at the inside. The second looked like the cut was made from front to back.

"This is a sagittal view, cut longitudinally." Karl pointed to the first screen. "And this is an axial, a lateral view. You'll get more comfortable with it as we go along." He pressed another button and spoke into a microphone. "You doing okay in there? We're about to get started."

"I'm ready when you are."

"Okay, Dr. Walker. Let's start with the Reid family. How did you meet them?"

"I, uh, I was Ridge's treating physician when—no, that can't be right." His fingers began to drum the armrest. "You know, to be completely honest, I can't quite recall how we met. I've known them for quite a while."

Cheyenne tried to protest but couldn't get the words out around the gag.

Karl winked at her and lifted his finger off the mic button. "Of course, you and I know where he really met the Reids," he said, "but if we told him, we'd ruin all the fun. Watch what happens next." He pointed to the images on the screen. Parts of Hamm's brain were highlighted in red and blue.

"As a result of my verbal cue, Dr. Walker accessed several memories involving the Reid family. Here, we see activation of the medial temporal lobe, which houses episodic memory. Even though his memory of meeting the Reids—which was intricately tied to his personal relationship with you—has already been erased, he has plenty of other memories that weren't linked to you." Karl tapped his finger on the largest areas of activity then pressed a red button on the control panel. There was a hum followed by a loud click. "Well, *had*."

He turned to Cheyenne for her reaction, looking disappointed when he was reminded that she couldn't respond. "Michael, go ahead and take that tape off her mouth. I think she's learned her lesson."

Cheyenne winced as Michael ripped off the duct tape, pulling at the fine hairs at the nape of her neck. He then plucked out the handkerchief. Cheyenne bent over, her hands on her knees, and coughed until her throat hurt. Once the coughing fit had subsided, she craned her neck upward to look at Karl. "So, what now? He's one of you?"

He sneered at her. "We're scientists, not zombies."

"What's that supposed to mean?"

Karl ignored her and activated the mic again. "Dr. Walker, tell me what you know about Ridge and Hendrix Reid."

Cheyenne looked at the computer screen. The brain images exhibited a few areas of transient activity then returned to the background level of stimulation.

"I'm sorry, can you tell me those names again?" Hamm asked.

Karl repeated himself.

"Yeah, I don't think I've heard of those people. Should I have?"

"Not necessarily, Dr. Walker." Karl once more nodded in the direction of the two-way mirror, and the metal bands that bound Hamm's arms and legs released their grip. "That's all we have for you today. You can leave through that door, there." Karl pointed to the back of the large room. "Thank you for your time."

The white helmet rose to the ceiling, and Cheyenne eagerly took in Hamm's face. The blank look he gave her in return confirmed what she already knew. Every angle of his face, every expression was so familiar to her, but she was nothing more than a stranger to him. He stood from the chair and slowly descended the platform.

She turned to Karl. "Why? Why can't you at least let him remember Ridge?"

Karl gave her a condescending look. "Don't be ridiculous, Cheyenne. It just takes one person, one memory, to compromise everything we've done. I simply can't have that."

"How do you know you haven't erased something important, a memory you didn't intend to get rid of?"

"Oh, that."

He turned back to his computer, and for a moment, Cheyenne didn't think he was going to answer her question. "It's been a work in progress, actually, but we've come a long way. Your friend, Dr. Isaacs, was one of the first guinea pigs." He opened a new folder and dragged a brain image to the top left of the large screen. He pointed to a large area that was circled in red. "They got too close to the basal ganglia, affected his procedural memory." He shook his head. "A shame, really. He was a fine surgeon before the incident. We were able to find another role for him for a while, but even then he just couldn't quit making a nuisance of himself."

Cheyenne's palms began to sweat, and her breathing became more shallow and rapid. This was really happening. Hamm was gone. He was never coming back, and she was quite possibly next. "Okay, you win." Her voice was high-pitched and shaky as she fought back tears. "You've proven your point. What do you want me to do?"

Karl closed his eyes and massaged the back of his neck. "Haven't you figured that out yet? I want you to forget you were ever here. That's the whole point."

"Deal. I won't say anything to anyone. I promise. Hamm and I will even move, break contact with anyone we've ever known. Like witness protection."

"Didn't you see? He doesn't know you."

"He will. We'll start over. I'm not leaving him behind." Even if she had to start over with him, it would be better than living without him. "He's part of the deal."

"Cheyenne, you seem like a nice person. You really do, but you know I can't trust a word you say. Why would you keep quiet?"

"Because," she looked at him desperately, "I'm scared of you. I'm terrified. What better reason is there?"

Hamm cleared his throat from somewhere behind Cheyenne, causing her to jump. "Sorry to interrupt," he said, "but can someone let me out? The door seems to be locked."

Karl and the guards looked toward Hamm's voice at the same moment, giving Cheyenne a split-second in which to act. She twisted her arms out of Michael's grip and lunged forward, reaching the gun in Karl's waistband just as he pressed a button to release the lock. She pointed the gun, hands shaking but mind alert, and backed away so that all three of the men were in her field of view.

"You can trust this, asshole. I am going to make sure that everyone on the face of this earth knows that you're a fraud, a thief, and a cold-blooded murderer. I am going to track down every patient, every family that was affected by your protocols, and make sure you stand trial for each and every one of them, and if you ever get out of jail, which I seriously doubt, then I will come after you myself and get justice for Andrew."

The three men reluctantly raised their hands into the air. For the first time since arriving here with Karl, Cheyenne felt in control.

Karl's eyes darted subtly to her left. The movement was so quick that Cheyenne almost missed it. As it was, she caught it a second too late. Just as she turned to see what had gotten Karl's attention, Hamm grabbed her from behind, forcing the gun out of her hands and then turning it on her.

"Sit down," he demanded.

"Hamm, what are you doing?"

He hesitated, lowering the gun ever so slightly before his expression hardened once more. "Stop calling me Hamm."

She lowered herself into a nearby chair, careful not to make any sudden moves. "I'm Cheyenne. You know me." She held her hands out to him, palms upward.

"All I know is that you have a weapon in a research facility and turned it on the people working here. What more do I need to know? I'm calling the cops." He turned toward the desk where Karl and the other men stood and reached for the phone.

Karl intercepted his hand before it reached the receiver. "That won't be necessary," he said. "I appreciate your getting control of the situation, Dr. Walker, but I can take it from here. This woman needs professional help, not a police record."

He walked up to Cheyenne and gripped her shoulders firmly. She winced underneath his grasp. "Walk with me, Miss Rose. I think I know how we can help you." He forced her toward the device that had erased any memory Hamm had of their last few months together. "After we're done, maybe I can interest you in a few cocktails, help you wind down a bit."

Karl stopped for a moment and looked back at his assistants. "Michael, Gary. Can you take care of Dr. Walker?" The men confiscated the handgun and escorted Hamm toward the back door.

Cheyenne ducked and tried to twist her body to face Karl's. Instead of letting go of her, he dug his thumbs into her back and forced her down to her hands and knees. Pain shot up her neck and to the base of her skull, and for a moment she could see nothing. She felt his foot dig into her back, and her arms threatened to give out.

She took advantage of his position and dropped her right shoulder. Just as she expected, Karl went tumbling over her and crashed headfirst into the staircase leading back up to the platform. Cheyenne heard a satisfying crack and looked to see Karl had a gash on his right eyebrow overlying his preexisting scar. That side of his face was already covered in blood.

"Bitch!"

Karl leapt toward her with fists flailing, making clumsy contact with first her stomach then her shoulder. As Cheyenne struggled to get back on her feet, the third blow hit her square on the nose. She felt a gush of warm liquid and brought both hands to her face. The bone protruded unnaturally, and her nose was already beginning to swell. The pain jabbed into her forehead, coming in waves, forcing her to brace herself on all fours until each moment passed.

Karl grabbed her arm, dragging her up the stairs and toward the chair Hamm had just vacated. Bright spots of light floated in her vision, but she could still see the blood pooling beneath her on the platform. It was a lot of blood. Too much.

There was a pressure under her arms, and she felt herself lifting from the floor. Then everything went black.

CHAPTER 49
Now
October 23, 2030

When Cheyenne woke up, the first thing she noticed was the sound of voices. She opened her eyes and immediately regretted it. Her head felt like her brain might be too swollen for her skull, and the sun from the breaking dawn blinded her. She was on the curb in front of the studio building, and the voices came from Ronnie and one of the other cameramen.

"I really thought she was getting better," Ronnie said, his voice hollow and disbelieving.

Cheyenne hated herself in that moment.

"It's a terrible disease, man. Terrible. My mom was an alcoholic. Other than in the mornings when we were getting ready for school, I never saw her sober the last five years of her life. Died of liver cirrhosis."

"Sorry, man. I hate to hear that."

"Should we wake her up? Get her inside?"

"I'm awake." Cheyenne's voice had that scratchy, post-binge quality to it. She wasn't sure the words she had spoken were even intelligible.

"Let's get you inside, Cheyenne, before anyone else sees you out here."

She moved to her hands and knees then laid her head down on the pavement. It felt cool, therapeutic. "No, just leave me here. I'll be okay."

"No chance." Ronnie's voice was stern, now, like he was talking to one of his children. "You're coming inside, even if I have to carry you. You'll feel much more comfortable in your dressing room. You can sleep it off on the couch."

"No, I like it here," she said. Cheyenne realized she was still a little drunk, which meant she was going to feel even worse later in the day. She groaned at that thought.

"Alright. I'm picking you up. Hold on." Ronnie put his hands around her middle, lifted her upper body, and propped her up on shaky legs.

Every step until she got to her dressing room felt like it would be her last. Her skin tingled all over as blood seemed to rush everywhere but her head. The room spun until she closed her eyes tightly and let Ronnie lead her the rest of the way. When they got to her room, he plopped her down onto the couch and poured her a glass of water. "I'll cover for you this morning, but we need to talk later. I really think you should get some professional help."

Cheyenne's eyes were still closed, but she pressed her lips together and nodded. She heard the door open and shut, and she was finally alone with her thoughts. She could no longer ignore the ache in her chest. She clutched her ribs and took several deep breaths, but it was still there. The disappointment of letting Ronnie down, letting herself down. She couldn't even remember what had happened the night before, where she was or how she had gotten blackout drunk. And who did she hang out with that would have dropped her off at work in that kind of shape? She had probably insisted, but still. They should've known better.

She picked up the glass of water Ronnie had left for her and took a big swig. Her stomach lurched sideways. *Okay, no more water for now.* When she went to put the glass down onto the coffee table, she noticed a note. She picked it up.

You missed a call from:
Isabella Reid

Cheyenne stared at the paper for a full minute. After racking her brain and coming up empty, she folded the note and set it aside. "Sorry, Ms. Reid. I don't know why you're calling, but it's going to have to wait until Monday."

She glanced down at the table again and noticed a brochure for a place called Healing Hearts. She opened the pamphlet, the letters swimming on its slick pages. She blinked several times, and the text steadied enough for her to understand that Healing Hearts was a rehab facility. Her eyes filled with tears, making the words indecipherable once more.

So this was rock bottom.

She lay down on the couch with the brochure still clutched in her hand. She stared straight ahead at nothing, the familiar tension settling in between her eye sockets as a hangover signaled the return of her sobriety. As the alcohol wore off, she noticed more aches and pains. *What in the world did I do to myself last night? And where did I leave my car?*

She closed her eyes, promising herself she'd get help once she woke up. It was a promise she'd made before, but this time she meant it.

She had nothing more to lose.

EPILOGUE
Now
November 20, 2030

"And never forget, friends: These are the stories that matter."

Cheyenne pressed the off button on the remote, then she chucked it across the room toward the TV. A counselor came running in response to the commotion. He glanced around the nearly empty room before his gaze settled on Cheyenne.

"Cheyenne? Everything okay?" His eyes were big and round, the whites standing out against his brown skin.

"Of all people, Doug, why'd they have to replace me with her?"

Doug relaxed his stance and took a seat on the couch next to Cheyenne. "You mean Claire McBee? She doesn't seem that bad."

Cheyenne gave him a sideways glance. "She's the devil incarnate."

The two sat in silence for several minutes before Doug said, "I have this for you." He held up a plastic bag for her to see. It contained all the personal belongings she relinquished when she checked into the rehab facility four weeks prior.

"Thanks." She accepted the bag from him and took a quick inventory: a change of clothes, a pair of earrings and matching necklace, a pair of shoes, a watch, and the contents of her purse.

"You ready to go home?"

She shrugged, fingering the necklace through the clear plastic of a Ziploc bag. "Nothing to go home to."

"Well, you can't stay here forever."

She blew a gust of air through her nostrils. "You don't have to worry about *that*."

"Well." Doug slapped his hands against his thighs before standing up, an act that seemed to represent both a beginning and an end. "Whenever you're ready, we'll call a cab."

He left her once more to her thoughts. She sat with the bag in her lap, staring at its contents and thinking about what had gotten her here.

She still remembered nothing of that night. She pieced together enough to know she started the night alone. Her car was found at a bar downtown with her cell phone and purse inside. She had several missed calls from someone named Isabella, probably the same woman who called the studio looking for her.

Had she tried to drive? Thankfully, someone must have stopped her from getting behind the wheel, but she had no idea who.

She picked up the blouse she wore that night, held it up and examined it. She closed her eyes and imagined putting it on.

Nothing.

Trying to remember felt like an itch she couldn't scratch. Thinking back over the last few months leading up to that night, there were moments of clarity and moments that felt like having a conversation under water. Then there were moments that were gone entirely. They were erased from her memory but left behind a vacancy, a notion something was missing, as if she'd forgotten what she was going to say.

She had just walked around like that for the past month, with something perpetually on the tip of her tongue. She felt like an amputee with phantom limb syndrome, only it affected her brain instead.

She dug through the bag and pulled out the watch. A warm feeling washed over her, and she smiled without knowing exactly why.

Cheyenne checked the time against the clock in the room. It was an hour fast. Made sense with the time change. She turned the watch over in her hand, examining the tiny buttons and knobs. She rolled her eyes. Everything was so much more complicated than it had to be. She pressed one of the buttons and looked back at the watch face to see that nothing had changed. She tried another button.

"Did you enjoy your ride?" The man's voice snaked out of the device and wrapped ice-cold hands around her heart. She pressed the button again to turn off the recording. She wasn't sure she wanted to hear any more.

She sat listening to the seconds tick by and clutched the watch with sweaty hands. She sensed that pressing the button would be like opening Pandora's box. She wouldn't be able to take it back, but she couldn't unhear that voice, couldn't unfeel the terror that had gripped her. There was only one option, and she knew it.

She pressed play.

About the Author

K.V. Scruggs is an internal medicine physician, blogger, and novelist. She is an alumna of Clemson University and received her MD from the Medical University of South Carolina in Charleston. She completed her residency in Internal Medicine at the University of North Carolina – Chapel Hill. She is currently working as a hospitalist and lives in Raleigh, North Carolina with her husband and two sons.

She enjoys writing about current medical issues, and uses her blog as a platform to educate patients and their families. She is also a regular contributor to The Huffington Post. In her fiction writing, Dr. Scruggs not only draws from her experience as a physician, but as a wife, friend and mother.

Visit her website at **https://kvscruggs.com/**

Visit NightLark Publishing at

www.NightLarkPublishing.com

"Down a dark rabbit hole we go, following headstrong Cheyenne Rose and her need for the truth. This suspenseful tale is an anticipatory tale as much as it is a thriller. Intriguing and compelling, the story dares us to consider what kind of medical care we want for our nation and what we're willing to sacrifice to have it."

- Nadia Hashimi, author of International Best Seller, *The Pearl that Broke its Shell*

"An exciting adventure into the world of futuristic medicine where nightmarish consequences await. There are clever and unexpected twists and turns, mixed in with murder and romance, and believable characters that command our sympathies."

- Leonard Goldberg, author of The *Daughter of Sherlock Holmes*

"This propulsive, dystopian thriller thrusts you into a terrifying, futuristic medical world, and leaves you with an ending you'll never forget."

- Sandra Block, author of *The Girl Without a Name*

89350389R00167

Made in the USA
Columbia, SC
13 February 2018